Courage
through
Time

ALSO BY ANN MARIE PICHE

Spiritual Journey of an Ordinary Girl

Journey Through Magic River

Book design by Jessika Hazelton
Printed in the United States of America
The Troy Book Makers • Troy, New York • thetroybookmakers.com

To order additional copies of this title,
contact your favorite local bookstore
or visit www.shoptbmbooks.com

ISBN: 978-1-61468-931-7

Courage through Time

Beyond the Magic River

ANN MARIE PICHE

Contents

Massachusetts 1935 1

Chapter 1: The Haunting Voice 3

Chapter 2: It's Not Over Yet 13

Chapter 3: Powers of the Mystic Guardians 23

Chapter 4: Into Thin Air 31

Chapter 5: Familiar Faces 35

Chapter 6: Back in the Military 41

Chapter 7: The Beggar Boy 53

Chapter 8: Hickam Field 63

Chapter 9: Death Curse 73

Chapter 10: Pearl Harbor 85

Chapter 11: Bad News 97

Chapter 12: Honorable Discharge 107

Chapter 13: Ghosts 117

Chapter 14: Saving Beth 125

Chapter 15: The Homecoming 133

Chapter 16: Telling the Truth 139

Chapter 17: Mysterious Message 143

Chapter 18: The Shack 149

Chapter 19: Into the Ashes 157

Chapter 20: Oasis 163

Chapter 21: Making an Amends 175

Chapter 22: Safe and Sound 181

Chapter 23: The Enchanted Cottage 187

Chapter 24: The Emerald Tear Drop 197

Chapter 25: The Way Home 201

Chapter 26: The Sad Detour 205

Chapter 27: Painful Reality 215

Chapter 28: Regrets 221

Chapter 29: A New Message 225

Chapter 30: Visions of a Seer 231

Chapter 31: The Hidden Clues 235

Chapter 32: The Easton Park Square 245

Chapter 33: The Gifts 253

Chapter 34: Magically Ever After 259

Epilogue 269

Ancestral Flow Charts 272

Acknowledgements 281

THE DARKNESS ENGULFED THE EDGES OF THE MARSHLAND, tucked into an unknown place beyond the long-forgotten graveyard. Mist seeped from the naked gravestones shrouded in evil, stones that had long since lost their names. Wickedness had consumed the soul of the one who had sought vengeance upon the enemy. The chant of three words settled over the land: "They. Will. Die."

Dread fell upon the land as the raindrops seeped through the crumbling dwelling as a door creaked open, allowing the dark secret on the other side to have air. The evil soul, hopelessly trapped in the dwelling, locked in by the soul's deadly deed, moved to an empty corner of the room. Consumed by darkness, the soul had no other alternative left but to destroy the one to come and escape the land and the murky waters beyond the Magic River.

THE HAUNTING VOICE

Maple Ridge, Massachusetts
Present Day

EMILY MILLER STUDIED THE LARGE STONE with its ragged edges and flat surface that stood just over the Shady Brook Bridge and near the entrance of Stanford Park Square. She looked forward to talking with the engraver. Stanford Park needed the real founder's name somewhere among all the other park dedications that included one to the anniversary of the 1918 Spanish flu pandemic and war memorials commemorating the Revolution and more recently the wars in Iraq and Afghanistan. Emily had had the stone placed in honor of the park's true founder, William Easton, and also in remembrance of her late husband, Lucas Easton, who had tragically died three years earlier.

Emily could feel the tears welling up. The emotions were always just beneath the surface, and it had been a long healing process for her. Dreams would sometimes creep into the night and seep into her subconscious mind. Always the same questions rattled her when she awoke. What had been Lucas's last thought? Was he afraid? And worst of all, did he suffer any pain when he drowned? Emily knew in her heart that he was in a good place now. That gave her comfort. Dealing with the loss was also made easier by her new husband's unwavering love. She felt extremely happy every day to have Rick Miller in her life.

As Emily bathed in blissful feelings about the man who had swept her off her feet, she suddenly became distracted by a strange breeze in the distance affecting the upper tips of the golden fall leaves on the nearby trees. With the flutter of the leaves a faint haunting voice called out, "Emily…Emily." Emily stepped back, putting her fingers in her ears, thinking the sound would disappear if she blocked out the voice. She looked into the swamp behind the large stone where a marsh area ran alongside the Magic River. The swamp wasn't very large, less than an acre, Emily estimated. The rest of the land gradually slopped upward into a thickly wooded area with a few old logging trails carved between birch, maple, and pine trees. She had never attempted to walk through the swamp area but knew it was a favorite spot for duck hunters.

The air became still, and she saw a heron perched on the edge of a rock with its long beak waiting for the unsuspecting bugs to surface from the calm waters. An eerie voice broke through the silence again, and Emily responded: "Who are you? What do you want from me this time?"

Suddenly, a ding sound came from her pocket, startling her. She reached for her phone and saw a text message from the engraver:

Sorry for the inconvenience, Mrs. Miller, but I'm afraid I will have to reschedule. I'm stuck on another job that's taking longer than expected. Let me know what's convenient for you.

Emily shot back a message and began to walk away when she heard the voice again. She felt a spike of fear grip through her and tried to ignore the sound. She continued to walk a little faster and let her mind go to happy thoughts of her handsome, blue-eyed, loving husband, Rick.

More than once, Rick had pulled her back from the brink of insanity from her strange experiences. Emily's thoughts wandered to the past as she walked over the Shady Brook Bridge and stopped in the middle, watching the sun's reflection shimmer off the waters of the Magic River below. She avoided looking to the right where the swamp met the riverbank.

The river was pleasant to look at, but it wasn't always that way. She had experienced the results of a curse on the river that an ancient Witch had cast, something Emily would rather forget. The curse had caused her to travel back in time to tell those affected by it that their Creator loved them. She accomplished that mission, and in the process, she and Rick fell madly in love throughout the adventure of solving the mystery of the curse. She settled on the latter part of those thoughts where she and Rick were madly in love.

"I don't need any more strange happenings in my life," she declared to the river. Emily continued to walk back to the town office where she worked as a columnist for the *Maple Ridge Gazette*'s historical page. She was sure her boss, Mark Johnson, had more assignments for her to tackle.

The door to the office was closed, trapping the heat that poured relentlessly from the old radiators. Although Rick and his plumber friend had worked on it, the old heating system continued to act up. Emily pulled off her sweater, revealing a T-shirt she wore on purpose for this very reason and then turned on her computer.

Emily concentrated on the computer screen, looking at all things related to World War II, when a file slid across her desk. She glanced up at Mark Johnson, who typically entered the office shouting orders with his booming voice.

"What's this?" she asked, tapping a finger on the file.

"Thought you could do a re-run of the 1918 pandemic story, seeing its October and the organizers decided to have a small dedication alongside two other programs coming up in two weeks."

Emily frowned as she opened the folder, not wanting to rehash her 1918-time-travel experience and another time period to which the Witch's curse had taken her.

"Why do you want to do a re-run? Don't you want something

new?" Emily sat up straight in her chair, eager to offer her own idea. "Hey, how about I do a war story of some kind?"

Mark sat at the desk opposite of hers, twirling his unlit cigar in the corner of his mouth. "What do you have in mind then?"

"WWII." But no sooner had Emily said that she slumped her shoulders and felt the enthusiasm of a war story evaporate into thin air. "The only problem," she continued, "there's nobody left in Maple Ridge to interview." Emily let out a frustrated breath as she twisted a strand of her long red hair around her finger. "Besides, even if there were anyone left, they may not remember much."

Mark walked over to a giant filing cabinet, opened a drawer labeled *Old News Stories*, and thumbed through some folders. Emily did many things the old-school way, but relying on a filing cabinet wasn't one of them. She tried kidding him about his method of Google searching, but Mark's attention was buried deep into the file cabinet. He finally pulled out the chosen folder and tossed it on her desk. She looked at the name.

"Joseph Miller?"

"Now, young lady, go ask your man about that guy," Mark said and then turned and walked out the door.

Emily stared at the name. A bead of sweat dripped down the back of her neck as a creeping chill ran up her spine, with only one thought lingering in her mind: more ghosts.

Emily drove down School Street, cleverly named because of the old school at the end of the road. Emily could see Rick's old Ford pickup truck parked in front of the school, pulled behind it, and shut her car off. She hesitated momentarily and then opened the car door and stared at the old building. For Emily, the school represented another time travel episode when she found herself in 1963 and where she met her six-year-old self. A bizarre experience at best, and one kept tucked away in the back of her mind. "Well," she sighed. "Bizarre experience or not, I must admit I've wanted to see Rick's progress."

Emily approached the large front doors and could hear faint

sounds of hammering. Rick had been working on the old school for the past three years, turning it into apartments. She followed the sound to one of the old classrooms and found Rick covered from head to toe in sawdust. She could see only the top of his head as he measured a longboard and then saw him glance up with a smile, clearly happy to see her.

"What's up, sweetie? Is everything okay? Mark being a pain in the ass today?" he asked with a bit of sarcastic humor.

Emily stood next to Rick, wiping the sawdust off his nose. "No, not exactly."

The two looked into each other's eyes, causing the usual reaction: Rick's arms slid around Emily's waist as he pulled her in close. Emily responded to his greeting by wrapping her arms around his neck and giving him a kiss that told him she missed him too. Rick ran his hand down her thigh, kissing her passionately, both lost in the moment until Rick pulled back, looking into Emily's eyes, and grinned. "I suppose I'll never get any work done this way."

"Later then?" she responded with a promise in her voice.

"It's a deal, besides, you know I could never resist those emerald-green eyes." He kissed Emily again, but this time on the cheek.

Emily strolled around the old classroom, with walls sectioned off for different rooms that would make a good-sized apartment. Rick also worked for the town as a building inspector, and she held back on asking him if he was qualified to inspect his own work. As far as Emily was concerned, his carpentry skills were pretty impressive for a guy with just one good hand and a prosthetic for the other. Rick had lost his hand shortly after 9/11 in Iraq and only recently had come to terms with his disability.

Rick picked up his level and bent over to watch the bubble drift to the middle. In the corner of her eye, she saw his attention move past the bubble and onto her as she wandered around the room aimlessly.

"You got something on your mind there, sweetie?" he asked.

Emily turned towards Rick abruptly. "Who is Joseph Miller?"

Sporting a surprised look, Rick set his level down and ran his hand through his thick, silver hair. "Well, he's my grandfather. Why?"

"Mark Johnson is why." She turned an empty bucket upside-down to sit. "I wanted to do a WWII story but have no subjects to interview, and Mark gave me your grandfather's file."

"My grandfather has a file?"

"Apparently," Emily said, pushing the sawdust on the floor with the tip of her boot, making swirling patterns.

Rick plopped another bucket alongside Emily and leaned forward, resting his elbows on his knees. "Joseph Miller was killed at Pearl Harbor. I never knew him, only heard stories. He was a mechanic at the Hickam Air Force Base and was killed near one of the hangers during the attack. My grandfather worked on the D3s, dive bombers, B-17s, P-40 Warhawks." While Rick rattled off statistics, Emily gazed at the ceiling, taking mental notes as she listened. Rick tilted his head as if he knew what she was doing, trying to conjure up a story in her head.

"It's okay, sweetie, we can get together later and write down all this stuff," he said, standing and stretching his back with a painful groan. "Oh, man, I think I'm getting too old for this."

Emily stood and pulled her sweater around her body to keep warm from the chill in the room. Rick's sore back recovered enough so he could hug her for more warmth. He walked her to the front door of the old school as she pressed herself snuggly against him in a cozy embrace.

"Keep this up, Mrs. Miller, and I'll have to quit early," Rick said.

"I'll be home waiting, and I'll even give you a back rub if you're a good boy," she said, kissing her finger and placing it on his lips. "In the meantime, think of more stories about your grandfather."

Emily walked to her car and glanced back at the old school. "Not sure if I could live in there with all those ghosts," she said as the memories flowed back to 1963. "Well, I suppose if I'm to be honest," she admitted while getting into her car. "Those ghosts haven't exactly ended at the school's front door now, have they?"

She glanced at the school once more and then drove off to her farmhouse with plenty of ghosts of its own.

Later that evening, Emily sat sipping hot tea next to Rick by the blazing fireplace. In her family for over two hundred years, the Queen Anne farmhouse had recently been undergoing renovations. Rick's daughter-in-law, Meghan, now seven months pregnant, was the interior decorator who had done the job. She had stopped by several times, implementing her skills for the Victorian decor Emily loved so much. Most of the work had ended, and Emily felt content with what she affectionately called "Sam's house."

Emily's beloved great-great-grandfather Sam was another ancestor Emily had met during her quest to defeat the curse. She had met him in one time period and again in another. Both young and old, Sam had become an ever-present part of her heart and home. It wasn't the past that bothered Emily at the moment, though; it was the voice she had heard in the park. She knew that talking to Rick would help ease her mind.

Emily lay her head back on the soft, comfy chair beside Rick, taking another sip of her chamomile tea. She set her tea down on a small table between them. "I went to the park today to go over the details of the new engraving," she said.

Although Rick's eyes were closed, she was sure he hadn't dozed off. "Oh, yeah, that's right, you said you were going today. What did they say?" He opened his eyes and looked at her.

Emily breathed deeply. "I never got to see the engraver. He couldn't make it, so I asked him to send me samples to choose from and that I would give my approval when I picked one out. I also told him there was no hurry, since the dedication won't take place until next summer and that he could check out the stone whenever he gets a chance." Emily leaned forward and massaged her temples, feeling uneasy. She then turned her attention to Rick. "There's something else."

Rick sat up and moved to the edge of his seat, focusing on Emily.

"When I was in the park," Emily began, "while standing next

to the dedication stone, I heard a voice coming from the swamp area beyond the stone."

Emily saw Rick's face show a look of worry. "What do you mean?"

"The strange thing about it—it was a man's voice calling my name, and it sounded so haunting."

"Maybe you thought you heard something. I know you still have some anxiety over the whole time travel thing."

Emily noticed that the worry Rick had in his eyes moments ago had turned into thoughtful consideration.

"To be honest, Emily, I don't think anyone would be completely normal after all that."

Emily sat back in the chair, crossing her arms in a pouting posture. She gave Rick an indignant look over his effort to make her feel better. "So, what you're saying is, I'll never be normal again?" As soon as she said those words, she realized she had acted like a child. Rick's mouth turned up in a half grin, and she knew he had read the regret on her face.

Rick gulped down the last of his tea and then got up, extending his hand, turning his thoughtful eyes into irresistible ones. "Come on, sweetie, let's go to bed."

Emily took his hand without resisting, and they went upstairs to their bedroom. The room was cozy with a king-size canopy bed, her grandmother's old dresser, and vanity. Meghan had done a beautiful job turning their bedroom into a quaint Victorian sanctuary.

Rick turned off the lights and clicked on the gas fireplace, which produced a simmering light across the ceiling. He approached her as she stood by the bed and moved his hand gently down the side of her shoulder, giving her goosebumps. He unbuttoned her blouse, and his hand caressed her erect nipples.

"Now," he said as he pressed his body against hers. "Let's forget all about strange voices, and by tomorrow you'll have a fresher perspective on the whole matter."

"So, what you're saying, Mr. Miller," she began, with no attempt to pull away, "is that sex will solve everything?"

"No, but I can make you forget for the time being." He grabbed her by the waist, pulling her tighter against himself.

She felt the hardness between his legs. She was unable to resist, aroused by the heat of his body. She placed her hand on his chest and ran her fingers slowly down to the zipper of his pants, releasing the hard source that seemed desperate to have her. She parted her legs slightly, feeling the same cravings and wanting him to fill the heat building between her thighs.

He kissed her hard, responding to her touch. Their tongues mingled, sparking the raging desire that took little to ignite. Within seconds, they were naked and fell to the bed.

His eyes gazed intently into hers as his hot breath whispered. "I know you need me, sweetie, but I'm thinking, I just might need you more."

She felt the weight of his body and the throbbing of his groin when he took her at that moment and performed what she craved as they made love. Then, finally, as they fell asleep in each other's arms, she had forgotten the strange, haunting voice that seemed to beckon her through the whispering wind that had floated along the top of the trees and beyond the Magic River.

The following morning came with a cool, foggy rain. Emily made her usual perked coffee and cinnamon rolls. She could hear the sound of water trickling through the old pipes as Rick took his shower. Emily noticed the garbage was overflowing, tied the bag, and then pulled on her muck boots and coat to take the bag to the bin out back.

She stood for a moment, looking out over the fog that blanketed her yard that led to the Magic River. It reminded her of the familiar mist she had entered when going through time and felt a chill go up her spine at the thought of it. She often wondered if she would ever get past her time travel experiences.

While turning to go back into the house, she heard the same haunting voice coming from the direction of the river. Emily took a few steps towards the sound and heard the mysterious man's voice again, "Emily...Emily." She could feel the hair go up on the back of her neck. She struggled to see through the fog.

Suddenly a more unmistakable voice came from behind her. This time it was a woman's voice. Emily flinched as if her heart were about to jump out of her chest and then turned and saw Sylvia Spencer Collins a few feet away.

"Oh, dear, so sorry. I didn't mean to scare you, Emily." A stunning brunette with brown eyes, Sylvia came from a long line of Spencer Witches.

Emily pulled herself together, closed her coat, and managed to smile. "Oh, it's you. I'm sorry I didn't hear you coming."

Emily noticed that Sylvia held a notebook of some kind in her hand.

"I hope this isn't a bad time?" Sylvia said.

Emily walked over, tucking her arm under Sylvia's. "How does fresh perked coffee sound?"

Chapter 2

IT'S NOT OVER YET

THE KITCHEN WAS WARM AND SMELLED OF CINNAMON. Emily poured coffee into two mugs and sat across from Sylvia at the kitchen table and sipped slowly, letting the caffeine seep into her bloodstream. That's when Sylvia laid the notebook she had been holding in front of Emily.

"What's this?" Emily asked.

Sylvia took a deep breath and exhaled slowly. "It's my great-great grandmother's original diary."

Sylvia pointed to the name on the bottom of the cover. Emily's eyes widened when she saw the name *Lily Spencer*. She had seen Lily's diary before, but it had been turned into a published book. Meghan had given her the book one day when she had stopped by the house, and Emily had since given it back after reading it.

"This diary looks different. The one I read was a published book." Emily picked up the tattered, old notebook with its frayed edges. She could hardly read the word *Diary* written on the front. She turned it over and flipped through several pages carefully.

Sylvia lowered her voice. "Lily Spencer used this diary as a reference for writing her published book. It was hidden away. That is until a couple of days ago." Sylvia fidgeted in her chair and leaned closer as though she was about to tell a secret. "I also found a magic spell book along with the diary. I discovered them while rummaging through my mother's old hope chest she had stored in the attic. Both the diary and spell book were hidden deep down at the very bottom."

"I don't understand. Why would she hide them?" Emily asked

when a scary thought popped into her head. "Wait. Are you telling me there's something in this diary about me?"

Before Sylvia could answer, a scuffling noise came from the hallway that led to the kitchen. Rick strolled in, putting a sweatshirt over his head, causing his thick, gray locks to fly in every direction. He looked at both women, seemingly unfazed by his appearance, and said, "Well, good morning, ladies."

As he always did when nervous or in deep thought, Rick ran his fingers through his hair. But this time, he used his fingers as a makeshift comb.

"Good morning, Rick." Sylvia said. "I was just telling Emily about my great-great grandmother, Lily Spencer, and how I had found her diary in an old chest."

Rick walked over, giving Emily a gentle kiss on the lips. "I thought you already read Lily Spencer's diary?" he said, walking over to the counter to pour himself a cup of coffee.

Emily had read Lily's diary from cover to cover, filled with so much information about the Spencer Witches, but that was a book called *Diary Of The Witches' Testimony*. This ancient-looking notebook was not that book, and by how Sylvia acted, this diary must hold other secrets that Lily wished to keep hidden from her family.

"No, I never saw this diary before nor any magic spell book," Emily said in answer to Rick's question. She was beginning to feel that dreaded weight on her shoulders. Something was up, and Sylvia was there to tell her what that was.

Rick sat down next to Emily, and from the look on his face, she knew he could read her mind.

"Spell book? Diary? Is everything okay here?" he asked, taking the diary out of Emily's hands. "Sylvia? Is there something in here we need to know?"

Emily abruptly stood and walked to the kitchen window, looking out into the fog. She didn't want to know. Emily feared the inevitable, knowing what needed to be done. She almost wondered how she sensed it—and then turned to face that fear. "What does Lily Spencer want me to do?" she asked.

Sylvia got up and walked over, touching Emily's arm. Her dark eyes softened with empathy. "It's Thomas, your grandfather. Something happened between him and one of Lily Spencer's granddaughters. Lily never really shared what that was other than her granddaughter Charlotte had cast a death curse on Thomas."

"Is this Charlotte your grandmother?" Emily asked.

"No, my grandmother's name was Kathleen. Charlotte was her sister."

"But what you're telling me can't be right. My grandfather died of cancer at the age of forty-eight," Emily said. "A little over a year after I was born. I have a letter from him proving that."

Emily roamed around the kitchen, shaking her head as Rick approached her. She put her hand up to stop him. "No, this definitely can't be right. Whatever happened, this...this Charlotte person's curse didn't work."

"Emily? Listen to me," Sylvia said. "It's because someone had stopped it."

Emily froze in place. She began to sway sideways slightly and then she felt Rick's arm go around her. She squeezed her eyes shut, hoping everything would make more sense when she opened them.

"Come on, Emily, sit down," Rick insisted, escorting her over to a chair.

"Maybe I should go," Sylvia said regretfully.

"No!" Emily protested as she looked up at Sylvia. "I need to know more."

Rick let out an irritated sigh. "Sylvia, I think you need to be clearer about this."

Sylvia opened the diary to a bookmarked page. "Here, read this. Lily Spencer has a better way of explaining it than I do."

Emily and Rick leaned down, peering at the page as Emily read it aloud:

My thoughts after reading the writings of Rebecca Spencer:

After hearing Sandra Easton's confession to a strange woman with red hair of an egregious curse set upon two unsuspecting families over two hundred and fifty years ago, Rebecca Spencer vowed this would never happen again. She then released her own spell, binding the powers of all the Witches in her bloodline if they were to ever cast an awful death curse such as this in the future. They and the rest of her descendants would lose their powers until such time when the cry from a new Witch could be heard on the darkest day in a new century, which would unbind the powers of the Spencer Witches.

With what little power left in my body, I received a premonition. It was my granddaughter Charlotte casting this horrible curse onto my stepson Thomas, and now Charlotte is missing, and the premonition has not revealed where she has gone. I'm an old woman and soon will no longer be here to protect Thomas. I'm in deep distress and pray somehow the Spencer Witches get their powers back to send the time traveler to defeat the most powerful and evil curse any Witch could cast upon an innocent—the death curse.

Lily Spencer, November 6, 1935

Emily was speechless. Her eyes continued to focus on the page in front of her. She could sense Rick's tension, filled with anger and disbelief.

"No, Sylvia! There's no way Emily's going back in time. No, no," Rick protested as he shook his head. "I won't let it happen."

Emily finally looked up, pointing to a line Lily had written.

"What does she mean by, 'would unbind the powers of the Spencer Witches'?"

Sylvia sat down and folded her hands on the table. "It means the only way you'll be able to go back in time is if my daughter or I regain our powers." Sylvia gave Rick a weary glance. "And just so you know, neither Meghan nor I possess any such powers. We never did."

"Well, that's fine with me. Let's keep it that way," Rick said, with a resolute nod towards Emily.

"And the magic spell book? What does that say?" Emily asked.

"I haven't even attempted to try to read it, Emily. I am aware of how powerful those spells can be and to be honest, I'd just as soon not open it at this time."

Emily stood up, and without looking at Sylvia or Rick, she took two steps forward, still feeling wobbly on her legs. She wanted to run as far away as possible, but where would she go? "Would you excuse me? I need some air," she finally said as she went to the mud room to put her coat and muck boots on.

Emily reluctantly walked through the yard with the fog still hovering near the ground. She stood at the river's edge, watching tiny ripples caused by fish feeding on insects floating on the surface. The water ripples brought back a haunting memory from a time long past. It was something an old Native American seer named Catori had said, and Emily repeated it out loud: "A curse is like a stone hitting water as it ripples through time until it meets its end."

Those ripples were now flowing towards her from the Magic River. An unsettling dread inched its way into Emily's gut. She needed answers, yet at the same time, she feared what would be discovered if she were to get those answers. Emily mulled over what Sylvia had said and what Lily Spencer's diary had just revealed. She could feel Rick's presence as he caught up with her and stood by her side, yet he remained silent.

"I heard the man's voice again earlier when I brought the garbage out," she said as she gazed out over the river. She felt Rick's arm come around her shoulders. A gesture that would usually make her feel safe, yet now, she felt vulnerable. A bit of panic crept in as she turned to look up at Rick. "What does this all mean?" she asked, knowing he would have no answer. "And who is this young Witch who cries on the darkest day?"

For the past two months, Emily had kept herself busy with writing for the *Maple Ridge Gazette* and finalizing the dedication stone in the park for what Emily had petitioned for the town to rename *Easton Park Square*. Following the town's approval, all that was left to do was have the large dedication stone engraved.

Emily would come to the park only when it bustled with people. Even today as the park stirred with excitement over the yearly Christmas festival, she chose to stay at her desk in the town office. It was the beginning of December when the festivities of decorating for the holiday season were underway. Emily had spent very little time in the park and by the river running through her backyard, avoiding the voice that continued to beckon her. She also avoided Lily Spencer's diary, having buried it deep inside one of her desk drawers at home.

Instead, Emily focused on an article she had just started and needed to finish before the anniversary of the bombing of Pearl Harbor. A yearly commemoration ceremony was held during the winter festival every December. The article's angle was a tribute, honoring the local heroes of Pearl Harbor. She scanned the computer screen to review what she had written so far:

"Heroes of Pearl Harbor"

By Emily Miller

Men have fought and died in many wars throughout the centuries. The Revolutionary War brought independence. The Civil War brought freedom and human rights and ended slavery. But what about World War I? A prelude to World War II?

Nazism aimed to dominate the world, while Japan had ambitions for global expansion. This was the double whammy facing the United States: On one front, Germany; on the other, Japan. But it wasn't Nazi Germany that struck first. Japan had launched a devastating blow on the United States Naval Base and airfields in Hawaii, killing 2,403 Americans and wounding 1,178 others. This attack would change the course of history and bring the United States into World War II.

One soldier, Joseph John Miller, had thrown himself over two of his fellow airmen as an incoming bomb exploded within a foot of the men. Joseph was killed while saving his two comrades. Joseph John Miller is among the thousands of brave airmen, sailors, soldiers, marines, and coast guardsmen who sacrificed their lives on that infamous day. The reason for their sacrifice is the same as it was in every other war for which Americans have fought and died: Freedom.

Emily pushed herself from her desk, leaned back in the soft leather office chair, and felt a headache coming on. She rubbed her temples, taking a deep breath when the door abruptly swung open, with Rick hastily tossing a chart on the desk opposite Emily's.

"This job sucks," he said in frustration as he plopped himself in the chair in front of Emily's desk.

"What happened?" she asked.

"How about turning your friends in for a stupid technicality, is what happened." He ran his hand through his hair. "I have a mind to quit this job. Building inspector, my ass. Ratting out your friends is what I call it."

Emily stood and came around, sliding herself onto Rick's lap and hugged him. "Then quit," she said, cupping his cheeks in her hands.

Rick lifted one eyebrow with a slight grin. "You know, Mrs. Miller, keep up the touchy-feely stuff, and I might forget my frustrations after all," he said, sliding his lips gently across Emily's.

She knew his move was an invitation to an act they couldn't play out at that moment. "If it makes you feel any better," Emily offered and then changed the subject. "I'm almost finished with my article mentioning your grandfather." She reached over, turning the laptop in their direction.

Rick leaned forward to get a better look at the screen without letting go of Emily. "Hmm," he said, protruding his lower lip and nodding in approval. "Not bad. You should probably add some of the stories you've heard over the years from all those WWII vets from the nursing home. I'm sure you must have heard a lot of them," Rick suggested.

"Yeah, I thought of that," she agreed. "The problem is I'd have to go on my fuzzy memories of those conversations. Regardless, I'll complete the article by the end of the day. Mark needs it before December 7." Emily gave Rick another affectionate squeeze. "Now, in the meantime, we need to get our Christmas tree from the Maple Sugar Barn later."

Rick got up from the chair, helping Emily to her feet. "I'm on it, sweetie, and later will continue this," Rick said, pointing to the chair where a few moments ago they both had to tame those sexual desires.

Emily playfully kissed him on the nose. "It's a date, Mr. Miller."

Later that night, Emily lay awake listening to a faint whistling sound from a tiny hole along the edge of the old bedroom window. She turned to see Rick curled up in the fleece blanket, peacefully asleep. Their lovemaking had lingered through her body, and she felt a sudden need to awaken him for more. It had surprised her how intense the sexual attraction was between them. Rick was handsome, after all, and incredibly charming, which most likely fed that strong attraction.

She was beginning to forget what it had been like between

her and Lucas. She was losing track of time and felt as if she had somehow lived another life. Part of her didn't want to forget, yet how could she when the loss periodically manifested itself in her dreams. This is ridiculous, she thought, swinging her legs over the edge of the bed, deciding that chamomile tea would be a better option than letting her thoughts run away with her.

She put her robe on, sliding her feet into a pair of sippers. She hesitated at the top of the stairs and instead walked through the hallway leading to her office. She sat at the desk and opened her laptop. She typed Ancestry.com in the search bar, then typed in *SPENCER*, and scrolled through the results.

Emily found Lily Spencer. "Let me see here," Emily said to the computer screen. "Lily had one daughter who died of tuberculosis in 1930. Lily also had two granddaughters, one named Charlotte and one named Kathleen. Charlotte had no children. Kathleen had one, a daughter named Beth, born in 1934. Beth had one daughter named Sylvia born in 1959."

Emily continued searching and found that Beth had died on December 24, 2020. A chill spiked through her when she saw the date -- the exact date her husband Lucas had died. "That's unbelievable," Emily said as if someone was in the empty room to hear her. "Sylvia's mother died on the same day as Lucas."

Emily continued to read and found a newspaper clipping about Charlotte as a missing person and another clipping of Lily Spencer's obituary. Emily looked at the date of her death—November 6, 1935. She jerked her head up from the screen, realizing she had seen that date before. Emily opened the drawer of the desk where Lily's diary was hidden beneath a pile of papers. She went to the last entry that she and Rick had read, and there it was: November 6, 1935. "Oh, my God! Lily died the same day she wrote this!"

Emily turned to the inside back cover of the diary and saw something written in tiny letters at the bottom. She hadn't seen it before because she had refused to look further at Lily's diary out of fear of discovering the very thing that was right in front of her eyes at this very moment. A reference most likely to herself. At the bottom of the page was another person's handwriting:

I fear our powers are lost, and until the time traveler comes, I must leave my child in the care of the Mystic Guardian.

November 6, 1935. Entry from Kathleen Spencer

Emily glanced at the computer screen again, and she saw another obituary listed just below Lily's. It read Kathleen Spencer—November 6, 1935.

Emily stood. She felt dazed, and her steps felt heavy as she walked to the window. She looked out towards the Magic River. Her head was beginning to hurt again. She could feel her breathing quicken and her hands sweating as the realization sunk into her mind. Lily and her granddaughter Kathleen died on the same day.

"What the hell happened to them?" Emily said, staring out into the darkness with only one remaining question that begged an answer. "And who in God's name is the Mystic Guardian?"

Chapter 3

POWERS OF THE MYSTIC GUARDIANS

A FEW DAYS BEFORE CHRISTMAS, Emily had walked into Owens's Drug Store, looking for a bottle of pain reliever. She had been getting what she thought were stress headaches from all the uncertainty that had crawled back into her life. Emily had kept the information about Lily and Kathleen's strange same-day demises from Rick. She also didn't mention Kathleen's cryptic notation about the Mystic Guardian. Emily didn't want to worry him and certainly didn't want to talk about it.

Christmas time was at least a pleasant distraction with all the Christmas lights, decorations, and shoppers with their arms filled with holiday treasures as they hustled from one place to another throughout the small town. Even the drug store was festive with silver Christmas trees and red and green garlands draped everywhere.

As she browsed through the aisles, she heard the door swing open, ushering in a big gust of wind that blew the red and green garlands off anything within a foot of the door. She glanced over at the store window and saw heavy snow beginning to fall. She quickly paid for her items and hurried out the door and down the main road past the Stoney Brook Bridge.

Once again, Emily found herself at the bridge entrance leading to the park. She spotted someone crossing the now snow-covered bridge. The woman struggled to walk against the snowy wind that swirled around her. It wasn't until the woman was almost on top of her that Emily recognized who it was.

"Sylvia?" Emily said, surprised.

Sylvia approached Emily and gave her a friendly hug. "Emily! Fancy meeting you here," she said.

Emily scooped her hand under Sylvia's arm. "Come, let's get out of this snowstorm."

They reached Emily's car, not far from the bridge, and got in as Emily started the engine and cranked up the heat. She pulled her gloves off, allowing the hot air to blow into her hands as she shivered uncontrollably. "What are you doing in the park?" Emily asked through her chattering teeth.

Sylvia shot Emily a grin. "As long as I was in town to do some last-minute Christmas shopping, I decided to check out the big dedication stone first. It's going to be nice when it's finished and will be a great honor to your late husband's family."

"Thank you, Sylvia, for your kind words."

Sylvia shifted to face Emily. "Besides, I thought I'd get out before the storm. I guess the weather report's timing was off."

"Yeah, you're right. I didn't realize the storm was going to start this early either," Emily rubbed her hands together and glanced out of the driver-side window. The snow was beginning to cover Emily's car, and she put the wipers on, which had little effect on the ice accumulating quickly on the windshield. "This doesn't look good. You should come home with me and not try to drive to your place in this stuff," Emily suggested. "Besides, my house is closer than yours. Better to be safe than sorry."

Sylvia nodded. "I think you're right and just to let you know, Meghan and Derek are at your house right now anyway. I guess Rick needed his son's help with something."

Emily put the car in gear. "Well, then let's get back to them, shall we?"

After a short yet icy trip home, Emily pulled into the farmhouse driveway and saw Rick come out the front door waving, clearly happy she was home safe from what now appeared to be a blizzard. The two women came through the back door, taking off their snowy coats and boots. Rick greeted Emily with hugs and kisses.

When she spotted her mother, Meghan let out a gasp. "Oh, my goodness!" she said happily, giving Sylvia an awkward hug caused by Meghan's swelling belly. "I can't believe you're here."

Meghan was well past her due date, and her pregnant belly got in the way of almost anything within half a foot. Emily smiled at the sight and felt a sense of joy, knowing she would soon be a grandmother.

"Well, darling," Sylvia said with a sigh and glanced at Emily with uncertainty. "I'm afraid by the way it looks outside, I'll be here for a while."

"You're welcome to stay as long as you want," Emily said, taking the kettle and placing it on the burner.

"Sure," Rick agreed. "Of course, you should all stay. Hey, we'll even make a night of it if the snow keeps piling up out there." He craned his neck to peer out the kitchen window. "And by the looks of it, it's already doing just that."

"All right then," Sylvia said. "I should at least call my husband to let him know where I am."

"Well, then, it's settled," Emily said, opening the refrigerator. "And I happen to have a leftover roast with all the fixings."

Later that evening, Emily walked into the living room with a tray crowded with mugs of hot cocoa and a plate of Christmas cookies. Meghan and Sylvia sat on the couch by the fireplace, soaking up through their toes the warmth of the glowing logs. Emily set the tray on the coffee table and then took her mug of cocoa over to the window. "I guess it's no place for man nor beast out there tonight," she said.

"Oh, Emily, these cookies are delicious," Meghan swooned.

Emily turned from the window, smiled at Meghan, and then had a worrisome thought: Meghan might give birth at any moment. If she did, there would be no way they could make it to the hospital in the raging snowstorm. She certainly had more than her share of bringing babies into the world, but she was also well aware that things could go wrong.

"I must say, my dear, your hot cocoa is to die for," Sylvia added.

"Well, ladies, thank you both for your kind words, but I didn't make the cookies. They came from the Maple Sugar Barn, and the hot cocoa—" Emily lifted her mug of the steaming chocolate. "It's instant." She grinned and took a sip.

Both Sylvia and Meghan giggled. "You sure fooled us," Meghan said.

The women sat quietly while sounds of Rick and Derek yelling at the TV in the other room over a bad football play gave Emily the opportunity for which she had been waiting. Emily put her mug on the coffee table, sat on the edge of couch next to Meghan and Sylvia, and leaned towards the women. "I found something in Lily Spencer's old diary last night."

Emily noticed that Sylvia's relaxed position on the couch changed to a straight posture, and she seemed nervous as she tucked a strand of hair behind her ear. "What is it that you found?"

Emily retrieved the diary from a bookshelf in the corner of the room and returned to her seat on the couch. She opened the diary to the inside back cover and handed the diary to Sylvia.

Sylvia bit the side of her lip and met Emily's eyes. "So now you know."

"Know what?" Meghan asked, taking the diary from her mother.

"What happened to your grandmother Kathleen, Sylvia?" Emily asked. "She died the same day as Lily, and according to the diary, Kathleen feared losing her powers." Emily paused as mother and daughter stared at her recent discovery.

"Kathleen mentions the time traveler," Emily continued. "And how she felt the need to leave her child in the care of the Mystic Guardian. What does this all mean?"

Meghan popped her head up from the diary. "I've never seen this before," she said to her mother.

Sylvia stood without a word and walked over to the window with her arms crossed, seemingly staring at the snow sticking to the pane.

"Lily Spencer and my grandmother Kathleen were found dead in the swamp," Sylvia finally said. "Their bodies lay side by side. Neither one had any injuries. It was as if their hearts had just stopped beating." She turned to look at Emily. "Their deaths remain an unsolved mystery till this day."

"Do you mean the swamp alongside the Magic River not far from the bridge?" Emily asked.

Sylvia nodded and continued. "As far as the Mystic Guardians, they have great powers, even more powers than Witches. In fact, they protect Witches from any evil powers brought upon them. My grandmother Kathleen asked a Mystic Guardian to protect her daughter Beth from such evil powers." Sylvia gazed into the fireplace. "She must have felt at least her baby girl would be safe. As far as her sister Charlotte, her death curse had ended the powers of the Spencer witches, and as long as Charlotte was alive, the curse would remain. Not only that, but all the Witches were in danger without their powers." Sylvia sat down again.

Emily could see Sylvia was frightened by how she nervously twisted the ring on her finger.

"I'm afraid even Rebecca Spencer hadn't thought this whole thing through because her spell left all the Witches with no way of defending themselves against the death curse. I have my own suspicions of Lily and Kathleen being victims of Charlotte's curse," Sylvia said.

"You said as long as Charlotte was alive the curse remains. Wouldn't Charlotte be dead now? I mean, that was well over eighty years ago."

"Somehow Charlotte hadn't been completely stopped; otherwise, Meghan and I would have our powers right now."

"So, your grandmother Kathleen found a Mystic Guardian that would help?" Emily asked.

"Yes, but now there are no more Mystic Guardians. They're all gone. The day my mother Beth died was the day the Mystic Guardians ended."

"So, who is this Mystic Guardian that took your mother in as a child?" Emily asked.

Sylvia got up and began to pace back and forth. Meghan managed to get herself up off the couch while holding her belly.

"Mom? Who is the Mystic Guardian?" Meghan asked.

"That's the thing," Sylvia struggled with her words. "My...my mother never told me. No one knows who the Mystic Guardian was. My mother never let on who had raised her. I knew for sure the Mystic Guardian wasn't my grandfather. He had cut his hand fixing an old saw blade. The cut turned into an infection, and he died of sepsis soon after. My mother was barely two months old at the time." Sylvia sighed. "It was as if she had no family at all. With her mother Kathleen gone and her father dead from a nasty cut, she had no one other than this Mystic Guardian to care for her. My mother never talked about him to me or anyone else. So, there you have it: my great-great-grandmother, Lily, and grandmother, Kathleen, died mysteriously, and the Mystic Guardian never existed as far as my mother was concerned. Whoever he was, my mother kept his secret. And the strange irony is that my mother died on the same day the Mystic Guardians ended."

"How do you know the Mystic Guardians ended on the same day?" Emily asked.

Sylvia walked towards Emily, stopping within an inch of her. "Because the last words my mother said to me on her death bed were: 'Be careful, for today is the day all the Mystic Guardians cease to exist,' and with those words on her lips..." Sylvia swallowed hard. Emily could see she was on the verge of tears as she choked out her words. "She took her last breath."

Emily touched Sylvia's arm and then hugged her. "I'm so sorry about your mom. Did you know she died on the same day as my late husband. I saw it when I was looking at the Spencer ancestral site."

Meghan rubbed her back, looking painfully uncomfortable. "Your late husband wouldn't happen to be the last Mystic Guardian?"

Meghan's question only added to the peculiar irony of the two deaths on the same day. Emily was beginning to doubt everything, especially with all the newfound mysteries surrounding her. After spending over thirty years of marriage with Lucas, she would have known if he had been a Mystic Guardian. With all those powers, he would have used them to get so many of his difficult jobs done in record time, making it a breeze to run his construction business. Or at least, she thought, it was what she would do.

"No, Lucas was not a Mystic Guardian. That I can tell you for certain," she said as she watched Meghan's face pinched with pain. She had witnessed that same look multiple times, and she knew right away what was wrong. "Are you having contractions?" Emily asked.

Meghan bent over and cried out in pain as Emily leaped towards her, gripping her arms and darting a look at Sylvia. "Get the boys. We need to get her into the bedroom."

The bedroom across from the basement entrance was under construction, but the room still held a bed with a small dresser and a shade on the window. Emily turned on the ceiling lights as Rick and Derek helped Meghan into the bed. Meghan's water had broken, and she was screaming in pain.

"You're going to be okay," Emily said in a soothing voice.

She nodded to Rick, mouthing the word "towels" as she took one from the dresser. Rick nodded back and ran out to get what Emily needed.

Derek stepped forward and held a protective position alongside Meghan. "Is she all right with not going to the hospital?" Derek asked with a look of uncertainty.

"Stay by her side and she'll do just fine," Emily assured him.

Sylvia seemed more in control than Derek and spoke in a calm voice. "Is there anything I can do?"

"Yes, Sylvia, you can hand me things as I need them."

Just then Rick entered the room with extra towels, rubber gloves, a big basin, and a large water pitcher. Emily slipped on the rubber gloves to see how dilated Meghan was. Meghan began to whimper, gripping Derek's arm as Emily examined her.

"About eight centimeters," Emily said, pulling the gloves off, throwing them into the wastepaper basket, and smiling at Meghan and Derek. "You have a little time, but it won't be long."

"Won't be long!" Meghan grumbled. "It feels like the baby is coming any minute."

Sylvia came to Meghan's side with her tranquil words and a cool cloth that she placed on her daughter's forehead. "Hush, now, honey," she said as though lulling Meghan to sleep. "Babies come when they're ready."

Emily smiled as she watched the tender moment between mother and daughter, turned to look at Rick and then lifted her chin towards the door.

Emily and Rick huddled quietly outside the bedroom door. "Well, what do you think?" Rick whispered. His unsettled gaze towards the front door seemed to question whether Meghan could make it to the hospital or not.

"She doesn't have enough time. Besides the EMTs won't make it through this storm fast enough."

Rick moved closer to Emily, gently running his hand down her cheek and touching her lips. He leaned in as their lips met, and she glanced into his comforting eyes.

"Well, sweetie, you're certainly no stranger to this are you?" he said.

"That's the truth," Emily agreed. She took Rick's hand and looked at him. "I love you so much."

"I love you more," Rick responded.

Their gazes stayed locked together. They gave each other reassuring nods, and then Emily entered the bedroom and closed the door behind her.

Chapter 4

INTO THIN AIR

RICK PACED BACK AND FORTH from the kitchen through the hallway and into the living room, stopping at the bedroom door and pressing his ear against it. He returned to the kitchen, fiddled with papers on the table, and thumbed through an old car magazine, looking for anything to distract him from the impending birth of his first grandchild. He lingered by the side of the refrigerator, looking at a calendar. He noticed the date: December 21.

"Hmm…guess my granddaughter will be born on the winter solstice," he said, considering what that meant. "Fewer hours of sunlight, the shortest day of the year," he concluded.

Just then, Rick felt tension creep into every muscle of his body when he realized the meaning of the winter solstice. "The darkest day," spilled out of his mouth at the same time he heard a cry from the newborn. Rick's first reaction was joy over the baby being born, but within seconds, that joy dissolved as he continued to stare at the calendar, as he felt the increasing tension. One thought nagged him: the passage in Lily Spencer's diary. He recalled the words: 'the cry from a new Witch could be heard on the darkest day in a new century, which would unbind the powers of the Spencer Witches." He felt his throat tighten as if he would choke at any moment.

"Holy shit! Does this mean what I think it means?" He blinked at the calendar questioning himself. "No, it can't be."

As soon as the words came out of Rick's mouth, a thundering sound shook the floor beneath him as the lights flickered and then went out completely. He grabbed a flashlight out of the kitchen drawer. He could still hear the baby crying and went to the door but heard no one else. When he opened the door, he saw several lit candles surrounding the bed where Meghan sat up, holding her baby. The glow of each tiny flame revealed a look of shock as its light flickered across the faces of Sylvia and Derek. Rick slowly walked toward Meghan and peered down at the little bundle as he tried to make sense of what he saw. It was a spell-binding scene that looked like some ancient ritual, and then he realized: Emily was not in the room. Rick felt the adrenaline shoot through his body as his heart was about to jump out of his chest. He came within inches of Sylvia and saw an unsettling shock in her eyes.

"Sylvia?" he said sternly and touched her arm with more than a gentle grip. "Where the hell is Emily?"

A short while later, Rick stood by the fireplace with its smoldering remains and stared at the hook where his hand once was. He was feeling defeated and afraid for Emily. Rick needed to be with her, knowing she was frightened by a voice that had haunted her for several months. He also knew she was sent back to break the curse caused by some disgruntled Witch. Rick didn't care what happened to him but cared a great deal about what happened to Emily. He never loved anyone as much as he loved her. This time, he would be part of the solution, not someone waiting around for his wife to come bouncing back from the past in shock and stricken with terror.

Rick felt a presence and looked over his shoulder. Derek stood by the living room entrance as though hesitant to walk in. "Is the baby okay?" Rick asked, half interested.

"Fine. Sylvia's tending to them."

Rick sat in the chair by the fireplace. "Got a name?"

Derek came over and sat in the chair next to his father. "Yeah, Melanie."

A slight grin came across Rick's face as he nodded in approval. "That's nice...beautiful name, son." He gave Derek a soft pat on the back, which abruptly turned into a firm grip on his shoulder. "What the hell happened in there?"

Derek looked at the floor as if avoiding his father's eyes, ran his fingers through his thick, dark hair, and released the breath he had apparently been holding.

"I don't know, Dad. One minute Emily was cleaning the baby and then handed her to Sylvia to bundle up. Sylvia laid the baby in Meghan's arms, and that's when we heard the thunder and the floor beginning to shake. Emily was still in the room when the lights went out."

Derek looked at his father, and Rick saw the bewilderment on his face. "Then what happened?" Rick asked.

"All of sudden these candles appeared out of nowhere surrounding the bed and lighting themselves and then…" Derek hesitated. "That's when I noticed Emily was no longer in the room."

Rick remained quiet. He pressed his lips together, bowed his head, and then lifted his eyes. "You know what this means don't you?"

Derek said nothing, still looking bewildered.

"It means your mother-in-law and your wife are now full-blown Witches—powers and all." Rick stood, looking towards the entranceway, paused momentarily, and then made a decision. "And your mother-in-law is going use those powers to send me back in time to find Emily."

"It's not quite that simple." Sylvia strolled in with her serious dark eyes and bleak expression.

"It's a pretty powerful spell for someone who's never used their powers before."

Rick walked up to Sylvia, speaking with as much determination as possible. "Don't you have a spell somewhere in that magic book of yours to send someone back in time? Because no matter what it takes, I'm going back to find Emily."

"You don't understand, Rick. There are consequences when using Witchcraft. You can end up in another place and possibly somewhere in time you hadn't expected or worse yet, something physical could happen to you."

"Physical? What do mean physical?" Rick asked.

"I mean you could be younger, older, sick or...dead," Sylvia said firmly.

"Then it's a chance I have to take."

"Are you crazy, Dad?" Derek yelled. "Do you know what you're saying? You can't do this. It's too risky."

Rick planted his feet firmly in a demanding posture with his arms crossed and gave Sylvia and Derek his clear intentions and resolve. He could see Sylvia soften as Derek slumped into the chair with a sound in his throat that offered a hit of disgust.

"Well, Sylvia?" Rick said with sheer determination in his voice.

Sylvia's arms hung loosely at her sides, apparently signaling her intention to give in to Rick's request. "All right, I'll do it, but I can't do it alone. The spell is going to take more powers than I have on my own."

"What does that mean?" Rick asked, annoyed.

Sylvia looked towards Derek. "I'm going to need Meghan."

Derek jumped up like a jackrabbit, ready to hit something, but his words were hard-hitting enough. "No! No! I don't want her involved in any of this. For God's sake, Dad, she just had a baby." Derek approached his dad, pointing a finger in his face. "And you're crazy for even considering putting not only your own life at risk but also my wife's."

Rick grabbed Derek's finger, pushing him back two steps. "What would you have me do, Derek?" Rick asked in a raised voice. "Huh? Tell me. What if it was Meghan out there somewhere in danger fighting some evil Witch who may have every intention of killing her. Huh! What do yah got to say, son?"

Rick let go of his son's finger, which caused Derek to stagger back. Rick walked to the entranceway and then turned, giving his son an unwavering and definitive declaration. "I told Emily once," Rick said, slowing his words. "I told her I would never leave her behind and that I would always protect her." Rick looked straight at Sylvia. "Get yourself and your daughter ready, because no matter what it takes, I'm not about to leave Emily behind."

Chapter 5

FAMILIAR FACES

Is it a dream? Emily thought without opening her eyes as she lay on what she thought was her own bed. She heard sounds from an old staticky radio. A man's silky-smooth voice sang "Green eyes, I love you." Is he speaking to me? she wondered as she opened her eyes in a familiar room surrounded by unfamiliar wallpaper and window drapes from another era—the same era as the orchestra that played on the radio. Emily had never heard the song before. Still, she recognized the vintage sound of the old radio. She sat up in the bed, and her eyes began to focus on what she recognized: her grandmother's old dresser and a full-length mirror in the corner of the room.

She didn't recognize the headless mannequin wearing a half-made dress with pins holding the seams together. She swung her legs to the side of the bed and realized she was wearing a dress similar to the one on the mannequin. With wobbly legs, Emily walked to the mirror and ran her hand over the dress's fabric. Emily could dimly remember her grandmother wearing one just like it yet wondered if it was an actual memory or a dream. Suddenly, another fuzzy memory came into focus: her grandmother at the candy store, placing penny candy in a tiny brown bag and handing it to her. She couldn't have been more than three or four years old at the time. Her mind slowly began to process her surroundings. Emily heard a voice coming from the same direction as the old staticky radio.

"Now, my dear," the pleasant voice said. "That dress fits just perfectly. Why, I have one just like it and have to say it looks much more flattering on you."

Emily slowly turned towards the woman and gasped: "Grandma?"

"Oh, my, you really did hit your head," she said, taking Emily's arm and escorting her to a vanity with a chair that faced a round mirror.

As Emily lowered herself into the small chair, she looked at the reflection of the woman standing behind her. She was slender with strands of strawberry blonde hair pinned up with two decorative bobby pins as the rest traveled down to her shoulders. She wore a white dress with black polka dots. When Emily turned to look up at her face, she noticed the same green eyes as her own staring back at her. But it wasn't until Emily smelled the floral fragrance of her perfume that all the confusion disappeared. It's my grandmother, Emily thought. She is so young and flawless and no more than twenty-five.

"How long have I been unconscious?" Emily asked as she looked into the mirror and rubbed the side of her temples, feeling the pressure of a slight headache coming on.

"My brother-in-law found you lying in the snow by the side of the house," the woman pointed in the general direction. "Good thing, too, that Billy went to the side of the house to clear the snow from the shed roof." She shook her head, making a clicking noise with her tongue. "I swear that shed would collapse with a single snowflake landing on it." The woman hesitated, reflecting sympathy in her eyes. She reached out her hand, turned her pink lips into a welcoming grin, and said: "I'm Grace Stanford."

It's settled, Emily thought: My twenty-five-year-old grandmother is formally greeting me. Emily still felt disorientated as she offered her hand. "I'm Emily. It's nice to meet you."

Grace's hand was warm. Emily wanted to hug her. She missed her grandmother or at least what she remembered of her grandmother. Grace Stanford died when Emily was fourteen, yet here she was. It seemed impossible, but time travel wasn't impossible for Emily. The one thing she knew for sure was why she'd been sent there: a curse that only she could break.

A few hours later, Emily sat at the kitchen table. Grace offered Emily a pleasant smile and a much-needed cup of coffee and excused herself saying she would be right back. While Grace was gone, Emily listened to a Duke Ellington song playing on a vintage Victrola. The needle scratched out a static sound of a song called "In a Sentimental Mood."

At the moment, Emily wasn't sure if she felt the same sentimental mood. She was missing Rick desperately and thought he must be going out of his mind with worry. The only thing that felt sentimental at the moment was being with her grandmother, even though this version of her was not the middle-aged woman she remembered.

Time travel can be confusing for sure, but Emily kept her wits about her and had to find out what happened to the Witch called Charlotte. She knew she needed to figure out how to save her grandfather, Thomas, and possibly others including her grandmother and maybe even her father.

Just then, Emily became aware of the possibility her father might be alive right now. She saw a calendar hanging on the back of the pantry door and went over to find out what year it was. Upon looking at the calendar, Emily felt the blood drain from her face. She covered her mouth to stifle the shock, knowing the significance of the month and year. It was a countdown-to-Christmas calendar. Grace had circled each day, something Emily dimly remembered her grandmother doing at Christmas time. It took her breath away when she saw the circles had stopped on Saturday, December 6, 1941.

"I can't believe it!" Emily said out loud. "It's the day before the bombing of Pearl Harbor."

Then she realized something else. Her father was, in fact, three years old at that very moment, causing her to scan the kitchen for any signs of a small child. In the corner was an oak highchair with a picture of a teddy bear painted on the back. She walked over and touched the wooden tray that held small amounts of crumbs left from a previous meal.

"Would you mind pulling the highchair over to the table?" Grace asked, startling Emily.

Emily turned around and found her grandmother holding her three-year-old son. Emily lingered by the child's chair awkwardly rubbing her arm nervously. Grace seemed to notice.

"Are you all right, dear?" she asked.

"Er...yes, ah...of course, sorry," Emily said feebly as she waved her hand, swatting the empty words away. She dragged the highchair to the table and watched Grace seat her son and then hand him a cracker she magically took out of her apron pocket.

"Now you be a good boy," Grace told her little boy while patting him on the head and then looked up at Emily. "This is little Matthew, named after his grandfather, a brave soldier in the Great War," she said, kissing Matthew on the top of his head.

Emily lowered herself slowly into the chair next to the child in amazement. She vaguely remembered her father, dying when she was ten. He was a young man of thirty when he was killed in Vietnam. The thought of seeing the three-year-old and knowing the child's fate pained her. Once again, she had to pull herself together, reminding herself of where she was.

"Mommy make me pancake," he said, blinking his eyes at Emily.

Emily leaned in as though she was going to whisper a secret. "They're my favorite too," she told him.

"There now, honey, you eat up all your pancakes like a good boy," Grace said, pouring syrup on the little boy's plate. She turned and held up the spatula, balancing two more pancakes before Emily.

"Yes, please. Thank you," Emily said, holding her plate up.

Emily watched her grandmother with interest as she maneuvered around the kitchen. The younger version of her grandmother possessed the same traits as the older version, such as swaying to music playing in the background as she hummed softly to herself, which was what she was doing at that moment. Emily looked towards the hallway and wondered if her grandfather, Thomas, would pop up around the corner at any moment.

"Is your husband around, or did he go to work already?" Emily asked in a casual voice.

"Oh, he's working all right," she said, sitting down and drowning her own pancakes in syrup.

"For Uncle Sam and stationed in the most beautiful location in the world, I might add."

Emily had known her grandfather had served in the Air Force but thought it wasn't until later in the war. "Where is he stationed?" Emily asked.

"Hawaii. Can you believe it? Right next to a naval base called Pearl Harbor."

Emily jumped to her feet. "WHAT!"

Grace looked baffled over Emily's outburst. "Oh, dear, Emily. Did I say something wrong?"

Before Emily could respond, the back door flew open with a man stomping the snow off his boots. He looked at Emily and gave a familiar smile. She was still confronting the fact that Thomas was about to encounter one of the most horrific attacks in history. She lowered herself in the chair, staring at another revelation she wasn't quite sure of—the man who just walked in looked a great deal like her late husband, Lucas Easton.

"Emily, I believe you already know Billy Easton, the man who found you on the side the house last night."

Emily felt numb. Her mind was trying to process something impossible. First Thomas, now Billy. Her mouth fell open, but nothing came out. She struggled to find words, but none came. It was Billy who spoke first.

"It's been a long time, Miss Emily," Billy said, walking up to her and squatting down to meet her eyes. "And if you don't mind me saying so, you don't look a day older than the last time I saw you."

Chapter 6

BACK IN THE MILITARY

The breeze blew something gently across Rick's face. He opened his eyes and found himself among stalks with long, grassy stems brushing across his forehead. He could hear the rumbling of an aircraft in the distance in one direction and waves crashing onto rocks in the other. He sat up, trying to make sense of where he was.

The last he remembered, Sylvia and Meghan had cast a time travel spell. Sylvia had called it Magick, a form of magic that taps into unseen energies. She told him the Magic River still possessed these energies that any Witch could harness.

Although Meghan was in no condition to get out of bed after giving birth, the modern technology of FaceTime brought her and Sylvia to the edge of the Magic River to perform the spell. Sylvia and Meghan created a portal next to the river where Rick had stood armed only with a pocketknife tucked in his back pocket. Rick wasn't about to go to an unknown place without some weapon.

As he stood waiting to be thrust back in time, he felt a suffocating feeling in his chest as they cast their spell, and within moments he was lying on his back looking into a sunny, blue sky.

He glanced down and found that he was wearing a government-issued military shirt. He ran his right hand across his chest, and his mouth fell open. He felt the fabric with the hand that had been missing for twenty years.

"What the--? Holy shit!" Rick stared at his restored right hand. He knew it had been blown off in Iraq, yet there it was, as if nothing had ever happened to it. Rick touched each finger in disbelief. "If this is the dreaded physical change Sylvia was talking about, you sure won't get any complaints out of me." Rick was mesmerized as he sat in the swaying, sword-shaped leaves of a sugarcane field. He made a fist, then opened it, trying to decide whether the hand was real. He reached into his back pocket, checking to see if his pocketknife had made the trip and found that it had.

As Rick looked around, trying to assess his surroundings, a B-17 bomber flew overhead, telling him within seconds that he was on a World War II military airfield. He got to his feet for a better look. Just beyond the leafy stalks and brush, Rick could see an army Jeep approaching with the backdrop of other B-17s getting ready to take off. A man was frantically waving his arms in a panic, shouting something, but Rick couldn't hear him until he was within a few feet.

"Hey! You!" the man yelled. "Are you crazy or something? You wanna get yourself killed?"

Rick stepped out of the tall grass and waved as the Jeep came to a screeching halt beside him. The man looked flushed, bug-eyed in disbelief as he leaned towards the passenger seat, trying to get a better look. "Hey, there, old flyboy, somebody clip your wings or something?"

"Something like that," Rick said dryly, looking down the runway toward the wings in question. He felt awkward, standing in the middle of an airfield with no excuse. "I...ah...can I have a lift back to...?" he asked, pointing toward a large set of buildings with no idea where he was.

The man was young, clearly Air Force maintenance from the badge on the upper shoulder of his overalls. He jerked his head towards the passenger seat. "Get in."

As soon as Rick sat down, the maintenance worker jolted the Jeep into gear and sped the vehicle down the runway, swerving into a pathway safe from the outbound planes taking off. Rick looked at the man's tight grip on the steering wheel, as he maneuvered the

Jeep in and out of the narrow path with precision. The narrow path ran alongside the turquoise blue ocean and led to several aircraft hangers. The Jeep finally stopped in front of an officers' quarters with two military police officers waiting by the door.

The driver faced Rick. "I believe headquarters might want to look you over." He leaned in with a smirk that looked so familiar that Rick could swear he was looking at his own reflection in a mirror. "They gotta make sure you're not cuckoo in the head," he said tapping the back of his hand on Rick's arm. "Can't have any crazies running around, if you get my meaning."

Rick nodded and then considered the man's familiar smirk. "What's your name, soldier?" Rick asked.

"They call me J.J. I just happened to be in the officers' quarters when a call came in that some lunatic with a head full of silver hair was detected near the airstrip." J.J. gave Rick a smug look. "So, I offered to retrieve the suspect."

"Well, J.J, sounds like you pulled off a mighty dangerous mission." Rick was about to get out of the Jeep when he glanced over at J.J., giving him his own smug expression "Maybe I'll see you around. That is, if they don't find me to be cuckoo, crazy or a lunatic."

The smirk on J.J.'s face grew wider, and he shifted his body in preparation for speeding off. Rick got out of the Jeep and watched as J.J. whizzed past other soldiers who jumped out of the way. Rick shook his head and then turned and stared at the two MPs. He gave them a wild-eyed look, put both hands up as if pretending to be surprised, and then said. "Okay. Okay. Take me to your leader."

The two soldiers led Rick through large double doors into a lobby filled with military personnel hustling around from one room to another. One of the MPs disappeared into the room ahead of them while the other stayed with Rick. Rick considered the man guarding him and thought: Should I ask where the hell I am? The MP looked to be just shy of his sixteenth birthday, which made it that much easier to ask the question without causing too much suspicion, Rick thought.

"Hey, there, buddy, can you tell me where I am?"

The soldier became rigid and looked at his watch to avoid eye contact with him. Suddenly, Rick caught a glimpse of something over the young MP's shoulder. In big letters on the bulletin board was a sign that read *Hickam Air Force Base, Honolulu, Hawaii.* Then Rick saw the date that horrified him the most: Saturday, December 6, 1941. "You gotta be shitting me."

Just then, the other MP came out of the room. "The officer and medic will see you now," the MP said, lifting his chin toward the room he had just left.

Rick slowly walked in, uncertain what would happen next. If his military background told him anything, he would face a long line of questions about whether he was a nut case or not. If not, they would at least make him clean the latrines for the next week and a half.

The room was all gray down to the chairs and desk with the head MP officer sitting behind it. The windows had no shades or curtains, with a clear view of a large hanger in the distance with men working on military aircraft. Behind the officer was a large, locked gun case with every kind of weapon of its time. The officer stood and gestured towards a chair for him to sit as the medic looked on suspiciously. Rick remained standing and offered a respectful salute.

"So, what do you have to say for yourself, soldier?" The man behind the desk was clearly waiting for an answer.

Rick shuffled his feet nervously and began to understand how Emily felt, trying to navigate through a time not her own. Rick looked into the officer's eyes with resolve.

"If I told you, you would never believe me," Rick said, stalling for time.

The officer narrowed his eyes. "That is an unacceptable answer, soldier," he said, sounding almost surprised that someone would talk to an officer like that. The officer sat down and leaned forward with his hands folded on his desk. "How about we start with your name," he said, pointing to the chair again, indicating for Rick to sit.

Rick sat down, and instead of answering the officer's question, he asked one of his own: "How about you tell me who you are first, sir." Rick knew that talking this way could get him at least a month of cleaning latrines or possibly land him in the brig.

"All right. We'll have it your way, as long as I get answers out of you. I'm Second Lieutenant Thomas Stanford in charge of the MPs and also in charge of keeping the rest of the men in line," he said sharply.

Rick's mouth drop opened. He sucked air in and held it for a second. "Thomas Stanford from Maple Ridge, Massachusetts?" Rick let out his breath as he felt shock waves go through him.

"Why do you ask? Are you from Maple Ridge?"Thomas asked.

Rick moved to the edge of his chair and gave the medic a sneering glance. "Get rid of him," he said, jerking his head in the medic's direction. "And I'll tell you who I am."

Thomas lifted his chin towards the door. "It's fine. I got this," he said as the seemingly disgruntled medic returned Rick's sneer and left the room. Thomas then stood with his arms crossed in front of his chest. "How old are you, soldier? You look old enough to be in a higher rank, and what the hell are you doing roaming around in the sugarcane field just inches from an active runway?"

"It's not important to know how old I am right now or why I was out by the runway," Rick said.

"Not important!" Thomas's face flushed with anger as he stepped toward Rick, holding up two fingers an inch apart. "You're about this close to being court martialed, and that's your answer?"

Rick stood, leaning over the desk in Thomas's direction, closing the gap between them. With a commanding look of determination, Rick asked. "Do you know a woman by the name of Emily Stanford?"

Thomas lowered his arms, taking two steps back. He blinked several times as if trying to come to grips with a name he clearly knew. Rick could sense Thomas's shock by his slumped shoulders. He was a man trying to process the information.

"Emily Stanford is my wife," Rick added as he put his hand out to shake Thomas's. "I'm Rick Miller, a retired United States Marine."

Thomas looked up and nodded slightly, offering a weak handshake as he tried but failed to respond.

"Sorry, buddy. I know it's a lot to take in, and how I got out on that landing strip is a long story. If you want to know how old I am, I'm older than you, or at least at the moment, but I'm young enough to fight if I have to," Rick pointed to the gun case behind Thomas, indicating he knew how to use them.

Rick returned to the chair, leaned back with his elbows on the arms, and casually folded his hands in front of him. "After your father and mother died, your grandfather Sam raised you. Then, when Sam died of the Spanish flu, Lily Spencer became your adopted mother. Lily also took in Billy Easton, whose father also died of the same flu minutes before your grandfather."

Thomas lowered himself to his chair. "I don't understand," Thomas said with a look of dismay.

"Emily's a time traveler. Are you also one? And why are you here?"

"So, you do know Emily?" Rick asked.

"Yes, my grandfather told me about her. Mostly on the morning of the day he died. I remembered her when I was sick with that God-awful flu. She was kind." Thomas showed a hint of a smile as the memory flashed across his face and then glanced at Rick. "She was also beautiful, and I know enough to know—she's my granddaughter, or she will be in the future," Thomas admitted.

Rick took a deep breath. Just the thought of Emily gave him a sensation of desire for her. He knew he had to erase that thought from his mind for now and concentrate on *The Twilight Zone* he found himself in. He sat on the edge of his seat, giving Thomas a friendly grin.

"Like I said, it's a long story. So, ah, you got a chow hall around here? Because I'm starving."

Rick downed a juicy hamburger with all the fixings and guzzled a cold glass of milk, plopping the glass on the table. As Rick looked around, he felt he was back in the military. The mess hall was bustling, but Rick knew all military mess halls were busy feeding hundreds of military personnel at any given time during the day.

It was a brand-new facility larger than a football field. The gigantic hall was staffed with at least fifty food handlers, serving all kinds of food from beef, chicken, and seafood to potatoes, salad, and vegetables. A dessert line served assorted cakes, cookies, and ice cream in every imaginable flavor.

Thomas sat across from him, slurping chicken soup, and Rick could see he was looking a little dismayed over discovering a person from the future. "So, ah, you gonna turn me in and make me do KP duty until I get snatched back to my own time?" Rick joked.

Thomas put his soup spoon down, seemingly unamused and leaned his elbows on the table. "You still didn't tell me why you're here."

"I don't know, Thomas, maybe you can tell me."

"What do you mean? What would I know?"

"How about we start with a girl named Charlotte Spencer. Do you know her?"

Thomas's face had a look of suspicion. "Yes, she's my stepmother's granddaughter. Why?"

Rick leaned in and spoke in a low voice so the two soldiers sitting beside them couldn't hear. "Apparently—and I'll use one of today's expressions: She's got some beef with you."

Thomas's gaze shifted to the men at the table. Thomas nodded a friendly hello at them with a forced smile and then looked at Rick. "Come on. I know a better place where we can talk."

Rick and Thomas made their way in a Jeep, passing red-roofed houses with palm trees shading the front of each home. Each house was landscaped with tropical flowers of all colors. Thomas pulled into the driveway, jumped out of the Jeep, and stood with his hands on his hips. "What do you think, Miller, mighty nifty or what," he said proudly.

"How in world did you get to stay in a place like this?" Rick asked.

"The plan was to bring my wife, Grace, and our little boy, Matthew, here for a nice vacation for my final two weeks before my tour of duty is up. Grace thought it would be better for her to stay home with our son seeing it was so close to Christmas." Thomas leaned toward Rick with a crooked smile. "Grace would never admit it, but I think she's afraid of flying. Besides, I'll be home in time for Christmas anyway."

Rick was well aware of the significance of that decision. He was glad Thomas's wife had made that choice because death and destruction would rain down from the sky everywhere in Pearl Harbor within twenty-four hours. He tried to push the unsettling thought deep within the back of his mind along with why he ended up in Pearl Harbor at this exact moment in time.

Thomas motioned to Rick. "Come on in and have a beer," Thomas offered.

Rick followed Thomas through the front door. "I'm afraid beer and I don't get along so well theses days. Soda, juice, or water would be fine if you got it," Rick said, remembering his vow never to take a drink again. Booze had almost destroyed him after he was wounded in Iraq.

The house was pleasant, although the place felt empty. Rick didn't see any family pictures or mementos displayed anywhere. He spotted a large gun case in the corner of the room that was stocked with weapons. Rick peered through the glass, noticing several hand grenades.

Thomas smiled and then chuckled, obviously noticing Rick's reaction. "Don't worry. They're not live. Just for display."

"These guns all yours?" Rick asked.

"They belong to the officer who usually stays here. He's a pal of mine. His rank is slightly higher than mine which afforded him these accommodations. We went to boot camp together. Turns out he lives only three hours west of Maple Ridge in a sleepy little town called Hoosick Falls. Normally I stay in the main barracks with all the other guys. This is just a two-week deal, I'm afraid." Thomas tilted his head to the side. "What kind of weapons do future soldiers fight with?" he asked.

"Let me see," Rick said. "We have so many. There's a wide variety of machine guns, many with a long firing range. There are the semiautomatic snipers, but some are being phased out. Then there's the M203 launcher, a secondary weapon attached to the M4. The 203 launches—" Rick glanced at the grenade in the gun case. "Well, let's just say, you don't have to shoot your gun while trying to throw one of those at your target anymore." Rick watched Thomas's face light up when hearing about the future innovation in weaponry.

"Guess I'll never be around to see that," Thomas said while walking to the icebox, taking out two bottles with the word *Beer* on the label. He grabbed a bottle opener from one of the kitchen drawers, flipped open the tops, and handed one to Rick with a mischievous grin. "Don't worry: It's beer all right—root beer."

Rick and Thomas sat at the kitchen table by a window, watching men from various branches of the service come and go. Rick was still reeling from the realization of being in the place where World War II began. He could think only about the famous words that had gone down in history: "a date which will live in infamy."

Rick regarded Thomas's role in all this. Emily had never spoken of her grandfather being in Pearl Harbor. She must not have known, Rick thought. Otherwise, she would have mentioned him in her article. Rick could tell Thomas was mulling over something because he kept rubbing his chin as he looked out the window. Finally, Thomas nodded slightly and then landed his gaze on Rick.

"Charlotte was sweet on me," Thomas said, taking another sip of his root beer. "I wasn't interested. My heart was set on another girl, and we had an intense romance. She was young, beautiful. I loved her, wanted her in every way. I thought she loved me too."

Thomas shook his head. "Then one day, she was gone and without a single word. She had lived with her mother. Her father died before she was born. When she left town with her mother, I tried finding her, but she had just disappeared." Thomas reached into his back pocket and pulled out his wallet, showing Rick a black-and-white picture of a beautiful woman.

"She's pretty. Is that her?" Rick asked.

Thomas looked adoringly at the picture. "No, it's my wife, Grace. I had put that first love affair behind me, and soon after, I met Grace. We fell in love almost immediately." Thomas took a deep breath, closing his eyes as if savoring the thought of his beautiful wife. "Of course," he said, opening his eyes to look at the picture again. "You can't see it in the picture, but she has the most beautiful red hair."

Rick felt his heart flutter at the mention of red hair. He missed Emily with each passing moment and was uncertain where she was. He hoped she had ended up in Maple Ridge in 1941.

Rick pointed to the picture. "Emily has her grandmother's red hair. I guess we both miss our wives," Rick said, taking a long gulp of his root beer, setting the bottle on the table, and giving Thomas a serious look. "So, not to change the subject, but what happened to Charlotte?"

"She disappeared too."

"So, what you're telling me is, Charlotte disappeared around the same time this first girl left town?" Rick asked.

"Why? Do you think there's something to it?" Thomas asked.

"Maybe, but whatever it is, it's beginning to sound like Charlotte might have been a woman scorned and had a mind to put a death curse on you. Hopefully, it's just on you and not on anyone else."

"Death curse?" Thomas hesitated as he glanced back at his wife's photo. "This can't be good," he said in a voice so low Rick could hardly hear him. Rick could sense by Thomas's demeanor that he knew about the existence of a death curse.

Then Thomas looked up at Rick with certainty in his eyes and a stronger tone to his voice. "In that case, I'm sure glad Billy is back home with Grace. I trust him with my life and my family's lives. He'll look after them until I get back home," Thomas said with confidence and then added. "Besides, I doubt we should worry too much about Charlotte. She's been missing for more than a few years now."

Rick nodded slowly while sorting out in his mind the situation at hand and then added: "The question is, where did Charlotte disappear to?"

Chapter 7

THE BEGGAR BOY

Emily leaned against the cherry tree in her grandmother's yard as cold drops of water dripped from a branch onto her coat, spraying tiny ice crystals across her cheeks. Mist floated near the surface of the waters of the Magic River, reminding her of how the first deadly curse had held its grip on this time and place.

Emily took a deep breath as she tried to come to terms with one of history's most tragic attacks coming in a few short hours. "I'm not going to be able to help Thomas," she said to the river. "Why am I here then?" Emily's conflicting thoughts darted back and forth in her mind. Having knowledge of the future could be a curse in and of itself.

Emily stared into the river's misty waters when a haunting whisper of a man's voice drifted beyond the river. She recognized the voice as the same one she had heard back in her own time. Emily stayed calm and strained her ears to listen carefully to the faint sound of someone calling her name.

She wondered if it could be her imagination. Sylvia had told her about Lily and Kathleen's mysterious deaths in the swamp. Could the voice she heard have anything to do with that mystery? The trees swayed in the wind, carrying the haunting voice as it repeatedly said her name. Emily put her hands over her ears. "No, please leave me alone, whoever you are," she said to the drifting breeze. Then, another sound came from the house. It was one object hitting another.

Emily followed the sound that came from the side of the house. As she came around the corner, she saw Billy hitting ice off the gutter as he mumbled obscenities under his breath at the stubborn frozen water that seemed to be clogging the drain. She walked to the ladder and looked up, catching Billy off guard, causing the hammer to suddenly slip from his hand and tumble straight for Emily's head. She tried to jump out of the way and saw Billy's hand reach out as he yelled "STOP!" commanding the hammer to halt, change direction, and float gently into the snow beside her feet.

Emily's gaze traveled up the ladder, and she saw the dumbstruck look on Billy's face. She was sure it was the same expression on her own face. Billy seemed nervous, clearing his throat as if stalling for a sensible answer to what she had just witnessed.

"Are you all right, Miss Emily?" he finally asked, descending the ladder.

Emily met his eyes. "What in the world was that all about?"

Billy bent down, picked up the hammer, and tucked it back into his tool belt as he raised one eyebrow at Emily. "I'm surprised my stepmother, Lily, didn't go further in her writings about men like me."

"Men like you? Billy, you just made that hammer stop in midair. What's going on?"

Billy looked up at the ladder and paused. Emily could tell he was withholding something.

"Billy? It's okay...after all, I'm trusting you with my secret," she reminded him.

"Well, ah...I, ah, I'm a Mystic Guardian," he forcefully admitted.

It all came rushing in. The last entry ever written in Lily Spencer's diary. An entry Kathleen wrote: *"I fear our powers are lost, and until the time traveler comes, I must leave my child in the care of the Mystic Guardian."*

Emily backed away. It was all coming true. She felt danger, worried that Charlotte's curse would somehow kill her, too. She pictured herself lying in the swamp, dead, just like the two Spencer Witches. It wasn't until Billy took a step forward and touched her arm that she felt warm and had a sense of calm as if Billy was some sort of a refuge.

"You don't need to be afraid of me," he said. "I have the power to protect. I can give you that protection."

Emily could easily surrender her fears to Billy, yet she still had questions. "Does Grace know?"

"No, Thomas and I thought keeping the secret between us would be best. Thomas didn't want Grace to have such burdensome knowledge."

"If Grace doesn't know anything at all then what did she say when you found me in the snow? She must have looked for some kind of explanation?" Emily asked.

"I just told her you're an old friend of Thomas's grandfather." Billy had a less than convincing tone.

"And she believed you?" Emily said with suspicion. "Sorry but, if it were me, it would sound like a lame excuse. I know I'd be wondering why a mysterious woman showed up, passed out in the snow outside my window on a cold, snowy night."

Billy looked at the ladder again and then back at Emily. "I suppose it was better than the truth for now."

Emily knew that Billy and Thomas were right in keeping all of this from Grace. Sometimes she wished the same for herself, but Emily was already up to her neck in the strange world thrust upon her—the time traveler who had the power to right the wrongs of Witches. But there was one more question on Emily's mind, a question that would solve another mystery not only for her but for Sylvia and Meghan as well. Emily gave Billy a firm look. "What happened to Beth?"

Before Billy could answer, a rustling noise came from the back porch with the screen door opening and shutting. Emily and Billy looked simultaneously and saw Grace come around the corner of the house, stepping through the fresh snow.

"Ah, there you are, Emily," Grace said. "I was wondering if you could do me a favor, which I hope won't be too much to ask."

"Of course. "What is it, Grace?"

"I fear I ran out of a few things I need for dinner tonight. Could you go into town to the grocer's shop and pick them up for me? I already phoned in an order and don't worry about the bill; the grocer will put it on the family account." Grace moved closer as she regarded Emily with her sympathetic green eyes and then gave her an awkward pat on arm. "I also noticed that you showed up here with nothing but the clothes on your back but don't worry," Grace assured her. "I can lend you one of my pocketbooks and with extra money just in case you need it."

Emily was immediately grateful that Grace had interceded before she had to come up with an explanation for her lack of personal possessions. "That's very kind of you, Grace."

Emily glanced at Billy. "I guess we can talk later." She turned towards Grace. "Just point me in the direction of your car."

Relief came over Grace's face, clearly glad someone would help her. Emily was about to head to the garage Grace had pointed out when Grace addressed Billy. "Be sure Beth has her special baby doll with her later. That poor child cried her eyes out when she forgot it last Saturday."

Emily looked in Billy's direction. He ran his hand across the back of his neck as he cleared his throat. "Yeah...um—Beth?" Billy said, pointing to his left as if the little girl would pop out from the other side of the house at any moment. "She's my niece and now my daughter, who is under my protection."

Emily drove down Main Street, fascinated by the sights and sounds. The engine of Grace and Thomas's 1940 Oldsmobile sedan was just as loud as all the other huge cars chugging down the road. As she gripped the bigger-than-usual steering wheel, she thought of Rick and his love of classic cars. "If Rick were here right now, he would be out of his mind with nostalgic bliss," she chuckled.

As she drove along the central thoroughfare, she noticed that most men wore heavy overalls and rain jackets with fur collars. Other men wore suits and fedora hats that matched their suits.

The women, with meticulously groomed hair, wore floral dresses under wool coats. Some women wore fancy hats adorned with colorful ribbons and little flowers. Emily could tell they were women of means by the fur coats and the hats with veils that partially covered their faces. She vaguely remembered her grandmother getting all decked out in her best. Shopping on Saturday and attending church on Sunday brought out the best attire in the old days. Well, these are definitely the good old days, Emily thought. It was a time of innocence—an innocence that will soon be shattered, and America will shift into a fighting mode.

Emily pulled in front of the grocer's shop and into one of the only remaining parking spots. Next to the grocer's shop was Owen's Drug Store. In her own time, it was still Owen's, but the original family had sold it.

In 1941, it was a drug store and also a diner. In front, Emily noticed a big sign advertising the Maple Ridge High School band playing that night. According to the schedule, different musical bands and singers performed every Saturday night. Then, she noticed a little boy standing by the sign with a can in his hand with only the occasional passerby tossing coins into his can. The child's clothes were dirty and so was his little face. She couldn't help but feel sorry for the little guy and thought it was a pity the child stood in the cold begging for money. Emily got out of the car and slowly approached the boy.

"Hello, little one," Emily said, squatting down to the child's level. "What brings you out on such a cold day?" The boy said nothing. Emily glanced up the street. "Where is your mommy?"

The beggar boy blinked his eyes through his disheveled brown hair that hung over his forehead. Emily sensed his hesitation. By the way people hustled past him, she figured not many of them paid much attention to him.

"It's okay, honey. I won't hurt you. I'm just worried." She noticed his ungloved hands clinging to the cold can. "Your hands look so red. You wouldn't want to get frostbite now, would you?"

The child shook his head timidly, still not speaking.

Emily reached into the pocketbook Grace had given her and pulled out a shiny dime, dropping it into the can. "If you would like, I can buy you some lunch." Emily pointed at the big store window, showing all the patrons inside sitting at the lunch bar. "A juicy hamburger...or how about a hot dog with French fries? How's that sound?"

The little boy placed his hand over his belly. "I'm hungry. My tummy keeps making noises."

"Well, then, it's settled. How about we go in and get rid of those pesky old noises?" Emily stood and offered her hand, and he reached up to hold hers.

Emily held his ice-cold hand, leading him into Owen's. She lifted him onto an empty stool next to a small vent with warm air flowing out. As they waited to order lunch, the waitress placed a large mug of cocoa in front of the child and gave him a friendly wink. "On the house," the waitress said. Emily offered a nod of appreciation and placed their order.

Emily looked over and watched the boy sip his cocoa. She noticed that he appeared to be in much better spirits. "My name is Emily. What's yours?"

"Walter," he said, wrapping his hands around the warm mug while slurping the cocoa.

She felt a spike of adrenaline shoot straight through her. She had cared for and loved a man named Walter in her own time.

"I used to know someone by the name of Walter. He was very special to me. He was like a father to me." She watched Walter finish his cocoa and then asked him the next obvious question. How about you? Do you have a Dad?"

"No, don't got no Ma neither. Just Grammy and she's real sick." Walter stared at all the sweets in the glass case behind the lunch bar.

"What's wrong with your Grammy?"

Walter shrugged his shoulders, saying nothing as he continued to look at the glass case.

"Well, Walter, maybe we can bring some of those back to your Grammy," Emily said, lifting her chin towards the assorted cakes and cookies Walter had been staring at. "Maybe I can help her. Do you know that I'm a nurse?"

Walter finally gazed at Emily with tears forming in his eyes. "My Grammy is going to die. Can you make it stop?"

"I'll see what I can do, honey," Emily said as the waitress placed a plate in front of Walter. The plate held a giant hot dog topped off with all the fixings and a big mound of French fries. Walter's face lit up, and he licked his lips in delight.

"Wow, that sure looks yummy," Emily said, giving Walter a little nudge on his arm. "You eat up now, and then we'll see what we can do for your Grammy."

After Walter finished his lunch, Emily walked down the busy street holding Walter's hand when, out of the corner of her eye, she caught a glimpse of an older woman standing by the Shady Brook Bridge. Wearing a buckskin shawl and with her hair braided to her shoulders, the woman stood out among all the other pedestrians. Walter pulled on Emily's hand, distracting her for a second, and when she looked back, the woman was gone—more strange things, Emily thought and then dismissed it.

Walter led her into a run-down apartment building and up two flights of stairs. One single light dangled on the ceiling of the stairway, giving off a dim glow that barely cast enough light to see the dingy wallpaper streaked with water stains. Emily remembered the town had taken the building down when she was a child. It was rumored to be a house of prostitution at one time, and the building desperately needed repair when the townspeople finally voted to demolish it. Although she saw no signs of any ladies of ill repute, she could see the deterioration of the building had already started.

"This way," Walter said, opening the door to a small apartment with a living room, kitchen, and one bedroom, into which Walter disappeared.

Emily looked around and could smell stale food and then immediately found the source of the odor in a sink full of soiled dishes. She opened the ice box and found the shelves mostly empty, except for a half-eaten sandwich and a glass milk bottle. She opened the top of the bottle and wrinkled her nose from the sour milk when Walter suddenly appeared behind her.

"My Grammy wants to talk to you."

Emily placed the bottle in the sink with the dirty dishes and decided she would clean up the mess before leaving.

Upon entering the bedroom, Emily immediately recognized the woman lying in bed. The woman had given birth during the 1918 Spanish flu pandemic. Emily had helped her through the pain of childbirth and then soon after helped her through the pain of losing her husband from the terrible virus.

"Lucy?" Emily said with a mixture of happiness and sorrow at the sight of her condition.

"Oh, my Lord, have mercy...is that really you—Emily? Why, I haven't seen you in…what, twenty-three years now," Lucy said.

Emily sat beside Lucy and felt the small veins beneath the skin of her withering cold hand. Lucy's face showed signs of malnutrition. Emily wondered if it was from a lack of food or the illness Walter had mentioned.

"Lucy, it's so good to see you," Emily looked at Walter and smiled. "I found a new friend who tells me you're sick."

Lucy waved her bony hand for Walter to come to her side. She gave her grandson a loving hug. "You go play, my darling, and let Emily and me talk a bit."

"Emily's a nurse," Walter chirped. "She'll make you all better, Grammy."

"I'm sure with Emily just being here, it will cheer me up and make me feel much better, darling. Now, you be a good boy and go play."

Walter skipped happily from the room as Lucy took a deep breath and heaved a weary glance towards the door. "I fear I can no longer take care of him."

"Lucy? What do you have? Why are you sick?"

"I'm afraid it's the last stages of leukemia."

Emily wondered what that meant in 1941. Surely, they would have had some chemotherapy. By Lucy's appearance, it didn't seem to matter now. Whatever treatments Lucy may have had, it was too late. Her skin was gray, and her cheeks were sunken in. It was clear to Emily that Lucy was dying.

"What can I do to help?" Emily asked.

Lucy's hand tightened over Emily's as she reached for her ruffled hanky with the other and wiped the tears from her eyes. "You might not know this, but my precious Laura is dead. She died giving birth to Walter."

Emily couldn't let on that she knew this information. Ironically, it was eighty-six-year-old Walter who had given her that information when he lived in the Maple Ridge nursing home.

"I'm so sorry, Lucy. So, you've been caring for Walter ever since?"

"Oh, yes, and gratefully so. I love that boy more than life itself." Lucy tried sitting up, and Emily helped to lift her into a more upright position. She straightened the blanket to make Lucy comfortable, and Lucy gripped Emily's arm. "That's why I came back into town," Lucy said with conviction in her voice. "I think it's time for Walter to know his real father."

"Who is the father? If you don't mind my asking."

Lucy patted Emily's hand. "A very kind man and a very married man, I'm afraid. I worry the news of Walter's existence may drive a wedge between him and his wife. From what I understand, she's a lovely woman."

"So, this man doesn't even know Walter's his son?"

"No, he doesn't know." Lucy waved the problem away as she seemed exhausted suddenly. "For now, we need not speak of it."

Lucy's head drooped slightly, and she lifted it again as if fighting to stay awake. Emily decided to be respectful and stayed quiet to allow Lucy to gain more strength to speak again. Emily felt she needed to make things better for Lucy and Walter and could think of only one way to help.

"Lucy?" she finally said, caressing Lucy's arm. "I think I have an idea. I just need to make one phone call first—then I'll be back.

Chapter 8

HICKAM FIELD

RICK WALKED AMONG THE OPEN SPACES of several hangers, each bigger than the next, and was amazed by the vast number of them. Railroad tracks ran alongside the hangers, leading into Honolulu about nine miles away. Far enough away, Rick thought, from the devastating blow on Hickam Field tomorrow morning. He calculated it might be safer in Honolulu than where he stood with Thomas as they watched a plane take off into the deep blue sky.

"Come on," Thomas said. "I'll show you where the enlisted men's accommodations are and the many ways they keep busy during their off-duty time."

He showed Rick the barracks. Next to that was a recreation hall where Rick saw a game room, a large bar, and a formal dining room with a small stage for bands and other entertainment. As Rick and Thomas came out of the facility, Rick saw a Jeep approaching at a high rate of speed, heading straight for them.

"Jesus," Thomas yelled as he and Rick jumped out of the way. "I swear I'm going to wring his neck. I don't know how many times I've told J.J. to slow down."

As J.J. came to a dead stop in front of them, Rick saw he was the same guy who rescued him from the runway.

"Hey there, old flyboy. Did Lieutenant Stanford find you to be crazy yet?" J.J. said, glancing at Thomas and smirking.

"Nah," Rick said, patting Thomas on the shoulder. "I was just saying to Lieutenant Stanford here that he ought-a give you a speeding ticket. That way, I wouldn't have to be alone cleaning all the latrines."

"Oh, a smart ass. Well—"

"Stop it, you two," Thomas interrupted as he walked to the Jeep. Rick saw the dirty look he gave J.J. "What the hell is the big rush, J.J.?"

"I'm late for duty, so ah...thought I'd stop and see if you're going into Honolulu later. What-a you say?" J.J.'s eyebrows wiggled up and down, and his face showed a mischievous grin. "Saturday night… lots of pretty girls, and I know you said you're off duty tonight." J.J. gave Rick another devilish look. "Maybe this old man could come with us. That is if he can keep up with us, if you know what I mean."

Rick approached the Jeep, narrowing his eyes as his blood pressure rose. The guy was a punk, a wise-ass, and had way too much confidence for his own good. "Listen, you little bastard. I could outrun, outjump, outgun, and outwit you long before you were the spit in your old man's mouth. So, if you wanna give it a go with me, you would do well to think twice, unless you don't mind getting your ass kicked."

Thomas put his arm in front of Rick. "All right, all right— enough. J.J., get to work, and Rick, we have more to talk about."

"Suit yourself there, Tommy boy and mister whoever you are because I'll be at the Black Cat Café, bellying up to the bar and getting my picture taken with a couple of hula girls." J.J. wiggled his eyebrows up and down again. With another mischievous gleam in his eyes, he put his hand up to his forehead with a salute, and then he sped off towards one of the hangers.

"Who the hell is that guy?" Rick asked.

"He's my best friend from Maple Ridge. I suppose that's why I put up with his shenanigans," Thomas said. Suddenly he gave Rick a strange look.

"What is it, Thomas?"

"You don't happen to be related to J.J.—are you?"

"Why would you say that?"

"Because he has the same last name—Miller? His name is Joseph John Miller."

Rick's heart pounded, and he felt the blood pulsing in his ears. He jerked his head towards the hanger where the Jeep darted through the giant entrance. "Holy shit!" He shifted his eyes toward Thomas. "That wise-ass—is my grandfather."

A couple of hours later, Rick and Thomas hopped into one of the MP vehicles heading towards Pearl Harbor. Thomas wanted to show Rick around the harbor located west of Honolulu.

The experience was surreal to Rick. Every ship was anchored peacefully in the harbor's waters. One particular battleship caught his eye. Rick sighed, gazing at the ship's mainmast with its large American flag waving leisurely in the ocean breezes: the soon-to-be-famous *USS Arizona*. A watery tomb by this time tomorrow. It sickened him to think that so many sailors would die within a few short hours. He felt the horrible burden of what was to come. He turned his head, taking his eyes off the magnificent ship and looked at Thomas who seemed to read his face.

"You okay there, Rick?"

"Yeah, I'm okay. Let's just get out of here."

Thomas nodded with concern. Rick could see by the look on his face that he suspected something, yet Thomas said nothing.

When they returned to Hickam Field, Thomas suggested taking a bus to Honolulu instead of driving through the busy streets where most of the Saturday night action took place. Rick felt slightly relieved that his grandfather would be in town instead of at Hickam Field. He formed a plan in his mind that, at all costs, he would keep Thomas and his grandfather away from the airfield.

Was he messing with time and history? Rick wondered. He knew J.J. was supposed to die at Pearl Harbor, specifically at Hickam Field. Did he have the power to stop that from happening? Rick knew he couldn't stop the bombing, and even if he tried, who in God's name would believe him? They would surely put him in the brig for being crazy. Rick felt he could at least save his grandfather, whatever that would mean, and hopefully, it wouldn't cause some cosmic force to go awry. He would have to worry about that later. For now, getting them to stay overnight in Honolulu was his top priority.

Honolulu was hopping with lively sailors and beautiful women. Rick thought it had the same atmosphere as the old Atlantic City without the boardwalk. There were various concession stands with every kind of food from hot dogs to seafood. One place served up steak and mushrooms costing only a dollar. Thomas suggested getting one of Honolulu's best hot pork sandwiches. Rick looked at the price of the sandwich and stifled a laugh.

"What's so funny?" Thomas asked.

"Twenty-five cents," Rick said, leaning toward Thomas and whispering. "In the future, you'll pay up to six bucks for the same sandwich."

"What! That's highway robbery," Thomas huffed.

"Yeah, well, so is a lot of stuff in my time."

They sat at a picnic table, chowing down their pork sandwiches. Rick was fascinated by all the people walking by all decked out in their best. It was an innocent time, at least for the next few hours. He almost felt sorry for them and wondered how many enlisted guys walking past would be dead within the next four years of war. He thought of his own time in the military, glad he had no idea what was to come. It was better that way, better for Thomas and his grandfather, too. *I just need to keep them away from the danger and safe somewhere,* he thought. But how? He had to figure a way.

Rick finished his sandwich and guzzled down the rest of his soda pop when he saw Thomas giving him a curious stare while tapping a finger on the tabletop.

"What?" Rick said.

"Charlotte? What's the deal with this death curse?" Thomas asked.

Rick leaned forward, resting his arms on the picnic table. "Did you know your stepmother, Lily Spencer, kept a diary?"

"Sure, it was what she used to write her book. Why?"

"Emily and I read Lily's last entry. It was about her ancestor Rebecca who had put a spell on her own descendants over two hundred fifty years ago. Rebecca stated that if one of the Spencer Witches were to cast a death curse on anyone, the Witches would lose all their powers. Lily had a premonition that Charlotte cast this horrible curse on you."

"Me? But why?" The muscles in Thomas's face tightened as though weighing the information in his mind. "So, wait a second. What you're saying is that Charlotte put this curse on me and now all the Spencer Witches lost their powers?"

"Yup," Rick said.

Thomas rubbed the back of his neck. "The last time I saw that diary was when I was a kid. Can't say I ever saw that entry. Although I have to admit, I had little interest in reading it to begin with." A look of concern remained on Thomas's face. "You think Charlotte was jealous of this other girl, or maybe jealous I got married, and set out to get both Grace and me?"

"I don't know but it makes sense," Rick ran his fingers through his hair, reluctant to talk about the danger Thomas's wife and son could be in. "There's something else, and I know it's a long shot, but I think Emily time-traveled to1941. She disappeared when our granddaughter was born. Rebecca also said that when the cry from a new Witch could be heard on the darkest day in a new century, the spell will be broken, and the Spencer Witches would get their powers back. Thomas, my son married a Spencer Witch who gave birth to our granddaughter on the winter solstice."

Thomas's stared at Rick and nodded slowly. "The darkest day."

"That's right, and to make a long story short: It was my daughter-in-law and her mother, both of whom are Spencer Witches, who sent me back in time to be with Emily. I think she may very well be at your house right now. And if that's true, well, Emily is the only one who can break the curse, at least that's what Lily wrote in her diary."

The lines on Thomas's forehead deepened. "I've always tried to keep my family from all this supernatural stuff. I let Billy deal with it, especially after all the strange occurrences from the past. Billy being back home does give me some reassurance. He is the protector after all."

Somehow the word "protector" jumped out at Rick. "Protector? What does that mean?"

"You're saying you didn't know?" Thomas asked.

Rick shook his head.

"Billy is what's called a Mystic Guardian. He has more powers than Witches, and Mystic Guardians are known in the magical world as protectors."

"Wow! I never heard that one. Is he like a Warlock?"

"No. Warlocks are considered evil," Thomas leaned in with a slight grin. "Mystic Guardians are like…well, they're kind of like Glinda, the Good Witch of the North."

"Then I'm glad Billy's there to protect your family," Rick said.

But if what you're saying is true about Emily being in Maple Ridge, isn't she also in danger?" Thomas looked concerned.

"Yes, and somehow I gotta get to her."

"Billy's there to protect my family and Emily, as well. I'll have to send word and let Billy know what I've learned about Charlotte." Thomas's attention was drawn to a scuffle that broke out across the street by the Black Cat Cafe. Rick squinted his eye, focusing on a sailor getting his collar pulled by another man who clearly had too much to drink. It only took a second for him to realize who the drunk was.

"J.J.? What the hell!" Rick said.

Thomas jumped to his feet as he saw the exchange between the two men. "Now, I'm really going to wring his neck."

Rick and Thomas crossed the street to break up the fight. Rick grabbed J.J.'s arm, leading him to the front of a candy store next door to the Black Cat Cafe, where fewer people were around. "What the hell's going on, J.J.?" Rick yelled.

J.J. jerked his arm away from Rick as he made an attempt to talk without slurring his words. "Ah, don't be a killjoy. I'm just having a little fun with the hula girls, and that drunken sailor had to put his nose in my business, is all."

Rick grabbed J.J.'s arm again. "Don't you have a wife at home? I happen to know she's a good woman, and you want to dishonor her this way? What the hell is wrong with you?"

"All right, all right, yeah, I got myself a beautiful wife, Mr. Know It All," J.J. muttered while staggering and then caught himself from falling. "Whom, by the way there, pal," J.J. pushed his finger into Rick's chest and swayed to one side. "I haven't seen that beauty in almost a year. She probably doesn't even remember what I look like, maybe even got herself a new fella by now."

Rick looked over at Thomas, who nodded as if feeling sorry for his friend. Not Rick. He wasn't having it. He didn't like the tone of disrespect in J.J.'s voice. He felt the surge of anger shoot through his body and wanted, in the worst way, to punch him in the face. Instead, Rick pushed J.J. against the brick storefront.

"You know what, you little shit? I used to be just like you. Cocky, a man around town, getting any girl, drinking up a storm, and not giving one shit about my family. I was you until I got wounded in a fucking war! I couldn't get past myself. Just kept drinking until my wife and son wanted no part of me. It wasn't just a year for me. I spent twenty years alone." Rick released his grip on J.J. and took a step back. "So, tell me, J.J. Is that gonna be you?"

J.J. leaned forward, putting his hand on Rick's chest to hold himself up from falling over. Rick could see he had turned a sick shade of green.

"No need to get so sore there, old flyboy," J.J. mumbled. Suddenly, he lurched his head forward and threw up, just missing Rick's boots.

Rick reached under J.J.'s arm as Thomas took the other. "Come on. I know a place where he can sleep it off," Thomas said as they led J.J. across the street and down a long alleyway.

The location looked like a miniature barracks with ten beds. Thomas dropped his friend onto one of the cots as Rick pulled his grandfather's boots off. Within moments J.J. was passed out and snoring.

"Well, that ought-a do it until morning," Thomas said.

Rick glanced around the room and noticed how empty it was. He guessed it was most likely used for the sick or injured, but he was unsure. "What is this place?"

Thomas sat on the cot next to J.J., letting out a long sigh. "It's for guys like him," he said, pointing to his friend. "Being an MP has its advantages and its disadvantages. Tonight J.J. is lucky it's not some other MP dragging his ass in here."

Rick sat on the other side of J.J. in another empty cot. He put his hands over his face, rubbing his eyes, feeling a sudden surge of fatigue. He had started his day lost in the sugarcane on the runway of Hickam Field. Now, a few short hours later, he found himself with Emily's grandfather and his own in a time and place where he didn't belong. Everything felt strange, but nothing could be more unsettling than the worst yet to come, with bullets and bombs raining down from the skies in a few short hours. In the morning, it won't be the rising sun everyone expects. Instead, the rising sun will be displayed on the wings of hundreds of aircraft bombers racing across the skies.

"What you said back there," Thomas spoke, interrupting Rick's concerning thoughts. "You being just like him. You'd be right. But not in a bad way," Thomas glanced at J.J. "Your grandfather is no bum, and it might not seem like it, but he's a swell enough guy. And...so are you."

"Well, I appreciate those kind words, Thomas, but if he's anything like me, I can only feel sorry for his wife and son."

Thomas gave Rick a lingering look of appreciation. "So, tell me, what's this about you being wounded in a war?"

Rick looked at his newfound hand, rubbing his fingers over the palm. "I got my hand blown off, lived for twenty years feeling like half a man." Rick looked at Thomas with a crooked smile. "Until I met Emily. She...she made me feel whole again, made me feel like a man again."

"But your hand…It's not gone. How do you have one now?"

Rick took a deep, weary breath and was on the verge of yawning. "It's hard to explain, but all I can say is, not all Witches are bad."

Thomas looked around the room and then back at Rick. "Well, you look pretty tired, and I could use some shut-eye myself. I don't think anyone will bother us here."

Rick lay down on the cot. "You won't get any arguments from me," he said as a big yawn finally escaped. Then he turned his head towards Thomas. "Hey, how about we take our time in the morning and get breakfast."

Thomas lay down, putting his arms up, and resting his head on his hands. "Sounds like a plan."

Rick felt relieved, glad none of them would be in harm's way. At least, he didn't think so. He tried to remember if the bombing affected this part of Honolulu. The thought made him wish he had paid more attention in history class. All he knew was the ships out in the harbor would take the brunt of the attack. As far as Hickam Field? Devastation was the only word that came to mind. He yawned again, did his best not to think about the day to come, and fell asleep within seconds from sheer exhaustion.

Chapter 9

DEATH CURSE

EMILY PULLED UP TO THE FARMHOUSE with the Oldsmobile filled with groceries, extra blankets, and pillows she had purchased after calling Grace on the pay phone in Owen's. She also brought Lucy and Walter and a small suitcase containing all their worldly possessions. Walter opened the back door and jumped happily out of the car with an adventurous gleam in his eyes.

Lucy sat quietly, not making a move, as she glanced at the big house. She seemed uncomfortable, and Emily wondered if it had anything to do with the accommodations that were being offered. "Are you all right, Lucy?"

"This is your family?" Lucy asked suspiciously.

"Well, yes, sort of...for now anyway, until I return home," Emily said, leaving out the part where home meant far into the future. "You needn't worry, Lucy. I assure you Grace Stanford is more than happy to help out." Emily hoped her words would reassure Lucy.

Lucy continued to stare at the farmhouse. Emily couldn't see her face but noticed the tension in her shoulders. "I'm sure she's a fine woman and a good mother," Lucy finally said.

Emily saw Grace come out onto the front porch holding Matthew in her arms. There was another young boy who looked older than Matthew standing alongside a little girl cradling a doll in her arms. Grace waved at Emily as the young boy and little girl ran off the porch to play in the snow. Walter glanced at his grandmother with a look that clearly said: May I play?

"Go on, darling," Lucy said, waving him in the direction of the laughing children.

Walter darted as fast as he could, picking up snow, and forming a ball as the other boy made another.

"It'll be nice to see a snowman in the front yard," Emily said, gently patting Lucy on the shoulder. "Come. Let's get you inside where it's warm."

After Emily made quick introductions, Grace prepared tea and biscuits for them, but Lucy had been so weak from the trip that she declined Graces's offer. Instead, Emily and Grace helped Lucy up the stairs to where Emily had slept the night before. After Emily got Lucy settled, Grace brought a tray with her previous offer of tea and biscuits.

"I don't know how to thank you for all the kindness," Lucy said to both women who stood by the bed.

"Now you hush. It's no trouble at all. Later, I'll have a nice dinner for you," Grace said. She gave Emily a nod and left the room.

Emily walked over, glanced out the window, and took in the sight gratefully as she watched the children play. "When it's time for the children to come inside, we might have to pry Walter away from the snowball fight." Emily looked over her shoulder and regarded Lucy's condition.

Emily walked to the vanity, picked up the small chair, and set it next to the bed. She watched Lucy sip her tea and barely take a bit of the biscuit. She reached for Lucy's hand and felt her thankful grip. There was no strength, only skin and bones. Emily leaned in. "Don't worry about Walter. I have it on good authority that he will do very well for himself."

"You read the future then?" Lucy asked with a weak smile.

"I'm just saying, don't worry."

A moment of silence fell between them, with the only sounds in the room coming from the sparks popping within the logs nestled in the fireplace. Emily's thoughts wandered to the gas fireplace in the future, needing only a simple push of a button to ignite the flames. That convenience could never replace the smell of wood burning and the soothing sound of logs crackling.

But what was real? She didn't belong in this time or any other time she had drifted through. With each experience, she had a task to save lives and to tell her and Rick's ancestors that their Creator loved them. That love was strong enough to break any curse, yet here she was again. Would she be able to find Charlotte? Could she simply tell her that the Creator loves her, too? Would it be enough? So many questions without answers. For now, Emily thought, I'll take care of Lucy and Walter.

Emily looked at Lucy's dark gray eyes. The skin sagged around her jaw, and her face was tired and drawn. Despite Lucy's painful appearance, Emily could see gratitude in her gray stare.

"Thank you, Emily," she whispered. "Just like before, you're an angel who showed up at the right time," Lucy's voice trailed off, and she fell fast asleep, leaving Emily to conclude that maybe she was supposed to be there after all.

After leaving Lucy to rest, Emily walked down the staircase and reached the bottom step just as the children darted past with Grace on their heels. "Take those boots off, or I'll have your hide, Marty!" she yelled.

"Marty?" Emily asked.

"Oh, yes, of course," Grace said while catching her breath. "You haven't met Marty yet; he's Billy's son. He's usually well-behaved, but I swear that boy has ants in his pants." Grace gathered the children, lining them up in front of Emily. "Of course, you know my little one, Matthew," Grace placed her hand on her son's head and her other hand on the little girl's head. "And this is Beth."

Emily leaned forward and reached out her hand. "It's nice to meet you, Beth."

Beth took her hand, giving Emily a shy smile.

Grace put her hand on top of the other boy's head. "And this is Marty."

Emily offered the same handshake, but this time, the electric spark ran up her arm. She ignored the sensation, knowing he was probably a little Mystic Guardian in the making. "Hello, Marty."

"Now, children, this is our guest, Emily. How do we treat our guests?"

All three children spoke in unison with the answer. "With respect."

"It's nice to meet you all," Emily said.

She noticed Walter off to one side, watching the introductions. Emily reached her hand out for him to come over. "This is my friend, Walter, and I'd like to thank you for including him when making your lovely snowman outside."

"Gee whiz, if it weren't for Walter that snow man would have no head," Beth chimed in as the other children giggled.

Grace waved the dish towel still in her hand. "You go play now till supper." Doing as they were told, the children scurried off.

"Do you need some help in the kitchen, Grace?" Emily asked.

Grace put her arm around Emily's shoulder. "Always," she said.

At dinner time, the children sat at the table, licking their lips, and complaining that they were starving. Grace walked behind each child, plopping a big spoonful of stew on each plate.

Emily fixed a tray for Lucy, walked up the stairs, and pushed the bedroom door open with her foot while balancing the tray in both hands. Lucy was sitting up in a rocker by the front window.

"I brought you some of Grace's famous stew, or at least that's what Marty called it," Emily said, placing the tray on a small, round table by the rocker. Lucy smiled.

"You're looking a bit more chipper."

"I suppose at the moment," Lucy said, leaning forward and touching the tray of food. "Is Walter behaving himself, I hope?"

"I'm sure he's happier than a bear cub with a jar of honey and no doubt chowing down his bowl of stew at the moment," Emily said.

"Well, thank Grace for me," Lucy reclined back in the rocker and closed her eyes as she took a shallow breath. "I need to tell you something, Emily." She opened her eyes, which showed unease. "It's about Walter's father."

"Yes, you said you wanted to find him."

Lucy's serious gaze settled on Emily. "I did."

"You found him? Where?"

Lucy sat up, holding onto the arms of the rocker. "Right here. I knew the moment you pulled up to this farmhouse and told me that Grace Stanford was more than happy to help out," she said.

Emily walked over, grabbed the small chair left by the bed, and placed it alongside the round table next to Lucy. "I don't understand. What do the Stanfords have to do with it?"

"It's Thomas Stanford. Walter is Thomas's son."

Emily felt as though the air just got sucked out of the room. She stared at Lucy in disbelief. Emily knew that Thomas was eight years older than Laura. She had tended to Thomas when he came down with the 1918 Spanish flu. At the same time, Emily had helped Lucy give birth to her baby girl, Laura. She never thought that Thomas and Laura would be together someday. "Thomas? Are you sure?" Emily asked.

"Positive. I've seen them together. Thomas was a fine boy. I realized he was older than Laura, but she seemed so happy. Both of them were so much in love. It wasn't until Charlotte came into the picture."

"Charlotte?"

Emily wondered if this was why Charlotte had cast a death curse. She must have been in love with Thomas and jealous of Laura. It was starting to make sense. "What happened with Charlotte?"

"She's evil. The things that came out of her mouth I wouldn't repeat to the most hardened criminal," Lucy slumped back in the rocker. "Laura told me everything Charlotte said to her. But the most disturbing thing was how Charlotte threatened Laura with a knife by putting it to her throat. That evil bitch even drew blood. Charlotte told Laura that if she didn't leave town, she would kill Thomas with the same knife with Laura's blood. Laura wanted to tell Thomas what had happened between her and Charlotte. But more importantly about the baby," Lucy hesitated, placing her hand over her belly. "I was afraid if Charlotte knew about Laura's pregnancy, she would do something to her baby. So, I took Laura, and we left town.

Emily knew that it wasn't a knife Charlotte would use to try and kill Thomas but a death curse. "I'm so sorry, Lucy. That's awful."

"Laura was upset with me for a while, but I had to do it. There was something so evil about Charlotte. I just couldn't put my finger on it. Then when her sister Kathleen and grandmother Lily were found dead in the swamp, I knew I had made the right decision to leave town."

"So, you think Charlotte might have had something to do with Kathleen and Lily's deaths?"

"From what I know about Charlotte, I wouldn't put it past her."

Lucy looked exhausted, and Emily stood up just as Lucy attempted to get out of the rocker.

"Come. Let me help you back into bed," Emily offered. Once in bed, Lucy struggled to find a comfortable position. Emily covered Lucy with a blanket and rested a sympathetic hand on Lucy's arm. "You rest now. We can talk more later."

"Grace needs to know," Lucy whispered, "about Walter."

"You can wait to tell her," Emily suggested as she tucked the blanket around Lucy's frail body. "Maybe tomorrow. You settle yourself now, and I'll be back in a little bit to check on you."

After dinner, Grace settled the children to play in the bedroom off from the kitchen. Emily listened to the sounds of their laughter, and she also heard Grace humming a pleasant melody in the kitchen as she made bread for the following day.

Emily sat on the couch in the living room by the radio, listening to an orchestra's calm, relaxing music. She felt at ease for the first time since she arrived there until her mind settled on Rick.

She missed him, and the thought of him made tears well up in her eyes. With time travel, so much emotion had easily found its way into her soul. Emily could feel the pains of this generation of people who have long passed. Tomorrow, December 7th, would be the beginning of that pain for so many.

And then there were her own sorrows beginning to seep in, sorrows only Rick could replace with contentment. But he wasn't here yet; she sensed him all around her as if he existed in this time, in this year of 1941. Then there was Charlotte and what she did to Laura: driving that poor girl away. As a result, Thomas never knew he had another son. Emily suddenly felt a presence in the room. She looked over and saw Billy standing by the entrance.

"I guess we need to talk," he said.

Emily nodded, offering a weary grin.

"About my being a Mystic Guardian I—"

"It's okay, Billy," Emily interrupted. "I do know about Mystic Guardians. I just never expected you to be one."

Billy sat on the other end of the couch, resting his arms on his lap. They both stared at the radio with its mellow music drifting between them. Billy rubbed the palms of his hand as if nervous to say something more. Finally he spoke.

"Kathleen came to me one day and told me to protect Beth. It was a few days before Kathleen and her grandmother – my step-mother, Lily – were found dead in the swamp," Billy gave Emily a grim look.

Emily moved to the edge of her seat and turned towards Billy. "Did you know Kathleen wrote in Lily Spencer's diary about me, well, without mentioning my name, of course? She talked about a time traveler coming to break a curse that had been put on Thomas."

Billy gave Emily a sympathetic nod. "I am aware of this in-formation."

"Kathleen must have known about Charlotte putting a death curse on Thomas. If I had to guess," Emily raised one eyebrow. "I think Charlotte was pretty upset over his affair with Laura Green."

"What? Wait a second You mean you know about that. I mean about Thomas and Laura?"

"I do, and right now Laura's mother is upstairs dying, and Walter...well."

"So, Walter is Laura's son?" Billy whispered. "Then Walter?" Billy looked as if he was calculating Walter's age and matching it up with Thomas's love affair with Laura and then came to an obvious conclusion. "That would make Walter, Thomas's son?"

"He sure is. Lucy just told me everything and wants to tell Grace about it."

"Where is Laura now?" Billy asked.

"She died giving birth to Walter."

Billy stood and walked to the fireplace, placing both hands on the mantle as he gazed at the smoldering flames. He then turned his head to look at Emily. "Charlotte," he began. "She's pure evil. She was nothing like her sister, Kathleen." Billy lingered for a moment by the fireplace and then sat back down next to Emily as he continued. "She had a thing for Thomas, but he wanted nothing to do with her. At the time, I had no idea Charlotte had cast a death curse. Kathleen never told me. She just asked me to protect Beth, so I did. The next thing I knew, she and my stepmother were dead."

"After their deaths, did you think it might have been from a death curse?" Emily asked.

"Not for certain, but then I read my stepmother's diary. That's when I knew Charlotte must have done something because soon after, Kathleen and Lily turned up dead and Charlotte disappeared. I also knew that if Charlotte did cast this death curse, it would bind the Witch's powers. That means Kathleen and Lily must have lost their powers, and little Beth would no longer possess these powers either." Billy rubbed the back of his neck, his eyebrows drawn together with worry.

"Thomas never read our stepmother's old diary, not even her published book. But I sure did. When I became suspicious of their deaths, I dug out the old diary to see if I could find something in there. Sounds to me like you and I must've read the same passage."

"Does Thomas know about the curse or the Spencer Witches?" Emily asked.

"He knows about the Witches. As far as the curse, I kept that information to myself. He never was interested in reading the diary; I think he preferred it that way, just as well. I did my best to keep an eye on Thomas and protect him. When he went overseas, I figured he would be too far away for a curse to have any effect or at least I had hoped. I told him years ago I was a Mystic Guardian," Billy smirked. "At first he didn't believe me, and then I reminded him that nobody would have believed in a time traveler either."

"So, Lily told both of you then, I mean, about me."

"She did but not your name only about being the time traveler. It was Thomas who had filled me in about you. It was his grandfather who had told him everything."

"Sam Stanford," Emily said.

"Yes, and that's when I remembered you helping me through the woods towards the hospital that day during the Spanish flu outbreak. So, both Thomas and I have memories of you. Then, later on...much later, I told Thomas about Mystic Guardians having the power to protect. So, he asked me to protect his family while he was gone." Billy let out a long sigh. "Ironically, if he had known the truth, he might've not agreed to take his tour of duty so far away. He did have other options. Regardless, I would have looked after his family anyway."

"Billy, I think I've been sent here to break that curse, and as you had read in the diary, well, it's something only a time traveler can do." Emily leaned towards Billy, speaking in a low voice so no one else could hear. "I've also been hearing a man's voice coming from the swamp across the Magic River. He calls out my name, beckoning me."

Billy jumped up suddenly. "Emily, don't go anywhere near that swamp. I'm telling you it's cursed, which is probably why Kathleen and Lily died in there."

Emily stood. "Do you think Charlotte died in there too?"

"I'm not sure. Other than finding Lily and Kathleen, the authorities never found a trace of anyone else in there," Billy gripped both her arms gently. "Promise me you won't go anywhere near that swamp."

Billy seemed frightened. Emily could sense his fear and was confident it had come from something he couldn't control. "Billy? Why do I need to be afraid of going in there?"

"Because I can't go in there. If I can't, I won't be able to protect you from whatever curse is on that swamp."

"Why can't you go in there?"

"I tried to. I wanted to. I followed the police into the swamp one day to look for Charlotte or evidence as to what happened to Kathleen and Lily. I knew of an old hunting cabin...well, an old shack really. Thomas had used it on occasion during hunting season. I've never actually been to it, but I thought I'd go check it out. When I stepped into the swampy water my chest began to tighten, and I couldn't breathe. My legs were becoming paralyzed. It took all the strength I had left in my body to get myself out of there. I knew right then and there the swamp was cursed. I didn't even tell Thomas—another thing I kept to myself." Billy took a deep breath and walked over and leaned his hand on the radio with music playing that didn't match the haunting conversation.

Emily went to Billy's side and put her hand on his. "I'm starting to see the full picture now. If the police had no problem going through the swamp, then it must be cursed only to those with magical powers—like yours."

Billy stood tall, towering over Emily. Resolve filled his eyes as he spoke in an even tone. "I've spent the last six years protecting Thomas, Grace, Matthew, and little Beth. Now, I find myself looking after you. So, Emily, I'm asking you, please do not go in there and don't listen to whatever thing is calling you to go in there."

Emily smiled and touched Billy's cheek. "I'm so glad I have someone to look out for me. I'll stay away from that area, I promise. Okay?"

Billy pulled Emily in, giving her an affectionate hug, the same kind of hug a son would give to his mother.

Later that evening, Emily checked on Lucy and then sat in the rocker by the window, feeling uneasy. The realization of the death curse Charlotte had put on Thomas gave her increased anxiety, causing her to feel sick. She knew tomorrow would be a difficult day. The world would be at war, and she prayed that nothing would happen to her grandfather, Thomas. She had no way of helping him half a world away; for that matter, neither could Billy. Thomas's chances were already in peril and didn't need a curse on top of that. In just a few short hours, Thomas would be right in the middle of ground zero.

Chapter 10

PEARL HARBOR

December 7, 1941

RICK DREAMED OF EMILY. She was in a dark, misty wooded area trying to find her way towards something. She stood in water up to her waist and clawed for a tree branch just out of arm's reach. She screamed his name. Rick abruptly woke in a cold sweat. He looked around and saw several other guys sleeping on cots. It was early morning, and he caught the smell of bacon in the air. Rick got up and stood by the doorway.

The silent sky had not yet been pierced by the roar of the engines. Dew dripped from long blades of sugarcane. The brilliant colors of tropical flowers offered a glorious peace. Most everyone nestled in their slumber. All seemed normal except for Rick's heart pounding in his ears. Chills crawled up his back, and he wondered how this massive hit of adrenaline could engulf his body on such a peaceful morning. He looked over and saw that Thomas was sleeping, but when he looked to his right, a note rested on J.J.'s empty cot. Rick had a sinking feeling as he opened the message:

> Hey Thomas, and you, too, old flyboy. Guess I'm in enough trouble, so I thought I'd head back to the base where I belong before I get stuck helping the old man clean the shitters.
>
> P.S. Sorry, you got wounded, old flyboy. Nobody deserves that.
>
> Over and out, J.J.

Rick quietly walked towards the door. He needed Thomas to stay put. Keep him from the carnage yet to be released onto Pearl Harbor and Hickam Field. He glanced at the clock on the wall: 7:40 a.m. "Shit, I only have 15 minutes," he said under his breath.

Rick peeked around the corner just outside the door and saw an unused taxi with its driver nowhere in sight. He darted towards the taxi and jumped into the front seat. Rick looked at the dashboard, hesitating when he remembered his pocketknife. He reached into his pocket, opened the blade, and stuck the sharp edge into the ignition. The engine sputtered. Rick pleaded with the taxi to start, and suddenly the motor roared. "It sure ain't that easy in the future," he said, reaching for the shifter. Suddenly, he felt a firm hand grip his shoulder.

"Where the hell do you think you're going?" Thomas squawked.

"Thomas, you need to stay here. Trust me. I need you to stay," Rick implored.

"What the hell are you talking about, Rick?" Thomas jumped in front of the taxi with his arms up, blocking Rick from moving forward.

"Get the hell out of my way, Thomas!"

"Not until you let me in that car."

Rick was about to back up when Thomas darted to the passenger side door and hopped in.

"I don't have time for this, Thomas."

Rick gripped the steering wheel. He wanted to punch Thomas, knock him unconscious, and push him out of the taxi. It was better than getting shot or having a bomb fall on his head. Instead, he bit the side of his mouth and slowed his words. "J.J. went back to the base. If I don't stop him, he's going to get himself killed. Now, get the hell out of the car."

"Whoa, whoa, whoa—Rick. What do you know? And you better tell me the truth."

Rick ran his hand through his hair. "Look, I don't have time to explain. I'm going to get my grandfather out of harm's way."

Thomas's face turned red with anger. "RICK! THE TRUTH! NOW!"

Rick slammed the steering wheel with his two hands in frustration. "Okay. You want the truth? December 7, 1941. The bombing of Pearl Harbor and a date which will live in infamy. Thomas, the ships out in the harbor are about to be obliterated." Rick watched as the color in Thomas's face changed from red to white.

"Is that why you had that ghostly look on your face yesterday at Pearl?"

"Yes, and it's why I got to stop my grandfather before he reaches the airfield."

Thomas's horrified expression morphed into a look of determination. The muscles tightened around his jaw and with a steady but forceful tone to his voice, he said: "I'm going with you."

"Get out now," Rick said, pushing back on Thomas's insistence.

Thomas abruptly pinned Rick against the front seat with great force and with fire in his eyes. "I'm not leaving my post no matter what attack we're under. And I won't leave any of my men behind. Whether you like it or not, I'm going with you."

Rick stared at Thomas. Those exact words echoed in his mind. The day he, too, didn't leave his men behind when fighting in Iraq. He could see the resolve in Thomas's eyes, a sense of purpose that couldn't be stopped. At that very moment, he knew Thomas was a good soldier and one he would be honored to fight with by his side.

"Let's go then before J.J. gets his ass shot off," Rick said, stepping on the gas at the same speed as his grandfather and into a hell none could prevent. Rick held tight to the steering wheel, and Thomas gripped the dashboard while they sped franticly in the direction of Hickam Field to save J.J. from certain death.

"Why didn't you tell me about this attack?" Thomas yelled.

"Because I don't think I can change history itself. But maybe I can save people from it."

Rick saw Thomas's shoulders go limp as he looked out the window.

"Am I supposed to die today?" Thomas asked.

"What?" Rick said.

Thomas glared at Rick. "Do I get killed today?"

Rick shook his head. "I don't know." He glanced at Thomas for the second time. "All I know is there's a curse on you, and somehow I got sent here to save you. Or at least that's what I'm beginning to think. I…I just don't know."

"It's J.J. then, isn't' it?"

Rick cast Thomas a pained look. "My grandfather is supposed to die today. That much I do know." He stepped on the gas a little harder at the thought of J.J. getting killed. "As long as I'm trying to save you, maybe I can save him, too."

Suddenly, Rick heard a loud explosion off in the distance. The impact shook the ground, and Rick felt it vibrate through the steering wheel. Thomas stuck his head out the window, looking towards the sky.

"What the hell? It looks like the whole damn Japanese air force is up there."

They both glanced ahead towards Pearl Harbor as the Japanese planes dove downward, heading straight for battleship row, releasing the bombs from their bellies. Suddenly, a catastrophic explosion reverberated through the taxi, and it felt as though the tires had lifted off the ground.

"Christ, Almighty!" Thomas yelled. Rick and Thomas stared at the enormous plume of smoke over the horizon. "What in God's name was that?" Thomas said.

Rick looked at the cloud of black smoke. Once again, the sight was surreal. He had often seen footage of this event on television, yet now, it was happening in real-time. "I believe it was the *USS Arizona*," Rick said.

Thomas's eyes darted wildly, and his jaw slackened. He had no words.

Rick felt sorry for him. The attack on Pearl Harbor was not a shock to Rick, but it was to Thomas. Rick gave Thomas a weary glance. "It's why I had trouble looking at the ship yesterday. You know, with the full knowledge of its fate and all. Sorry, buddy, but it only gets worse, and Hickam Field is next."

With that, Rick drove as fast as he could. Along the way, they dodged bullets from the planes overhead. Finally, after passing the carnage happening in the harbor, they reached Hickam Field.

As they approached the hangers, Rick swerved the taxi around service members running for their lives just as ten were mowed down by machine gun fire. He slammed on the brakes to avoid running over the bodies. Rick and Thomas were within yards of the hangar where J.J. worked.

"Come on! We'll get some weapons in the MP building," Thomas said. Suddenly, the MP office was blown off its foundation, with the building erupting into an enormous plume of fiery, black smoke. It took a second for Rick to comprehend what he saw. Then he heard Thomas yell, "COME ON! I know another place."

As they ran, Rick and Thomas dodged bullets that spiked across the asphalt, shot from a Japanese Zero. The plane was so low it had to pull up at the last minute to avoid hitting the roof of the hanger. Rick saw the sneering grin on the pilot's face as he banked to the right, circling for another shot at them. Thomas stood frozen as the plane approached, his face stunned in terror. Rick grabbed him by the collar and pulled him back when a second round of gunfire from thc same plane ricocheted off everything around them.

"You're going to get yourself killed freezing up like that!" Rick shouted. He gripped Thomas by the arm, pushing him towards the hanger. Suddenly, the concussion from another bomb threw both Rick and Thomas onto the ground. Rick felt disoriented. Everything seemed to go in slow motion as he felt the hot, gritty pavement on his cheek. He quickly regained control and jumped to his feet. He helped Thomas to his feet just as another plane came at them, repeating the same hail of bullets that carved out a path leading straight for them. They made a mad dash for the hanger.

They found a blazing inferno inside, except for the far end where the parachutes were stored. Rick saw a man hopelessly tangled in the nylon lines of the parachutes. Black, billowing smoke shot to the ceiling of the hanger from a B-17 engulfed in flames. The firestorm inched towards the trapped man and a fuel tanker truck with two flat tires not far from the stored parachutes. When Rick looked closer, he couldn't believe who the man was.

"Holy shit! It's J.J.," Rick yelled as they ran towards the tangled man.

"Jesus, J.J.," Thomas squawked. "How the hell did you get yourself into this predicament?"

J.J.'s mouth turned up. Rick recognized the expression, the same expression he himself would offer when giving a sarcastic answer. "When the Japs decided to kick my ass," J.J. responded.

Rick assessed the situation quickly and could see he had only minutes to untangle J.J. He pulled out his pocketknife and started cutting the lines.

J.J.'s eyes widened. "Hey, old flyboy, you're handy to have around," he said.

His wittiness didn't fool Rick. He saw the sheer panic in J.J.'s eyes. "Don't worry. I'll get you out-a here," Rick said, mostly convincing himself.

"You really wanna save me after giving you such a hard time?"

"Yeah, well, even though you're a little bastard, I still need someone to help me clean the shitters," Rick said as he continued to cut the maze of lines wrapped around every part of J.J.'s body.

J.J. looked towards the tanker truck as Rick steadily cut each line and tried not to look in the same direction. Rick's military training kicked in, and he knew he had to keep himself as calm as possible in an impossible situation.

J.J. looked at Rick. "Hey, ah… I don't think I'm gonna make it, old flyboy." J.J.'s words were strangely calm, as if resigning himself to the fact that he was about to die.

"I'm not giving up on you yet." Rick cut the line wrapped

around J.J.'s throat as Thomas pulled it off, tossing it into the fire just inches away.

"I always wanted to wring your neck," Thomas said. "Just never thought I'd get the chance."

J.J. suddenly got quiet as he watched the parachutes over his head begin to melt. Rick saw his dull eyes and watched his chin tremble. "Hey there…Rick, is it? You said you knew my wife?" J.J.'s one free hand reached for Rick's wrist to stop him from cutting. "Tell her I'm sorry for being such a shitty husband and tell her that I love her more than words can say."

Rick pulled his wrist out of J.J.'s hand. "Tell her yourself." And with that, Rick cut the last line, freeing him. "Come on, let's get the hell outta here before that tanker blows."

The men ran full force. Rick yelled, "GET DOWN!" as the fuel truck exploded. Fire shot inches above their backs as they lay flat on the pavement.

"Holy shit!" J.J. said, as all three men stood and watched the area were J.J. had been trapped now consumed by flames. The shock of that moment quickly shifted when the men pivoted and saw the carnage on the airfield.

Rick saw bodies littered across the tarmac. Men in shock walked aimlessly. One man had blood oozing from the bottom of his pant leg. Another looked as if the side of his face had been blown off. Rick turned away from the carnage. Then suddenly, another massive explosion erupted in the distance.

The ground shook under their feet. A monstrous cloud of black smoke shot into the sky. Rick knew it came from the same direction as Pearl Harbor, where all the battleships sat in the harbor like sitting ducks. After he heard another explosion, Rick suspected that another ship had likely been blown out of the water. He felt the intense heat of the fire on his back and pointed to a large sandbag bunker with a machine gun. "We need to get to that machine gun if we have any chance of getting away from that inferno behind us."

Two more planes raced past them with bullets bouncing in front of them. "Let's make a run for it," Thomas shouted.

The three men darted towards the sandbags, with Thomas leading and Rick following. J.J. was on their heels when he abruptly stopped as one of the Japanese planes unleashed a bomb from its belly.

"INCOMING!" J.J. yelled. He lurched forward and shoved Thomas and Rick into the center of the sandbag bunker. Rick felt a sharp blow to his back. The force pushed the remaining air from his lungs, and then—everything stopped.

Rick's ears were ringing as he struggled to breathe. There were faint, muffled sounds of desperation in the distance from men who were wounded or dying. Am I dying? he wondered.

He saw Emily's face. She was smiling as if glad to see him. She was standing amid the carnage. Rick tried comprehending why she was there. His heart ached for her. He needed refuge from the chaos that only she could provide. Emily's lips were moving. She was saying something. He tried to reach out to her, but he couldn't move from the dead weight that had him pinned down. Smoke and debris crossed in front of Emily. She suddenly disappeared, replaced by cries of men calling for their mothers.

He felt crushed by the weight on top of him and tried to move. Warm liquid ran down the side of his head, and he reached up and touched the oozing substances on his cheek. His vision came into focus, and he saw blood covering his hand. Am I dead? Did I die in a war that's not my own? The thought seemed absurd to him. Then, there was movement beneath him. A small groan came from the man beneath Rick. The man pushed Rick upward along with the dead weight pressing down on Rick's back.

"Are you all right, Rick?"

Rick felt his chest with its strong heartbeat, pushing the blood to his brain, helping his mind to catch up. He was still alive. He looked at the man talking to him. Thomas? he thought and then stared at the other man. A sudden numbness took over his limbs, and he felt a tightening in his throat. "J.J.? Oh, no, J.J."

"He's dead, Rick," Thomas said.

Rick saw J.J.'s vacant stare. "No, no, J.J. I wanted so bad to keep you safe. I…I just couldn't." Rick took him in his arms and felt the blood-soaked shirt on J.J.'s back. Skin hung from the slashes in the fabric riddled with shrapnel. He held J.J. like a small child as he pressed his forehead against his grandfather's head. He felt the sting of tears welling up in his eyes. "I'm sorry. I'm so sorry." Rick swallowed hard, trying to get the words out. "I…I tried to save you." Rick felt a wave of despair. Defeated once again. He had tried to save men before in a future war, had held other dead soldiers in his arms, felt the same helplessness. His despair suddenly turned into rage. It billowed up in every fiber of his body when it suddenly reached his lips as he shouted, "WHY THE FUCK AM I HERE!"

Rick saw Thomas reach over to shut J.J.'s eyes, and then Thomas rested his hand on Rick's shoulder. "To save me, Rick—to save me."

Rick looked up at Thomas. A cut across Thomas's forehead caused blood to roll down the side of his head, reaching his chin as it dripped onto his shirt. Rick saw the look of despair in his eyes. Rick then realized that Thomas had also lost his best friend. Rick reached out to Thomas, and both men locked arms in solidarity as they carried each other's grief.

The bombing had stopped. The stench of death was all around them. And J.J.'s death moored Rick and Thomas to each other over the loss of someone they both loved.

It had been a few hours since they had put J.J. on a stretcher and laid him alongside all the other dead. Rick moved like a robot, going through the motions as he helped the wounded to the nearby hospital. He kept thinking how all this felt worse than Iraq. In the future, people will become desensitized by modern-day media exposure. But here in 1941, nobody was ever exposed to such graphic images and horror. It was more than even Rick could bear.

He sat on the ground across from the burning MP office, staring at the pavement pitted from machine gun fire. Blood had splattered over most of the area. Everywhere he looked, something was still burning, blown to bits, or riddled with bullets. A B-17 bomber sat on the tarmac with the whole back end blown off, its debris scattered in every direction. Even the railroad tracks alongside the hangers were damaged. Only one sight gave Rick hope. The large American flag still waved over Hickam Field, torn and tattered yet showing resolve. He felt an appreciation he would have never experienced in his own time—the enormous gratitude for the greatest generation.

Rick saw Thomas coming his way and stood as he approached. "I guess we're going to have to rebuild," Thomas said, looking at the remains of the MP office.

Rick said nothing, just stared at the burning pile.

"There's talk or…" Thomas instinctively put a hand on his revolver. "Rumor has it, the Japs might come back to finish us off."

"I wouldn't worry about it…they're done here," Rick said with an air of defeat in his voice.

Thomas took his hand off the revolver. "I know you already knew what was going to happen here but, why didn't the Japs just finish us off?"

Rick continued to stare at the pile of burning debris. "Because of Admiral Yamamoto." Rick turned towards Thomas. "He was the mastermind behind the attack on Pearl Harbor. He called off the third strike and then was famously quoted as saying, *I fear all we have done is to awaken a sleeping giant and fill him with a terrible resolve.*"

Thomas raised one eyebrow. "Well, I guess the Admiral wouldn't be wrong about that." Thomas looked off to the side where a large hole was left from one of the bombs. "Besides, I doubt we could've taken another blow, at least at the moment."

Rick nodded. "There was some controversy over whether a third strike was planned at all, or if the Admiral actually said the sleeping giant quote." Rick shrugged his shoulders as he breathed a heavy sigh. "Either way—it's over."

Thomas put his hands in his pockets and lifted his chin at the burning remains of his office building. "You know, I would have been in there if it hadn't been for you."

"What you mean?" Rick asked.

"The only reason I wasn't in there was because I took you to Honolulu to show you the sights." Thomas put his hand on Rick's shoulder, swallowing a couple of times as if to hold back his emotions. "I'd be in that heap of burning kindle right now, probably would have never known what hit me. So, as J.J. would say…you really did save my life, old fly boy."

Rick took a couple of steps towards the crumbling building and felt validated by Thomas's observation. He couldn't have saved his grandfather. And that's when it dawned on him. History showed that J.J. died that day, saving two of his comrades. "Well, I'll be damned," Rick said as his glance darted toward the American flag. Rick could have never imagined that those two soldiers were, in fact, Thomas and himself.

It wasn't his war, but here he was, sent through time, saving who needed to be saved—someone who was not supposed to die that day. Thomas will fight other battles in this war, saving other men. Thomas was part of that greatest generation, and so was his grandfather, men who fought freely and who sacrificed their lives.

At that moment, Rick turned, facing Thomas as the Stars and Strips whipped tirelessly in the wind. Rick lifted his hand in a salute. "It's been an honor to serve with you," he said, knowing somehow he had finished what he had been sent here to do—to save Thomas. "My mission is accomplished, sir."

Chapter 11

BAD NEWS

Maple Ridge, Massachusetts
On the morning of December 7ᵗʰ, 1941

EMILY FELT THE WARMTH ON HER FACE. The brightness of the morning sun seeped under her eyelids. She heard a faint sniffling followed by whimpers. The sound was coming from behind her. Emily opened her eyes and realized she had fallen asleep in the rocking chair in Lucy's room. She turned her head towards the whimpering and found Walter by his grandmother's bedside, holding her hand as tiny tears streamed down his cheeks.

"Walter?"

Emily walked over and placed a gentle hand on Walter's shoulder. She could feel the sorrow through his trembling body. She leaned forward to check Lucy's pulse but found none. Emily knelt at Walter's level. "Your Grammy is with your mommy now."

Walter looked at Emily with his puffy red eyes. "Why couldn't you fix her?"

"I wish I could have, but I think God wanted your Grammy with him and your mommy."

Walter remained quiet for a moment as he stared down, still holding his grandmother's limp hand. "Where do I go now?" he said through his tears and broken heart.

"Oh, Walter, honey, don't you worry about that right now. I'll be here for you and so will Mrs. Stanford. Don't you worry."

Emily took Walter in her arms and whispered soft comforting words and felt his tight grip cling to her as he cried.

A little while later, Emily and Walter entered the kitchen just as Grace was feeding Matthew. Emily held Walter's hand as he stared straight ahead with his red, swollen eyes. She knew by the look of concern on Grace's face that she was aware of something.

"Well, now, my sweet boy," Grace chirped, pulling out a kitchen chair. "You come right over here, and I'll get you some bacon and eggs. How does that sound?"

Walter slumped into the chair, making a tiny mutter of "Thank you." Emily lifted her chin towards the living room, and Grace responded with a slight nod. A couple of moments later, Grace entered the living room, still showing the same look of concern.

"What is it? Is Lucy...?" Grace's voice trailed off, and Emily answered with a slight nod. The two women sat down with sad, unspoken words between them.

Emily glanced at the silent radio when suddenly she was reminded of the day and date. Soon the whole country would get the frightening news of the attack on Pearl Harbor. In a few hours, information about death and destruction would blare out of everyone's radio, adding to the dismal news of Lucy's death. It was now up to Emily to tell Grace the truth about Walter. She gently touched Grace's hand. "Grace, I need to tell you something—something Lucy told me before she passed."

Grace shifted in her seat. Emily saw the look of worry on her face. "What is it?"

"Before you met Thomas, he was with another girl. Her name was Laura. Did he ever tell you about her?"

"Oh, yes. He had mentioned her, although not her name, and that's as far as our conversation went," Grace said, her words seeming to dismiss the girl and her name as though she hadn't existed at all. "Why, a handsome man like Thomas would certainly attract the women. I should know, I was one of them," she added logically in defense of her husband.

"Laura left town with her mother about six years ago," Emily began. "Thomas was in love with her. Laura loved Thomas as well. Several months after Laura left town, she died giving birth to a son. Her mother raised the child." Emily glanced towards the staircase to the bedroom where Lucy's body lay.

Grace followed Emily's eyes towards the stairs and then darted a look at Emily, clearly putting two and two together. "Lucy is this girl's mother?"

"Yes, which means..." Emily hesitated.

"Walter?" Grace sucked in her breath. "Are you telling me that Walter is Thomas's son?"

"Yes," Emily said. "Without his grandmother, he's all alone in the world. That's why Lucy came back to town in the first place. She knew she didn't have much longer to live." Emily held onto Grace's hands, giving them a gentle squeeze. "She needed to find Walter's father—to care for him after she's gone," Emily hesitated. "There is one more thing." Emily felt Grace's intense gaze. Her eyes showed fear, but she said nothing as Emily revealed the final piece of information. "Thomas has no idea Walter even exists."

Just then, Matthew started to cry for his mother. Grace abruptly stood. "I need to check on my son," she said and then darted out of the room.

Emily wasn't sure if Grace would be able to accept the news of Walter's paternity and wondered how she would feel in the same situation. The thought of her husband's love child showing up on her doorstep most certainly would have shocked her in the same way it had Grace. For now, though, the best thing she could do was make plans for Lucy to be buried alongside her daughter, Laura.

That afternoon, the funeral director came to discuss arrangements. Grace said no more about Walter, but to her credit, she agreed to have the calling hours the following morning at her home.

After Lucy's body was removed from the house, Emily continued to console Walter, and soon things began to quiet down. It wasn't until the late afternoon that word started to spread through the neighborhood about the attack on Pearl Harbor.

Emily sat in the living room with Grace and the children. Grace quietly did her needlework as Emily read a story to Matthew and Walter. In the corner of Emily's eye, she could see Grace glancing up every now and then at Walter and then dropping her head back down to her needlework.

Suddenly, several loud knocks came from the front door, startling everyone in the room.

"Good Lord, have mercy," Grace blustered, putting down her needlework. "What in the world is so urgent?"

As Grace got up to answer the door, Emily walked Walter and Matthew to the spare bedroom to play with toys. She knew what the frantic knocking was all about. Emily returned to the entranceway, where a woman about the same age as Grace stood on the threshold, gripping the hand of a two-year-old boy. The woman had a slight build and had blonde hair neatly done in a twist. Her pretty face reflected worry.

"Come in. Come in," Grace said as she escorted the woman into the living room. "Is something wrong?"

"Oh, yes. I'm afraid to tell you that something awful has happened in the Hawaiian islands. My poor Joseph is there with your Thomas in the middle of it all." The woman walked to the radio and turned the dial. "Here, listen."

A static sound came through with an upset newscaster delivering dire news from Washington. "Details are just coming in. There was an attack on naval, military facilities, and airfields in Hawaii. This Japanese attack will likely bring us into war." The news broadcaster continued his somber statement with Grace and the woman clinging to every word.

The woman's child seemed worried that his mother was upset. Emily walked over to the boy and leaned down with a friendly smile. "Would you like to go play with the other children?" Emily asked, but the little boy held tight to his mother's leg.

"Oh, dear, I'm sorry," Grace said. "Where are my manners? This is Emily, a friend of Thomas's grandfather."

"Hello," the woman said, holding out her hand to shake Emily's. "I'm Marion Miller, and this is my little boy, Randy."

At that moment, Emily knew who they were. She had heard Rick speak of his father, whose name was Randal. Marion was, in fact, Rick's grandmother, and the little boy clinging to her leg was his father. Emily stood dumbfounded, holding her hand out in slow motion to shake Marion's. "How do you do?" she finally managed to say.

As she regained her composure, Emily glanced at little Randy. "The other children are playing in the room down the hall," Emily said, looking at both Marion and Randy and hoping her eyes reflected less shock than she felt.

"Of course. Thank you," Marion said, leading her son to the makeshift playroom. "I'll make tea," Grace said.

While Marion tended to her son in the playroom, Grace went to the kitchen to make tea. Emily sat by the radio and listened to the sounds of Jimmy Dorsey's saxophone and Bing Crosby's rich, bass-baritone voice. The music was interrupted frequently with breaking news about the attacks.

She already knew that Marion's husband was killed at Pearl Harbor. Emily had written a story for the *Maple Ridge Gazette* on his heroism in saving two of his comrades. Having such knowledge was a terrible burden, and Emily knew all too well the heartache Marion would soon face.

December 8th, 1941

In the early hours of the following day, Lucy's body was returned to the Stanford home. She rested in a satin-lined, wooden box that was placed in the parlor. Calling hours were set from 9 a.m. to 11a.m. for anyone who cared to stop by.

Emily found Walter on the cushioned kneeler, staring at the side of the casket with his hands folded in prayer. He was too short to look into the coffin. She could hear his whimpering sounds, which broke her heart, and went over to join him. She, too, folded her hands in prayer. Lucy looked beautiful in a pale pink dress with her hair styled in finger waves.

Emily put her arm around Walter's slumped shoulders. "Walter? Would you like to stand on the kneeler so you can see your Grammy?"

Walter shook his head slowly and then looked up at Emily with sorrow. "I want to go home."

Emily peeked over her shoulder and saw Grace greeting two neighbors who kindly showed up to pay their respects. Although they didn't know Lucy, the few that did come seemed sympathetic with their food offerings and condolences. Emily suspected Grace had told her neighbors that Lucy was a family member of Thomas's. She saw Billy standing next to Grace and speaking to a man wearing a wool coat and a fedora. Emily glanced down at Walter. "Let me see what I can do," Emily said, giving Walter a pleasant smile. "I think we can fix it. Okay, honey?"

Emily led Walter to one of the chairs alongside the casket, where he sat swinging his short legs. He kept his hands folded on his lap and stared at the floor. Emily sat next to him and again put her arm around his shoulders. "I understand you're sad, and you're going to miss your Grammy so much. But I think everything will be all right. Do you trust me?"

Walter looked up at Emily and frowned. "But you couldn't fix my Grammy."

"No, honey. I'm so sorry I couldn't. But I think I can fix where you will live, okay?"

"Okay," Walter said.

Emily patted Walter on the knee, stood, and then made her way over to Billy. "Will you be okay greeting people on your own?

I'm going to steal Grace for a couple of minutes," Emily said.

"Sure, take your time," Billy said.

Grace had just finished talking with a woman wearing a fur coat and a large hat with feathers. Emily speculated the woman was with the man wearing the fedora.

"Grace, can we talk for a minute?"

Grace nodded, excused herself from the woman in fur, and then followed Emily into the kitchen.

"Is everything all right?" Grace asked.

"No, not really. Well, at least not all right for little Walter."

Grace shook her head and made a clicking sound with her tongue. "I know. That poor little thing. This has to be awful for him."

"That's what I wanted to talk to you about," Emily began. "You need to make a decision about what to do with Walter. Now, I know it's none of my business, but the reality is that little boy in there is Thomas's son who needs a home." Emily could tell by the way Grace chewed on her bottom lip that she was thinking. "Listen to me, Grace. This is not Walter's fault, and to be honest, it's not Laura or Thomas's fault either."

Grace lowered herself into one of the kitchen chairs by the table. Emily sat next to her. "Thomas loved Walter's mother. He was born out of love. Lucy came here so Walter could be with his father instead of ending up in an orphanage somewhere." Emily reached over and squeezed Grace's hand. "I know you think this will sound strange, but I know Walter will be a wonderful son. He will be smart, maybe even grow up to be a history teacher, and the best thing of all, he'll be a big brother to Matthew."

Grace took a deep breath and gave Emily a lopsided grin. "I know all of this, of course. I guess it's all a shock to me. Yes, certainly, I want Walter to live here with us." Grace hesitated as though gathering another thought and then gave Emily a gentle pat on the back of her hand. "I do know this much…I love Thomas with all my heart, and Walter is a part of Thomas. I have no doubt that Walter will be a part of my heart as well. Besides, that little guy in there… has certainly grown on me over these past few days."

"Well, then, Grace," Emily said, pointing to the kitchen door leading to the parlor. "Don't you think it's time you tell him that?"

It was after noontime when the few remaining neighbors had gone home after paying their respects that Emily found a quiet moment. She sat in the living room with a cup of tea and listened to the cheerful sounds of the children's laughter. Grace gave them snacks, and they played happily with their toys in the playroom. She glanced over and saw that Billy had closed the parlor doors until the next day's burial. He came into the living room and turned on the radio. "I wonder what the latest news is about the Japanese attack?" he said. He narrowed his eyes at Emily. "You must already know about all this."

"Yes, I do, and it's not good."

Billy turned the dial and sat in the chair beside Emily as the soft music began to play. "Does Thomas…" his voice trailed off.

"No, unless this stupid curse causes something to happen to him, but otherwise he survives Pearl Harbor," Emily said.

"Pearl Harbor?"

Emily leaned towards Billy. "History will record it as the bombing of Pearl Harbor and 'a date which will live in infamy'.»

Billy looked as if he was about to say something, but Grace walked in with her tea, set it on the coffee table, and sat on the couch. "Any more news?" she asked.

Before Emily or Billy could answer, the announcer on the radio suddenly interrupted the programming, saying President Roosevelt was about to speak. They all stared at the radio, but only Emily could envision the president standing at the podium in the halls of Congress. She heard applause followed by someone presenting the introductions. Once again, Emily was about to witness an iconic historical moment in real-time. Then came the familiar words she had heard many times before.

"Yesterday, December 7th, 1941-a date which will live in infamy-…"

Billy jerked his head towards Emily, and they exchanged a knowing glance. Then, the president proceeded with the devastating news.

"...the United States of America was suddenly and deliberately attacked by naval and air forces by the Empire of Japan...."

Emily watched the color drain from Grace's face. Billy went over and put his arm around Grace as they listened to how Japan supposedly was working to maintain peace in the Pacific. All lies, Emily knew, and now everyone here knows it, too. Billy and Grace looked stunned.

"...I regret to tell you that very many American lives have been lost...."

At those words, Grace stood, walked over to the entranceway, leaned on the door frame, and placed her hand on her stomach. Emily went to Grace and put her arms around the woman who would in the future be her grandmother. At the same time, Billy wandered aimlessly around the room, as if trying to comprehend the unfolding events. Although Emily wasn't sure of anything, given that Charlotte had cursed Thomas, she looked into Grace's teary eyes and decided to share what she did know to be true, at least in her lifetime.

"Don't be afraid, Grace," Emily said with as much certainty in her voice as possible. "Believe me when I tell you. I also have it on good authority that Thomas has survived this attack.

Chapter 12

HONORABLE DISCHARGE

Hickam Field

December 8, 1941

"...With confidence in our armed forces—with the unbounding determination of our people—we will gain the inevitable triumph—so help us God...."

The room erupted in howling applause. Rick and Thomas stood sardined between trucks, airplane parts, and wall-to-wall military personnel. President Roosevelt's speech blasted out of a loudspeaker near the ceiling of a maintenance garage. With every word, Rick could feel the momentum building in the guys.

"...I ask that the Congress declare that since the unprovoked and dastardly attack by Japan on Sunday, December 7, 1941, a state of war has existed between the United States and the Japanese Empire."

Again, the room cheered, enthusiastic fists punched the air, and resolve could be seen in every man's face. Rick was proud to be among this greatest generation of guys, ready to fight with their bare hands if they had to.

Thomas put his arm around Rick's shoulder, yelling into Rick's ear over the loud cheering. "Come on. Let's get some air."

Despite the tragedy of the attack, the day was beautiful with its deep blue sky and warm breezes coming off the ocean beyond the airstrip. The two men walked among the rubble and damaged aircraft. Rick was amazed at how much had been cleaned up already. Guards were posted everywhere around the airfield, with all military installations on high alert.

Rick had a gnawing sense of uncertainty in his gut. He had no idea what was next for him. Rick also had no idea how to return to the future. He looked around bewildered, not so much at the carnage that surrounded him but at the prospect of never being able to return to his own time and, even worse, never seeing Emily again.

"You look as though you have the world on your shoulders," Thomas said with a look of sympathy.

"Isn't that the truth," Rick said and then glanced at Thomas. "I don't suppose you know any local Witches who can send me back to my own time, do you?"

"Sorry, old fly boy, "Thomas said with a sly expression. "I'm all outta Witches."

Rick said nothing as he took several more steps forward before realizing that Thomas wasn't with him. He glanced over his shoulder and saw Thomas looking towards the post office, which had survived the attacks. "What's up, Thomas?"

Thomas smiled, and Rick noticed that he had an I-got-a-great-idea look on his face.

"Until I can figure some way to get you back state side, how about sending a letter to your beautiful, redheaded wife?" Thomas patted Rick on the back, apparently pleased with his brilliant idea.

The post office was bustling with men scrambling for every piece of stationery and envelopes and clamoring to get word to their loved ones. The clerk received piles of outgoing letters and stamped so many that he ran out of ink, prompting him to switch ink pads faster than the speed of light.

After obtaining his paper, envelope, and pen, Rick sat outside on a rock by a palm tree, leaning the stationery on a magazine he had grabbed off a table on the way out. He stared up at the blue sky for a moment, shifted his gaze to the blank paper, and then began to write.

December 8, 1941

To my dear, sweet Emily,

Can you believe it? I ended up in Pearl Harbor with your grandfather and got caught up in the bombing. How I got to Pearl Harbor is a whole other story, and we can talk about it when I see you. The good news is that your grandfather, Thomas, is well, and I'm here to ensure he stays that way. Then there is my grandfather, but I'll leave that for another day.

I pray you are in Maple Ridge at this time. Unfortunately, I have no idea if you are or not. I miss you, Emily, more than I can say and want desperately to hold you in my arms. I'm not sure what happens next, but at least I got your grandfather as a friend and soldier in arms by my side. I won't say anything about what I have witnessed here in Pearl Harbor. I will do what I can to reach you if you truly are in Maple Ridge at this time, and I pray that you are. Thomas is trying to figure out how to send me home, but just in case I don't get there and you receive this letter, write me as soon as possible and let me know that you are safe. For now, sweetie, please stay safe.

All my love, always

Your loving husband, Rick

Rick folded the letter, placed it in an envelope, and addressed it to the farmhouse where Rick was sure Thomas's wife and son were living. He gave it to the mail clerk and hoped for the best. She'll sure be surprised, he said to himself as he stared at the busy clerk stamping his letter.

"You done already?" Thomas asked, handing two letters of his own to the mail clerk.

"She'll be shocked, I think. More shocked to hear that, not only did I time travel, but that I ended up here with you."

Thomas waved his hand in a come-along motion. "Let's get something to eat. Tomorrow, we will say our last goodbyes to J.J."

December 9th, 1941

In the early hours of the next day, the air force base was in deep mourning. One of the few hangers left untouched by the attacks was filled with a multitude of flag-draped caskets. They were placed side-by-side for family and friends to say their goodbyes.

Rick stood at attention in a formal military Marine uniform that Thomas had borrowed from another soldier of the same height and weight as Rick. His grandfather lay among hundreds of the brave cut down in their prime. Rick's emotions came in waves of sorrow mixed with pride. He was honored to stand before the man who had saved his life. A name plaque that read *Joseph J. Miller* rested alongside a picture of J.J. with his wife, Marion. Rick picked up the image and remembered seeing it as a kid. It had sat on the fireplace mantel for years, and Rick never gave it much thought. His grandmother had died when he was fourteen, a mere teenager who had constantly gotten himself into trouble. He set the picture back on the casket and raised his hand in a salute. "Rest in peace, Grandpa J.J."

"He was a great friend," a voice said from behind. Thomas approached, placed his hand on the casket, and then bowed his head.

"Hi, J.J.," Thomas said with a slight tremble in his voice. "Tell God to leave room for me someday, my friend."

Rick placed his hand on Thomas's back, letting him know he was not alone in his grief. They stayed by J.J.'s remains for a while. Rick watched all the tearful loved ones file in and out with the lingering shock still in their eyes. He looked at Thomas, feeling a sense of loss even for him. Rick knew he would never see Thomas again when and if he could return to his own time.

Later that afternoon, Rick made his way over to what remained of the mess hall for lunch. The food choices were cut in half, so he opted for a ham and cheese sandwich. He wasn't hungry and mostly stared at the sandwich on his plate as his mind drifted toward Emily. It was the only thing that had made sense in *The Twilight Zone*. He looked up and saw Thomas quickly approaching, which snapped him out of his daydream.

"Hey! There you are. I was wondering where you disappeared to," Thomas said, catching his breath from the brisk walk across the room. He pulled out the chair next to Rick and sat down.

"Well, you know what they say," Rick responded with a bit of humor. "When in doubt, always check the mess hall when it comes to missing personnel." Rick tilted his head curiously. "So, ah, what's the big hurry?"

Thomas looked as if he had just won the latest sweepstakes. He reached into his pocket and set what looked to Rick like a winning ticket on the table. Rick squinted as he picked up Thomas's prize. "A plane ticket?"

"Yup, first thing in the morning—stateside. Boston, Massachusetts, to be exact." Thomas looked pleased with himself. "And with no delays in ground transportation, you just might find yourself in Maple Ridge, Massachusetts by 1200 hours the day after tomorrow."

"But how did—?"

"How did I pull it off?" Thomas finished Rick's question. "I pulled a few strings and obtained the ticket. I also made sure your identity was not revealed having to do with J.J when I filed a report on his death."

"What did you say in the report?"

"That I witnessed J.J. jumping on two airmen, saving their lives just as a Zero dropped its bomb." Thomas leaned in towards Rick. "I stated that I couldn't identify the airmen in all the chaos."

"Which is why there was only the mention of my grandfather saving two of his comrades in the military records," Rick concluded.

"That's right. And by what you just said, it sounds like we are in the clear of any suspicion over your appearance here as well." Thomas leaned back in his chair, looking proud of his accomplishment.

Rick turned the ticket around and flipped it back over again with excitement radiating through his chest. To think he might see Emily again. Hold her in his arms. Just thinking of her allowed a small amount of desire to pass through his body. He had held those feelings at bay, not knowing if he would ever see her again. But now? he thought. Maybe?

*Early morning of
December 10, 1941*

The sun rose over the horizon as Rick stood beside a B-17 aircraft—one of a few that had survived the attack. The plane was headed for the states to transport four officers, two service secretaries, himself, and two other crew members. He glanced at the ticket for the following day's date: December 11, 1941. It would be a long flight to California. Although he didn't need the ticket to get on the B-17, he would need it for the flight in California, which was scheduled to take off on the 11th at 2 a.m. Pacific Time. With all the time zones, Rick thought, I'll be back in Maple Ridge before noon tomorrow.

With sadness in his eyes, Thomas lingered next to him and handed Rick a khaki green backpack.

"What's this?" Rick asked.

"I packed a few things of importance to you. Oh, and seeing I might not make it home for Christmas with everything that's happened, could you give this to my wife and son? It's another letter, if you don't mind."

Rick swung the backpack over his shoulder. "No, of course not. I'll make sure they get it."

Thomas shifted from one foot to another with his hands in his pocket. "So…I suppose this is it."

Looking at the plane and then back at Thomas, Rick lingered for a moment, appreciating the man in front of him. "It's been an honor to know you, sir," Rick said, holding his hand out to shake Thomas's. The two men shook hands with a tight grip, which morphed into a manly hug of love and gratitude between friends.

"Tell my granddaughter I wish I could've seen her again." Thomas held back tears. "Tell her that I love her."

"Thomas?" Rick hesitated. He wanted to give his new friend comfort and words of encouragement for the long road ahead. "I want you to know that you will see Emily again. You'll hold her in your arms two days after she's born."

Thomas gave a meaningful nod. His voice trembled with emotion. "Thank you for telling me. It gives me great comfort." Thomas then grinned slightly. "Guess this means, I make it through the war?"

Rick leaned in towards Thomas. "Yeah, well, I'd still keep my head down if I were you."

The plane revved up its engine. It was time. Thomas took two steps back and raised his hand in a salute. "Yes, sir, I'll be sure to do just that."

Rick stood at attention, offering a salute back, he then turned and entered the plane toward an unknown future.

Rick sat back as the plane lifted off the runway of Hickam Field. He looked down at the island landscape, still smoldering with persistent fires. He glanced into the turquoise sky, its fluffy white clouds drifting in the distance. Rick had a strange sense of remorse for leaving Thomas behind. Rick knew it wasn't his time or his war, but the camaraderie of a soldier seemed to transcend time and space.

Rick opened the backpack and found two large envelopes, one for Grace Stanford, and the other for him. Inside his, he found a letter from Thomas.

> Dear Rick,
>
> I have given it a lot of thought and concluded that you, in fact, were sent here to save my life. I hope to earn back what you have given me and make you and Emily proud. Because of minor delays in the aftermath of the attack, your grandfather's remains should arrive home in a few days. So, for now, I thought you should have something of your grandfather's. I have every confidence that you will know what to do with it....

Rick reached into the bag and opened a small box. Nestled inside was his grandfather's Purple Heart. The last time he had seen it was in his grandmother's house. The medal was displayed next to a triangular case containing a folded American flag. Rick felt mad at himself for not taking the time to learn the true significance of his grandfather's sacrifice. Rick looked back at the letter and continued to read.

> ...I have enclosed another a gift for you. I've obtained a certificate, filling it out with your name, rank, and military branch. You probably already have one. Although you fought only one battle in this war, I know that the Pearl Harbor attack is significant. So, I thought you

also deserved to have one certificate from this battle and in this war. Thank you, my friend. I hope you and Emily find your way back to each other. It has been an honor to have known you.
with my deepest and heartfelt regards
Thomas Stanford

Rick opened the envelope, finding a certificate that read: *United States Marine Corps, Honorable Discharge.* Rick looked up, glancing out the tiny window as the Hawaiian islands began to disappear into the Pacific Ocean. He was stunned at Thomas's gesture and, without realizing it, expressed his thoughts out loud. "How the hell did he pull that one off?"

Chapter 13

GHOSTS

Maple Ridge, Massachusetts
December 9th, 1941

THE MORNING SUN ILLUMINATED the fresh December snow, and it glittered like sparkling diamonds alongside the old gravestones. Emily's mind struggled with the contradiction before her: a pleasant day contrasted with the sadness of death. How many more times, Emily thought, will I watch another person's burial from a time not my own?

The Trinity Church bell rang in honor of Lucy Green. Other than the bell and the murmurings of the small group gathered around Lucy's grave, the cemetery and church grounds were quiet. Grace held Walter's hand, and Emily was glad the two were bonding as mother and son. However, she had noticed who wasn't there—Marion Miller, Grace's good friend and Rick's grandmother. Maybe her little boy was not feeling well, Emily thought. Or perhaps Marion was sick with worry over her husband, Joseph.

Emily's wandering mind became focused again when the priest began reciting Psalm 23: *The Lord is my Shepherd.* A sudden movement over the priest's shoulder caught Emily's eye. An elderly woman with long gray hair draped over her hunched shoulders stood by the Magic River, which ran alongside the cemetery. The woman wore a buckskin shawl and had a picnic basket dangling from her arm. Is that the woman I saw a couple of days ago in town?

Emily pondered. She looked at Billy, wondering if he saw the same woman, but his attention was on the funeral. When Emily returned her gaze towards the mysterious old woman, she had disappeared. Emily turned her head, scanning the cemetery for any sign of the elderly lady, but she was nowhere in sight. Then she noticed Billy looking at her as he silently mouthed, "What's wrong?" Emily gave him an uncertain look as she shrugged her shoulders.

The morning had passed quickly between the services at the church and the gravesite; it was now noontime. The small group of mourners went to Owen's Drug Store for lunch, and the collective mood lightened.

Emily was amused by Walter's enthusiasm over his root-beer float and a thick, juicy cheeseburger. She felt a gentle touch on her shoulder as Billy slid past the crowd and sat on the stool beside her. "Are you all right?" Billy asked. "You seemed spooked at the cemetery."

Emily took a sip of coffee and set the cup down, staring at the plate of eggs before her. "When is this all going to end for me?" She looked into Billy's concerned eyes. "I mean…I've watched so many people lowered into the ground, and most of them long before I was born. Then I see some old woman standing by the river in the cemetery, and a moment later, she disappeared." Emily sighed, shaking her head. "Now, I'm seeing ghosts."

Billy put his elbows on the lunch bar, seemed to consider Emily's situation, and then glanced at her. "I'm sorry, Emily, not sure I'd wanna be in your shoes, that's for sure. But I'm sure whoever this older lady is, she's probably just a mourner herself. Maybe she was there visiting her own loved one," he suggested while shrugging his shoulders and then concluding. "Could be anything."

Emily went from a hunched-defeated position to sitting straight and turned her stool to face Billy. "So, how do you explain the fact that she completely disappeared?"

Billy tapped his fingers on the counter, letting out a slow breath, and then gave Emily a side glance. "Maybe it was a ghost then."

"Oh, great, thanks. That's encouraging," Emily huffed.

"Look, Emily." Billy lowered his voice to a whisper. "You're a time traveler. I'd be willing to bet seeing a ghost might be a common occurrence for you. You must have seen aberrations during your other adventures?"

Billy was right. The first time she saw a ghost was when Sandra Easton showed up in a cemetery in Salem to warn her of the impending danger Derek and Meghan were in. Then she appeared again to say goodbye to her and Rick on a snowy Christmas Eve. Sandra Easton also happened to be Billy's ancestor, and she was certain Billy had known this information. Sandra had also appeared to Emily with each episode of her passing through time.

"Yes, Billy, you're right," Emily whispered. "Guess anything is possible when traveling through time. I should expect it."

The diner became less crowded. Billy excused himself and walked over to talk to an attractive young woman who came in with the little girl Beth and with Billy's son, Marty. Emily could see the strong connection between Billy and the young woman, because her face lit up upon seeing Billy. Billy's posture was tall, and he stood close to the woman. Their closeness reminded Emily of the same way Lucas stood when he had greeted Emily.

The memories of Lucas had a way of catching Emily off guard. She still missed and loved him deeply. She had been with Lucas most of her adult life, enjoying a long and happy marriage until his tragic death. That was the past, or as Emily thought ironically, the future.

Grace had told Emily that Billy's wife worked long hours at the hospital as the head nurse in her nursing unit. Her long hours put Beth and Marty in Billy's care most of the time. The young couple approached Emily, and she immediately stood to greet them.

"This is Emily, a friend of Thomas's grandfather." Billy's features softened with pride. "And Emily, this is my wife, Marlene."

"It's so nice to meet you," Emily said as she reached out to shake Marlene's hand.

A curious look came across Marlene's face. "Why do you look so familiar?" she asked.

"Well, ah…I'm not sure," Emily said, not mentioning that Marlene looked familiar as well.

She was a little taller than Emily, a slender girl with light brown hair pulled up on one side with a pretty butterfly hair clip.

"Billy tells me you're a nurse," Marlene said.

"Yes, but mostly retired right now," Emily replied.

"Oh, really? Where did you work?"

Billy cleared his throat as if trying to deflect his wife's question. "Emily doesn't work around here, honey. Don't you have to get going? You'll be late for your shift."

Marlene tilted her head and seemed intrigued by Emily; either she was thinking of her next question or trying to capture an old memory. "I remember Sam Stanford, everyone called him Doc. He died of the Spanish flu," Marlene hesitated, then pointed at Emily. "I know. You're the nurse who cared for me when I was sick with that flu."

Emily saw that Marlene was beginning to put two and two together. Billy then gave Emily a look that warned *Don't say anything more*, but Emily felt the need to tell Marlene at least something.

"Yes, I helped many people during that time."

As soon as Emily said those words, she recalled how she knew Marlene. She remembered Sam's voice as clear as day, saying, *"Guess we've chosen our second lucky patient."* Marlene was the second patient to whom Emily had administered antibiotics. Thankfully, Emily had put enough antibiotics in her pocket at the Maple Ridge Nursing Home before passing through time. She had wound up at the Maple Ridge Hospital in the middle of the Spanish flu outbreak.

The spark of interest remained on Marlene's face. "I distinctly remembered you putting that ice-cold stethoscope on my back," Marlene recalled. "That was you, wasn't it?"

Emily shifted her weight from one foot to the other. "Er, I

suppose you could have been one of my patients. As I said, there were so many."

"And you helped Billy, too. I remember," Marlene added. "You gave us both some pills that made the symptoms go away. What were they?"

"Oh, wow!" Billy interrupted as he looked at an invisible watch on his wrist. "Look at the time. Honey, you're going to be late for work."

Marlene squinted her eyes at Billy, gave him a slight grin, and stood on her tippy-toes, kissing him on the cheek. "You're right as always, darling." She regarded Emily with a suspicious smile. "Well, Emily, it was nice to meet you. Maybe we can talk shop next time I see you." Marlene then looked towards Grace, offering a friendly nod, turned and then sashayed out the door.

Emily waited for the door to close behind Marlene before glancing up at Billy. "You never told your wife anything?"

Billy leaned on the lunch counter, letting out a sigh of relief. "No, both Thomas and I kept it from both Grace and Marlene. Not only is Beth under my protection, but dare I say, so is my beautiful, inquisitive wife."

Emily saw a slight blush forming on Billy's cheeks and gave him an appreciative smile.

Billy lifted his chin towards Emily. "What's that look for?"

"You just remind me of someone I knew long ago."

"Ah! And who is this person you speak of?"

Emily stood close to Billy and put a gentle hand on his arm. "If I told you, it would be like having your own ghost to deal with. Besides, it can be a burden knowing the future." Emily leaned in, speaking in a low voice. "And I doubt you really want to carry that burden."

"Well, I don't know about that. I suppose I could handle it."

Emily lowered her head, stared at the black and white tiles on the floor, and wondered if telling Billy anything about the future would be the right thing.

She then looked up into Billy's eyes. "Are you sure?" Billy nodded.

"The person I'm referring to is Lucas, my first husband and—your grandson."

Billy said nothing and lowered himself onto the stool, staring into space. Emily sat next to him and put a gentle hand on his shoulder. "I'm sorry, Billy, I shouldn't have told you."

Billy placed his hand over Emily's. "I'm not going to ask you what happened to my grandson, but now I just realized something." Billy gave Emily a look of regret. "I believe you're the one that's carrying the most burden."

After the luncheon, Emily and Grace drove back towards the house while Billy took the children to his home to play. Grace wanted to stop by to see how her friend, Marion Miller, was doing, since she hadn't been at the wake or funeral. Grace had told Emily it was uncharacteristic of Marion not to be there for people in time of need. As they advanced towards Marion's house, Emily could see a Western Union courier, getting out of a car in front of an old brownstone with a pale-yellow paper in his hand. Suddenly Emily heard Grace gasp. "Oh no!" Grace said.

Emily and Grace got out of the car and approached the courier as he walked up the front steps. They stopped a couple steps below him as he knocked on the door. Emily knew all too well what was about to happen. She had already known and had tried hard to tuck it deep inside her mind. Rick's grandfather, Joseph Miller, was killed at Pearl Harbor and died a hero. Emily had written an article about it for the *Maple Ridge Gazette* more than eighty years into the future. It was another painful reminder for Emily how time travel was nothing more than walking among the ghosts of the past. The man knocked for the second time when Marion opened the door.

"Are you Mrs. Joesph Miller, wife of Private First Class Joesph John Miller?" the courier asked.

Marion stood frozen for a second, unable to speak. She put

her hands over her face, and then her legs suddenly gave out, and Marion collapsed. Emily and Grace were by Marion's side immediately, trying without success to console her. Emily knew precisely how Marion felt. It was a cold December day, just like this one, when the police came to her door telling her that Lucas had been killed in a car accident. Only this time, the haunting words were for Marion Miller.

"This is Mrs. Miller," Emily confirmed as she held out her hand to take the telegram.

The courier looked down at Grace and then handed the telegram to Emily. "I'm sorry, ma'am." he said somberly. He then descended the stairs and returned to his car.

Grace held on to Marion as she urged Emily with a painful nod to read the telegram. Emily cleared her throat and did her best to stay poised as she saw the words *Western Union* on the top and read:

> "It is with deep regret that the United States Air Force informs you of the death of Private First Class Joseph John Miller. He died saving two of his fellow soliders as Japanese planes bombarded Hickam Field on December 7, 1941. Private First Class Joseph John Miller died a hero."

Marion stood with the help of Emily and Grace. She ran her hand down the front of her dress to smooth the wrinkles and stood tall and brave. Emily was astonished by how much composure Marion had at that moment. More composure than she herself had on the day she learned of her own tragic news.

Chapter 14

SAVING BETH

December 10, 1941

THE DAY AFTER MARION MILLER received the devastating news of her husband's death, the radio continued to broadcast updates about the attack on Pearl Harbor. For the most part, the day seemed to go by quickly and felt strangely normal, Emily thought. No strange voice or a ghost appearing as an elderly lady and then vanishing into thin air.

Even when Emily and Grace went into town, they enjoyed a pleasant day, shopping for what was needed to make cookies for the Christmas festival being held the next day. It had been three days since the bombing of Pearl Harbor, and there was no talk from the town officials of canceling the festival. Emily thought people were trying their best to carry on despite the realization that the whole world was now at war.

Later, after their shopping trip, Emily and Grace had gone to check on Marion, but Emily could tell she wanted no company. Being alone and trying to absorb the loss was something Emily understood, but Marion was gracious towards them anyway.

That evening, Emily lay in bed thinking about Rick. She felt homesick for him and for her own time. Emily worried about whether she would be stuck in 1941 indefinitely. Her tired mind gave up, and she drifted into conflicting dreams—dreams of holding a baby in her arms, feeling the comforting warmth of its body, and then being shocked when suddenly the child began to glow.

Then, the haunting voice again called to her from beyond the Magic River.

When the dreams evaporated, she awoke the next morning and sat up in bed as the sun rose on a new day. She looked around the room and then put her hands over her face in frustration, saying, "Why am I here?"

Thursday, December 11, 1941
Opening Day of the Festival

Emily pulled herself together after the restless night. She was glad to sit in the cozy, warm kitchen with the smell of vanilla and lemon from the Christmas cookies Grace was baking for the festival.

"I hated to leave Marion yesterday in such despair," Emily said while spreading the buttercream frosting on top of the cookies.

Grace opened the oven and pulled out the last batch of cookies, placing them on the cooling rack. "I know Marion well," Grace spoke with absolute conviction in her voice, "and believe me, we've been friends for a long time, and I know that she'll be fine."

Emily nodded. "Well, she did insist that she was okay. I just wish there was more we could do for her, is all." Emily said.

"I suppose giving her space is what's needed, no doubt," Grace added as she wiped her hands on her apron.

Emily couldn't help but think how Marion could ever be all right. But then Emily realized she had come to a place of acceptance after her loss, mostly because of Rick and how he had made her life complete again.

Emily also continued to worry about Thomas. She kept praying that Charlotte's curse had no power to reach as far as the Hawaiian islands. Just the thought of the telegram announcing the death of Marion's husband made her stomach feel queasy. Still, the thoughts nagged at her, especially after witnessing Marion's heartache the other day. Then again, she knew that Thomas didn't die in the war but of cancer many years later. Yet the curse, that damn curse, she thought. Emily did her best to compartmentalize everything before her. One thing at a time, she told herself.

"There," Emily said, holding up a plate of cookies, pleased with her masterpieces of frosting topped with green and red sprinkles. No sooner had she put the plate down than Walter, Beth, and Marty came running into the kitchen, lunging for the cookies.

Grace quickly pulled the dish towel from the hook and swatted the children on their behinds. "Get your little paws off those cookies! They're for the festival!" she yelled.

Grace's form of discipline amused Emily. Towel swatting was apparently her weapon of choice, and Grace used it with precision when annoyed with the children's lack of good behavior.

Billy strolled in behind the three cookie grabbers. "Hey, you hoodlums, I think you know better than that," Billy said, scooting them out of the kitchen. He lifted his chin in the direction of Emily and Grace. "You girls almost ready to leave?"

"As soon as I wrap up the cookies," Grace said.

Emily leaned over, looking past Billy. "Is Marlene going to be coming today?"

"Unfortunately, no. She's still at the hospital working a double shift."

Emily picked up the wrapped plate of cookies and smiled at Billy. "I guess we'll just have to save some for her to have later. Besides, we wouldn't want Marlene to miss out on Grace's famous Italian Christmas cookies now, would we?"

Come one, come all to the Annual Christmas Festival, beginning December 11, 1941, the banner proclaimed as Emily walked underneath it and over the Shady Brook Bridge, holding Beth's hand. Walter and Marty walked ahead, and Emily could tell the boys were eager to stop at the candy vendor just over the bridge and next to the swamp. Emily turned her head to avoid seeing the haunted swamp with its eerie sense of doom. Grace held tightly to Matthew's hand, as she made her way to her assigned place at the bake sale table.

It had been four days since the attack on Pearl Harbor. The festival tradition was still part of Maple Ridge in Emily's time. Each year, it typically kicked off on December 7, Pearl Harbor Day, as it became known, but in 1941, it was just another winter festival.

Beth tugged on Emily's hand. "Can we go see Santa?" she asked, pointing to a long line of children up ahead.

Emily bent down to Beth's level. The little girl had rosy cheeks and a sweet smile, and the steam from her breath circled her little face. "I think it's best to ask your daddy." Emily's eyes darted up at Billy as he looked over his shoulder.

"All right then. But stay with the boys," Billy told Beth.

The children scattered, anxious to check out all the vendors selling toys near the long line of children eagerly waiting for Santa. One vendor displayed handcrafted Christmas decorations, while another was a local women's group selling their latest patchwork quilts.

Emily set the plate of cookies on a long table for the bake sale. The table held a sign indicating that proceeds would be going towards the new wing of the Maple Ridge Hospital. She watched as people went by, all dressed warmly against the cold bite of the winter air.

Emily gravitated towards the roaring fire burning in an old, rusty barrel alongside the baked goods stand. She sat on a small bench next to the hot barrel and felt the Christmas spirit gain momentum over the turmoil of the past few days. She thought of Rick; he occupied her mind during quiet moments. She conjured up his face, heard his laughter in her mind, and giggled to herself when thinking about his silly jokes. Emily missed him but knew she had yet to accomplish something in this time and place.

The thought caused her to look towards the children waiting in line, and she suddenly realized that she could no longer see

Walter, Marty, or Beth. She reluctantly looked towards the swamp, and suddenly all the turmoil she thought had gone came rushing back. Beth was standing by the swamp's edge, talking to the same elderly lady Emily had seen in the cemetery. Emily jumped to her feet ready to run, but a woman's nasally voice interrupted her terror. "A dozen please," the woman said.

Emily wasn't sure the woman was speaking to her, since Grace was in charge of the bake sale table. Emily darted a look down the long table and saw Grace busy with a customer. Matthew held tightly to the side of his mother's coat. Billy was two vendors down, chatting with a guy selling tool belts. Emily's heart pounded, and as cold as it was, she felt beads of sweat roll down her back.

"I said a dozen please!" the irritating woman said louder.

Emily said nothing and quickly tossed cookies into a bag, shoving them into the customer's arms, and pushed past her. Emily ran towards the children in line, waiting to see Santa. Walter and Marty were near the front of the line, and when she looked towards the spot where Beth and the older woman had stood, they were both gone. She ran over, peering into the tall, dead brush on the edge of the swamp, forgetting her fears or her previous hesitation about the area. Getting to Beth was all she concentrated on.

"Beth? Beth!" she called. Emily thought she could see Beth going through the tall grass. This time, she thought, nothing is going to stop me. It wasn't just herself she had to think about anymore. Now, someone else was in danger. Then, Emily took a deep breath and entered the frozen swamp towards the mysterious old lady and a haunting voice that could possibly beckon to her at any moment.

Emily walked gingerly over the icy surface with long stems of cattails sticking through the ice. She turned her head towards the festival and noticed Billy and Grace looking on in horror. She waved her hand. "It's okay!" Emily yelled. "I think I hear Beth up ahead."

Billy inched his way in her direction.

"NO! Billy, you can't. It's okay, trust me, I can hear her."

Billy's posture stiffened, and Emily could see him tightening his fists as he reluctantly stood by helplessly. She knew this had to be awful for Billy. He was Beth's protector. Being unable to do his job caused obvious despair, which showed on his face. She was beginning to understand why she had time-traveled to 1941. With Thomas nowhere near Maple Ridge, Beth may have been the one she was supposed to save.

Emily heard the little girl whimper through the thick brush. "It's going to be all right, Beth," Emily said gently to ease the child's terror. "I'm here. Don't worry."

Emily saw Beth submerged in solid ice to her waist, strangely holding a candy cane in her little hand. She had stopped crying, which wasn't a good sign. Emily got down on her belly and began to crawl to distribute her weight evenly to keep the thinner sections of the ice from cracking. When she reached the little girl, Beth was hopelessly trapped in a solid patch of ice with a petrified look on her face. Clearly, the curse still had its icy grip on the swamp. Beth was nearly frozen. Emily checked to see if she was still breathing and saw a small amount of steam from her breath seeping between her narrow lips.

"Oh, my God, she's hardly breathing," Emily said in horror. Emily glanced over to Beth's side. Just a few feet away, she saw a stick with a sharp end resembling a spear. After crawling over to retrieve it, she made her way back and began to chisel the ice around the near-frozen child with the pointed edge of the stick. She loosened the ice enough to get hold of Beth under her arms and, with all her strength, began to pull her out. When Emily finally got Beth and herself away from the half-frozen swamp and onto a thick patch of ice. Emily knew she didn't have the strength to carry the little girl. Luckily, the Maple Ridge police who had been in the park for the festival reached Emily.

One officer grabbed Beth, dragging her little body across the snow toward Billy. He stood solidly in place with his arms out, ready to take over for the officer. Grace and the other children looked on in horror. Emily and the officer got Beth to the swamp's edge. Billy scooped Beth into his arms.

"Thank you, officer," Billy said and glanced at Emily. "Come on! We need to get her to the hospital quickly."

Grace ran over to Emily gripping her arm. "Are you all right, Emily?"

Emily began to catch her breath from her laboring task. "I'm fine. I'm going with Billy to the hospital."

Billy had already started walking fast over the Shady Brook Bridge towards his car.

"Tell Billy I'll look after Marty for him," Grace said.

Emily looked over and saw how scared Marty looked. Emily gave him a slight grin. "She's going to be okay, Marty, don't worry." Then she turned towards the bridge to follow Billy as he carried Beth's limp body.

Chapter 15

THE HOMECOMING

December 11, 1941

CRACKED ICE, FROZEN LILY PADS, and decomposed frogs lay scattered in the icy water alongside the trees. A delicate hand reached desperately for a branch. A woman breathing hard tried with all her strength to grab a limb. Then she yelled in a frantic voice, "DON'T GO OVER THE THRESHOLD!" She screamed his name, and he recognized her voice. It was Emily. As he ran towards the screams, he abruptly fell into the icy water. He could hear a beeping tone over and over as Emily called out to him. Rick jolted up in his seat as a blurry figure lingered before him. The beeping sound seemed to come from behind the looming presence. Then, a face came into focus. It was an attractive flight attendant leaning towards him.

"Are you all right, sir?" she asked.

It didn't take long for Rick to regain his senses. Still feeling slightly disoriented and most likely suffering from jet lag, he figured he had slept through the two-and-a-half-hour flight from Chicago, a refueling stop, to Boston. Although he remained awake through the four-hour, non-stop flight from California to Chicago, it wasn't long before sleep got the best of him.

"Can you tell me where we are?" he asked, still feeling dazed from his bad dream and unsure of his location.

"Yes, sir. We have just landed in Boston."

Rick felt uneasy in his gut, knowing it wouldn't be long before he found out whether Emily had made it to Maple Ridge, Massachusetts, in 1941. He stumbled out of his seat, grabbing the backpack from the overhead baggage bin.

Rick walked briskly through the airport and saw a long line of people waiting for the yellow taxis to take passengers to their final destinations. He overheard one of the baggage handlers say no more taxis were available and that the wait would be at least twenty minutes or more.

Rick looked over his shoulder and spotted a wall of phone booths with a much shorter line than the one by the taxi pick up. Well, maybe I can find out right away if Emily made it to this time, Rick thought as he stood waiting in line for his turn at a phone. Rick looked up at a wall clock: 11:45 a.m. Thomas's words echoed through his mind: *You might just find yourself in Maple Ridge, Massachusetts, by 1200 hours.* "Noontime," Rick said under his breath.

While waiting to use the phone, he took in all the sights and sounds around him. He could hear the familiar standards from the 1940s playing in the background as he watched fast-moving travelers trying to make their way to or from their flights. Now, there was a sight that hasn't changed, he thought. As he stood in line, he looked at the vintage phone booths and snorted as he realized that making a call would take forever. Without thinking, Rick found his words tumbling out of his mouth. "Oh, man, I could sure use a cell phone right now."

"What is that?" a man in line behind Rick asked. Rick turned around and saw a short, balding man in his late fifties wearing thick, dark rimmed glasses and holding a briefcase. The man looked skeptical.

Rick couldn't resist his usual off-the-cuff remarks that had a way of slipping past his lips. "If I told you, mister, it would blow your mind." Rick pointed to the phone booth. "And your next call would be to someone with a straight jacket to carry me away." The man looked indignant at Rick, just as the phone booth door opened for the next caller.

"Finally," Rick said as he closed the door behind him. He picked up the receiver, which carried the aroma of tobacco and a nasty case of bad breath. Ignoring the unpleasant smells, Rick reached into the backpack and took out a small notepad with Thomas's home number.

Rick was impressed with how well Thomas had packed all the right things Rick would need for the trip. Thomas had even put a small box wrapped in brown paper with the word *Biscuits* on the front and a canteen filled with apple juice. He also gave Rick spending money for the long trip home. Thomas knew what it took to be well prepared—a real Boy Scout, Rick thought. Rick put his finger in the hole marked zero and turned the dial of the rotary phone.

"Operator, I'd like to make a collect call, please," Rick said and then recited the number.

"Just a moment, sir. I will connect you," the operator said in a nasally voice.

His call rang at the other end with no answer. Rick hung up and tried again with no success. "Guess I better find myself a ride then," he said and opened the door. He found the nosy man still there and staring at him. Rick tapped him on the arm as the man approached the phone booth. "Hey, buddy, you don't happen to know where I could find an Uber?"

The man huffed his way into the phone booth, muttering something incoherent. Rick's mouth turned up in a playful grin. "Nah, I didn't think so."

No one was standing in the line for taxis, and he was able to catch one quickly. Rick was finally on his way with no idea what he would find when he got to Maple Ridge. The only sure thing in Rick's mind was his first stop. A place he was sure to find the same sorrow that had lingered inside him for the past few days.

After the twenty-minute ride to Maple Ridge, the taxi pulled up to a brownstone house with silver garland draped over the front entrance and a giant Christmas wreath on the front door. He reached into his pocket, pulled out several dollar bills, and handed them to the driver. The driver's eyes widened over the generous amount in the palm of his hand. Rick grinned at the pleased driver while opening the passenger door. "Merry Christmas, buddy. Thanks for the ride."

He lingered by the curb, studying the old row-houses. It looked the same as when he last saw it except for the oak tree in front that had shaded the dwellings in the hot summer months. In his time the old oak no longer existed. Rick took a deep breath and then swung his backpack over his shoulder.

The frigid air cut through him like a knife. That's when he realized Thomas had forgotten one thing—a heavy winter coat instead of the lightweight field jacket he was wearing. He moved slowly toward the steps that led to his grandmother's front door and looked up and noticed a flag banner in the window. It had a red border, a white middle, and a gold star in the center. The sight made Rick's heart sink. She already knows, he concluded.

At the top of the steps he stood by the door, looking down at himself. He ran his hand over his jacket to smooth out the wrinkles without success, ran his hand through his hair, cleared his throat, and then gently knocked on the door. He could hear a young child saying, "Mama! Door."

Then the doorknob turned as it slowly opened, and there stood a young woman carrying a small child in her arms. "Can I help you?" the young woman asked.

Rick cleared his throat again. "Ah, yes—I, ah...am looking for Marion Miller."

"Yes, that would be me."

The woman was beautiful, Rick thought. He had only known his grandmother with deep lines across her forehead and dark circles under her eyes. As he stood there mesmerized by her youthful looks, another revelation occurred. The child in her arms had to be his own father at the age of two. Rick composed himself quickly, putting the feeling of being in *The Twilight Zone* aside as he took up the critical matter before him.

"I served with your husband, Joseph, in Hawaii," Rick said with a catch in his voice.

Marion's eyes began to swim with tears. "You...you have seen my Joseph?"

"Yes, ma'am. He saved my life."

Marion looked as if she was going to drop her son. Rick's quick reflexes caused him to reach out, taking the child from her arms. The little boy smelled of baby powder and fresh soap, and he sported pajamas decorated with cowboys and horses. Marion held onto the door frame looking bewildered but seemed to regain her composure quickly as she waved her hand for Rick to enter the house without saying a word.

"I'm so sorry for your loss, ma'am," Rick said as he handed the child back to Marion.

"Please," Marion said, motioning her hand in the direction of the living room. "Have a seat. Can I get you anything, sir?"

"No, no, I'm fine, thank you," Rick said as he walked into the living room, sat on the couch, and put his backpack on the floor.

Marion set her little boy down on the floral rug next to a tower of alphabet blocks. "This is little Randy. He loves his building blocks," she said, sitting on the couch next to Rick. "My Joseph brought them for him last Christmas, and now…" she paused, her words strained. "There won't be anything this year."

Her beauty could not conceal the weariness evident in her bloodshot eyes. Sleep clearly eluded her. Marion pulled her hanky from her pocket and wiped her nose. "I'm sorry," she said and then gave an apologetic look to Rick. "I didn't quite catch your name, sir."

"Oh, I'm sorry. My name is Rick Miller." As soon as he said it, he realized how strange it sounded even to himself. He wondered how it would sound to Marion.

Marion seemed to be studying his face with uncertainty. "How interesting. Are you related to Joseph?"

Rick looked down at Randy, piling one block on top of another. If she only knew, he thought. "No, I don't think so. I guess there are a lot of Millers out there."

Marion let out a long sigh. "I suppose there are. It is, after all, a common name."

"The reason for my visit, ma'am, is to tell you how grateful I am for your husband's bravery. I was one of the soldiers Joseph saved just before he..." Rick's voice trailed off. Instead, he set his backpack on his lap and took out the box containing Joseph's Purple Heart. "Joseph would want you to have this, ma'am," he handed the box to Marion.

She opened the box slowly and ran her finger across the medal as her eyes filled with tears again. She said nothing, just gazed at the symbol of heroic loss and all that was left to remember her husband's sacrifice. Rick wanted to hug his grandmother, console her, and make her pain disappear, but he knew it would be impossible. He saw her look at Randy and then at him. "I will save this for Randy, and it will go to his son and then his son after that."

Her words settled heavily on his heart as he swallowed the hard lump in his throat. Rick contained his emotions and kept them steady in the presence of his grandmother. Marion reached in her pocket again for her trusted hanky. "At least then," she said between blowing her nose and wiping her tears, "Joseph will always be remembered for the hero he was."

Once again, Rick felt the guilt tumbling into his soul. He had been indifferent in the past regarding his grandmother and grandfather. The death of his grandfather was ancient history, and now Rick realized that he should have never dismissed his grandfather's bravery. He was seeing the hard truth in the face of his young grandmother. At that moment, he vowed never to let his son, Derek, or his granddaughter, Melanie, forget Joseph John Miller.

Chapter 16

TELLING THE TRUTH

EMILY LEANED HER FOREHEAD against the cold soda machine at the end of a long hallway in the Maple Ridge Hospital. She felt a bad headache coming on. The adrenaline she had three hours ago had subsided only slightly. "That damn stupid curse! Charlotte can go to hell for all I care," she barked in frustration to the soda machine.

"Did you get any good advice out of that thing?" a voice behind her asked.

Emily turned to find Marlene standing in her white nurse's uniform with a neatly placed nursing cap pinned to her hair. She had one hand on her hip, while the other held a clipboard.

"Oh, Marlene. I didn't know you were standing there. Is Beth all right?"

"I don't know. She's still alive, but her tests are inconclusive. It's as if she has polio, but somehow whatever this is seems different."

"How do you mean?" Emily asked.

"Well, her face is frozen. I don't mean frozen from the cold because her skin is warm and supple, not that discolored, waxy look. Her lips don't move, and her eyes have a dead stare as if she's in some sort of trance." Marlene shook her head. "None of this is indicative of polio. It's why I came out to see you. I need to ask you what happened in that swamp."

With Marlene's description of Beth's condition, Emily knew it must be the same thing that killed Lily Spencer and her grand-daughter, Kathleen – the curse – and Kathleen was Beth's birth mother. Emily walked past Marlene to one of the waiting room chairs and felt completely lost for words.

"I need you to tell me what happened in that swamp," Marlene said as she walked over to Emily and stood before her.

Emily sat in silence, as her mind wrestled with telling the truth. How can I explain this to Marlene and still keep Billy and Thomas's secret? Emily wondered.

Marlene sat next to Emily with her hands folded on her clipboard. "I'm not stupid, Emily. I know that you know something."

Emily could see her eyes filled with questions. Marlene seemed to have a suspicious nature—a person who needs proof beyond a reasonable doubt. Marlene was a critical thinker with an inquisitive mind—all good qualities for a head nurse in charge of a whole unit, Emily thought.

Marlene continued to press for answers. "Those pills you gave me back in 1918 were antibiotics, weren't they? That's why Billy and I recovered more easily, and now you show up twenty-three years later, looking as if you haven't aged a day. Then this happens." Marlene pointed in the direction of the emergency room.

Emily shifted in her seat and leaned in towards Marlene. "I can tell you this much," Emily finally said, touching Marlene's arm. "Beth is being attacked by the same thing that killed her mother and grandmother."

Marlene's face turned white, and she looked at Emily in disbelief. Within seconds, her demeanor quickly changed, and she narrowed her eyes. "They never could understand what they died from," Marlene said, tapping her fingers on the clipboard. "I remember being in nursing school where everyone had talked about it. They did autopsies on both women and found nothing wrong other than they stopped breathing and died. Oh, my God, could that happen to Beth?" Marlene's mouth dropped, and Emily saw panic in her eyes.

"I need to speak to Billy," Emily said standing and then craning her neck to see if he was nearby.

Marlene abruptly stood. She glared at Emily and grabbed her arms. "No, Emily, you're gonna give it to me straight. I already know Billy is keeping secrets from me." Marlene's nostrils flared, and she exhaled a breath that showed her frustration. "Whether you like it or not, Emily, you'll tell me the truth. That's my daughter in there. If there's something that I can do to stop her from dying, I need to know about it right now."

Emily pulled Marlene's grip from her arms and spoke with what truth she did control. "There's nothing that you can do," Emily hesitated and then said with determination, "but there's something I can do."

"What the hell is that supposed to mean?" Marlene shouted.

"What's going on!" a male voice called from down the hallway. Billy approached quickly, his eyebrows drawn together as he cut both women off from their heated discussion. Emily could see he was bewildered over the exchange between her and Marlene.

"Billy!" Marlene yelled. "It seems Emily has a cure for what ails Beth." Marlene glared at Emily.

Billy opened his mouth to say something, but Emily interrupted. "Billy, I think it's time you came clean with your wife. As for the cure to what is ailing Beth…" Emily said, glancing at Marlene and then at Billy, "I believe the swamp has something to do with this curse, and I need to go back there, and end this thing once and for all."

"You can't do this!" Billy said, holding his hand up to stop her from leaving. "Your chances of dying are good if you go in there. Emily, I can't protect you."

"What the hell are you two talking about?" Marlene interrupted.

Emily looked sternly into Billy's face. "Beth will die if I don't. It's why I'm here, Billy. I need to do this." Emily turned to Marlene and then focused her attention back on Billy. "It's time that your wife knows."

Billy stood helpless with sadness in his eyes and with his arms hanging limply by his side, as if in defeat. Emily realized at that moment how much Billy cared about her. He seemed to come to terms with Emily's fate. He reached into his pocket, took Emily's hand, and kissed it softly as he placed his car keys in her palm. "You're going to need a way to get there." He gently squeezed Emily's hand shut with the key safely tucked inside. "Be careful."

Emily gave Billy a look of resolve. The anguish on Billy and Marlene's faces was heartbreaking.

The thought of Charlotte's curse harming an innocent child went too far. Enough was enough.

"Don't worry, Billy. I'll take care of that bitch." Emily turned and walked down the long hallway. She looked over her shoulder and saw Billy holding Marlene in his arms. "It's time to make this right," Emily whispered at the sight of the grieving couple. With that, Emily began her journey of uncertainly towards a haunted swamp where she could face her own possible death.

Chapter 17

MYSTERIOUS MESSAGE

Rick spent nearly two hours with his grandmother, Marion, and her son, Randy. The thought of his two-year-old father sitting by his feet seemed ridiculous to Rick. He felt as though he had gone through the looking glass with *Alice in Wonderland*, but he mainly considered himself walking around in *The Twilight Zone*. He didn't mind. He was glad he had met his grandfather, Joseph, his grandmother, and now his future father.

When Rick inquired about Emily, Marion had told him that Emily was staying with Grace Stanford. He became excited and anxious to see Emily after what seemed like forever. Marion was trusting enough to let him take her car to the Stanford farmhouse. Rick couldn't believe someone would just let a stranger take her car so easily. It was a simpler time, for sure.

Rick chugged along in his grandparents' 1932 Chevy sedan. The three-speed shift was similar to the taxi he had driven in Pearl Harbor. He ran his hand across the surface of the beige wool seat beside him and felt a small amount of warm air drifting from a tiny vent below the dashboard. The vibration of the motor and lack of suspension made for a rough ride, and when Rick squinted at the gas gauge it pointed to empty. Rick gave the gauge a tap, and it popped back up to half full. "Oh, man, this is so cool," he gushed.

Rick drove through the main street and saw all the vendors in the park across the river. "Wow! Now that's a sight that looks familiar. It's nice to know some things remained the same," Rick said as he took in the sights and sounds of a time gone by. He drove a little farther, making his way just outside of town, and then pulled up to the farmhouse. He sat in the car and thought how all this was so strange.

The house looked the same; it hadn't changed much in nearly eight decades. He noticed a partially melted snowman in the front yard with its hat falling off and missing its eyes, nose, and mouth. A red knitted scarf around the melting figure was the only thing that looked intact. Children live here, Rick concluded. It almost felt as if he was coming home on any other ordinary day. But nothing here was ordinary, and Emily would be the only one who could ground him to his own time.

Without wasting another minute, he grabbed his backpack, exited the car, ran up the front steps onto the porch, and enthusiastically knocked on the door. When the door opened, Rick recognized the woman standing in the doorway. He had seen her picture just a few days ago. It was the day before the attack on Pearl Harbor when Thomas had shown it to him. She was Grace Stanford.

"Yes, may I help you?" Grace asked.

"Yes,..ah, I'm Rick Miller. I served with your husband, Thomas, at Pearl Harbor." Rick saw the immediate shock across her face. She barely held herself up while holding onto the doorknob.

"Are you okay, ma'am?" Rick asked as he stepped forward and took her arm. His mouth turned up slightly into a weary grin. "Sorry, I seem to have this effect on women lately," he said trying to lighten the mood. Then he became more serious. "I didn't mean to scare you that way. Your husband is fine, trust me. I'm telling the truth."

Grace looked at Rick, clutching her chest as she tried to catch her breath. "Oh, thank God. It's just. I didn't expect—"

"Of course, you wouldn't. I understand," Rick said. He pulled his backpack off his shoulder and took out the large envelope with Grace's name on it. "For you—from Thomas."

She looked doubtful as she took the envelope and then focused on Rick. "This...is really from Thomas?"

"Yes, ma'am."

"And Thomas is all right?"

"The last time I saw him he was as right as rain."

Grace tilted her head, darting her eyes from Rick back to the envelope and then at Rick again. "Miller. You said your name is Miller?"

"Yes, ma'am, I'm Emily's husband."

"Oh my!" Grace said as Rick saw her shoulders relax, all the doubt evaporating into the cold air. "Why, I didn't even know Miller was Emily's last name." Rick could see a hint of Emily's smile as Grace's face lit up with relief and joy. "Emily has told me so much about you."

Rick raised one eyebrow. "Well, I hope nothing bad," he said.

"Oh, no, not at all. She misses you fiercely. I can tell when she speaks your name," Grace said, gesturing a welcome with her arm. "Please, please come in. You'll catch your death out here. I'm Grace, by the way," she giggled. "But, of course, you must already know that. Can I get you coffee? Tea? I made fresh cookies this morning for the winter festival in the park."

"I thought that's what was going on when I went by there earlier and saw all the people. And thank you for the offer, but I'm more interested in seeing my wife at the moment."

Just then, two young boys and a toddler came running from the kitchen, chasing each other.

"Hey, hey, you little whippersnappers! Stop running in the house!" Grace scolded and then looked at Rick with sheepish eyes. "I'm sorry. They can get out of hand sometimes. This is my nephew, Marty, and that little guy is my son, Matthew, and, of course, my other son, Walter, " she said, winking at Walter.

Rick gave all three boys a nod, and he noticed Walter blushing from his mother's introductions.

"Who's that?" Marty asked, pointing to Rick.

"This is Mr. Miller, Emily's husband and a friend of Uncle Thomas. He was in the military with him."

"Did you ever get wounded?" Marty asked. Rick knelt on one knee to be at the boy's level. "I was wounded once, but I'm all better now."

"Do you have a gun, mister?" Walter asked.

"I do."

"Did you ever kill someone with your gun?" Marty chimed in.

Rick was about to answer when Grace took off her apron, swatting the boys. "You three go find something else to do other than bothering our guest."

"Hold on a second, guys," Rick said, reaching into his backpack and pulling out a little brown bag. "If you're good, I'll let you have a piece of my official military-issued chocolate." He glanced at Grace with a look that asked: *Is it okay?*

Grace nodded, the boys licked their lips, and Rick handed each of them a piece of candy that Thomas had packed for him.

"All right then, boys, you take Matthew into the playroom and don't get chocolate all over everything," Grace said breathlessly as the boys raced off.

Rick stood and looked around the room and up the staircase. "So, is Emily around somewhere?" he asked.

"Oh, dear," Grace said. "She's not here. She's at the hospital with Billy and little Beth, poor thing."

Rick clenched his jaw and felt his heart racing out of his chest. "What happened? Is Emily okay?"

"Oh, it's not Emily." Grace said with concern in her eyes. "It's little Beth. Emily pulled her from the frozen swamp a few hours ago. Beth was hardly breathing, so Emily and Billy took her to the hospital."

"Billy? Is that Billy Easton?" Rick asked.

"Yes. Beth is Billy's niece, and now he is raising her as his daughter. He's always been so protective over little Beth and now this." Grace sighed. "No doubt Billy is blaming himself right now, poor man."

Rick was beginning to feel uneasy. The fact that Emily had to go into the swamp to save a child who was hurt enough to land in the hospital caused a gnawing twist in his stomach. Rick started towards the door. "I'm sorry, Grace, to cut this short, but I gotta go. It was nice to meet you. I gotta find my wife."

The day was beginning to lose its light as Rick raced toward the hospital. He made his way down the main street, dodging festival goers getting in their cars as the day's events had ended. He spotted an old woman crossing the street wearing a buckskin shawl with her arm tucked under a basket handle. Rick swerved to avoid hitting her and slammed on his brakes, causing a loud screech. The woman just stood there unfazed, looking at him with penetrating eyes. He jumped out of the car and ran to the woman in the middle of the street. It was as if she had purposely stepped out in front of his car.

"Are you okay, lady? I'm so sorry. I hope I didn't scare you."

The old woman remained still. She seemed to be searching Rick's face. She spoke in a low, quivering voice, *"Don't go over the threshold."* This peculiar advice caused goosebumps to ripple up Rick's arms. And just like that, she continued to the other side of the street.

Rick stood in shock as he remembered his dream about Emily during which she had said the same thing: "Don't go over the threshold." Suddenly, a car horn blasted him back to reality.

"What the hell are you doing, bub? Get the hell out of my way!" a furious man yelled as he stuck his head out his car window.

Rick put his hand up. "Yeah, yeah, yeah. Take it easy. Keep your shirt on. I'm leaving."

Rick resumed his drive down the road, still shaking off what had just happened with the old lady. One thing he couldn't shake off—the feeling of doom gripping his gut. He knew what that swamp meant for Emily. She had heard a voice speaking to her on more than one occasion.

As far as some threshold—he had no clue. But he knew for sure something was happening; he could feel it. It was something terrible, deadly. The knowledge was absolute in his mind. How do I know this? he wondered. He had to get to Emily now before anything else happened.

Chapter 18

THE SHACK

EMILY'S STEPS MADE A CRUNCHING SOUND as she walked up a slight incline, pushing the dead branches aside. She came to an indentation that might have been an old road or path leading to somewhere. She stopped, looking at a deteriorated log covered in frozen moss. A squirrel poked its head up from a small hole in the old tree. "At least not everything is dead in here," she said to the squirrel, now frantically running away. Emily did her best to keep from walking over the icy parts, not wanting to fall in as Beth had.

The sun had gone down by now. She looked above and saw the full moon casting light on the frozen water and among the spooky shadows of darkness everywhere. She relied on the moonlight to guide her through the maze of dead trees. All Emily felt was dread. Her hands trembled; she did her best to stay calm, but fear had more of a significant effect. Emily found herself on a path that led uphill away from the wetland.

The trail took several twists and turns, and she decided to stay on it. A dead rabbit lay on the path, its fur scattered and its flesh picked over by the lingering vultures overhead. Up ahead, an old, rickety sign dangled from a rotted post. As she got closer, she could see the faded letters barely legible with the word *Cemetery*. Emily noticed a wrought iron fence with a broken gate just beyond the old sign. "What in the world?" Emily said, surprised, knowing she had never heard of a cemetery near the swamp. She pushed hard on the gate stuck in the frozen mud and squeezed through the opening.

Emily took several steps forward and stopped, peering into the brown, overgrown, snow-covered grass. She found rabbit and squirrel prints everywhere and morbidly wondered if some of those tracks belonged to the dead rabbit she had seen on the path. Emily wanted nothing to do with going further on the mysterious, ancient, hallowed ground.

When she turned to leave, she tripped over a broken gravestone. The sharp edges cut a large gash in her leg, knocking her off balance and causing her to land on the ground next to the old stone. "DAMMIT!" she screeched. She held her hand over the gash on her leg and felt the pain shoot across the bloody wound. "SHIT! SHIT!" she yelled, scaring away any remaining little creatures nearby.

Emily tore the slip underneath her dress into a long strip. Scooping her hand in the fresh snow, she wiped away the blood running down her leg, then wrapped the wound with the material tying it into place to stop the bleeding. Emily rested her head on her knees, trying to summon as much courage as possible. She lifted her head and saw an old oak tree alongside the broken gravestone that caused her to fall and injure herself.

The oak tree branch draped eerily over the grave as though bowing to its occupant resting beneath the ground. She leaned forward and cleared away the brown grass and snow from the stone when all her senses heightened. The sound of the howling wind whistled through tiny crevices of dead trees. Unearthly beams of moonlight cast menacing shadowy figures in every dark space around her. Emily felt the water trickling beneath the ice patches where she sat, and far away was the sound of a hawk waiting for its prey. She could even smell the blood from her wound. If I can smell it, she thought, so can other creatures.

It took all her courage not to let her imagination take over, and instead she tried hard to focus on the worn date and name written across the stone in front of her. She had just seen this name on a template ready to be engraved on a brand-new dedication stone placed in the park far into the future. But here and now, the ghosts were showing themselves again as Emily read the description of the old stone: *1756—1840, Beloved Husband and Father, William Easton.* She continued to stare at the stone curiously. "So, this is where you're buried. I had no idea," she said as though William Easton could hear her.

Emily lifted herself off the ground and hobbled her way out of the old hidden cemetery and stood in the pathway leading up an incline shrouded in darkness. Smoke from a wood fire drifted through the forest of decay. She started up the path, feeling the spikes of pain in her leg.

"Just my luck: the shin. Dammit, the most sensitive part of the leg," she grumbled and hobbled along the way.

Emily followed the smell of smoke, and as it got stronger, so did her fears. For Beth. I have to do this to save Beth, she said to herself. She kept thinking about Williams's grave, and how it made sense that he would have settled in this area close to the park he was inspired to create. She was, however, spooked over the sight of the gravestone.

Just ahead and over to the right, she saw a chimney sticking up over the gnarly brush. As she got closer, she found a narrow wooden walkway pitted with rot and slim. It seemed to lead towards the smoking chimney, and she followed it.

Emily stopped in her tracks upon seeing an old, broken-down shack sitting among birch trees surrounded by an ominous mist from beyond the structure. The moonlight had little effect in brightening the location's atmosphere as she approached cautiously. Other than the smoke from the chimney, the dwelling looked abandoned. She wondered if this was the hunting cabin Billy had told her about: a broken-down, old shack Thomas had used on occasion.

As Emily got closer, she could feel death looming, which caused her instincts to scream for her to run for her life. Emily slowed her breathing and fought off the fear as she did her best to move forward towards the shack and what she knew needed to be done. The door was slightly cracked open, allowing the dark secrets on the other side to have air.

"Hello?" Emily called out, but she heard no sound from inside. "Hello?" she called again and then spoke a little louder. "Is anyone home?"

Emily walked onto the crumbling porch, stepping around the rotted holes in the floorboards. She pushed the door open and felt the hair on the back of her neck go up. Everything inside her felt like ice running through her veins, but Emily willed herself to keep going. She walked into a small room lit by a single candle sitting on the table. To the right of the table was a bed of straw.

On the bed, Emily could see a crumpled-up pillow and a nasty sheet that might have been white once. The one-room shack had smoldering coals in the firebox of a cobblestone fireplace. The shack was so old she wondered if it had once been William Easton's home. Emily could hear faint breathing and movement from the room's dark corner.

"Hello. My name is Emily," she said, hoping to pry loose whoever it was, hidden in the shadows.

A silhouette of someone seemed to stand and linger in its place. A moment later, the strange dark figure spoke in a satanic whisper. "I know who you are."

Emily took a step forward, trying to get a better look, only to smell a nasty odor of rotted flesh.

Although Emily suspected the identity of the figure standing in the corner, she still proceeded with caution. "Okay," Emily said tentatively, "but I don't know who you are."

The mysterious figure stepped into the candle's flickering light, causing Emily to step back and let out a tiny gasp. The woman looked worn out, Emily thought, with leathery skin and black eyes sunk deep into their sockets. Her hair was matted. She wore a ripped dress stained with food and dirt and a shawl draped over her shoulders that looked as if it was made of old rags. Her lips were dry, and they parted with a wicked grin. "I'm Charlotte," she said in the same evil whisper. "I've been waiting for you."

Emily kept her wits about her. She didn't know whether to feel sorry for Charlotte or be appalled by the sight of her but quickly reminded herself of Charlotte's evil deeds: the curse on Thomas and what happened to Beth in the swamp. "Why have you been waiting for me?" Emily asked.

Charlotte laughed. "You're a fool for coming here. Don't you know you're going to die?"

Emily took three steps forward. She held her ground and mustered up all her courage with the knowledge of what she needed to do. "You have no power over me, Charlotte," Emily said. "Your curse didn't stop me from coming through that swamp."

"No, but it stops Witches and that self-righteous Guardian, Billy Easton." Charlotte laughed again, an evil laugh that showed all her rotted teeth. "Speaking of Billy, he must have hated the sudden inability to protect his precious Beth," she mocked.

Emily's anger rose. "Why, you little bitch."

Charlotte's satanic laughter resumed as she stepped toward Emily with only the table between them. Charlotte was close enough for Emily to see how the whites of her eyes had turned black and her pupils glowed red. Clearly, Charlotte was pure evil, just as Lucy and Billy had said.

"I even took care of that whimpering little mouse Laura. You know, the one Thomas convinced himself that he loved. I followed the two despicable lovers here one day. Peeked right through that window and watched them go at it like rabbits in heat."

"What do you mean 'took care of'?" Emily asked, ignoring Charlotte's version of Thomas and Laura's love affair. Emily then moved close enough to touch the table where the lit candle flickered.

Charlotte's lip curled up in a sneer. Emily refused to let Charlotte intimidate her.

"You just don't get it, do you, Emily?" Charlotte tilted her head downward, yet her eyes remained fixed on Emily with a penetrating stare. "I cursed the whore. It was easy really...used her own blood to do it."

Emily remembered what Lucy had told her. Charlotte had threatened Laura and drew her blood with a knife. The thought of it sickened Emily.

"That same day," Charlotte continued. "I called Thomas, told him to meet me here in this dingy, old shack. Show him what a real woman could do for him, but he never showed up. Then that wretched Guardian, Billy, got in the way, stopped Thomas from coming here."

Emily's anger had far outweighed her fear. "You mean Billy protected Thomas." She narrowed her eyes at Charlotte. "You used the death curse three times, didn't you?" Emily's voice grew louder as she confronted Charlotte over her deadly deeds. "First, on Laura and then on Thomas. Then you cursed the swamp and the land that surrounds it just to keep Billy out!" Emily leaned forward and placed her hands on the table in front of her. "And in the process, you killed your own sister and grandmother with your sick, twisted curse! And you did all of this out of jealousy! What kind of demented person are you?"

Emily could see she hit a nerve. Charlotte pulled her raggedy shawl tighter around her shoulders. It must have stung to hear the truth for the first time, yet Charlotte refused to back down. "Well, Miss Know-it-All. I see you're finally catching up," she said. "I was beginning to think you were stupid, Emily."

"The only stupid one here is you, Charlotte. Look what the curse has done to you. You allowed evil to take control and to the point where your whole body is rotten away. Don't you have even an ounce of remorse over what you've done?"

Charlotte leaned forward this time, her cynical grin and demonic voice caused Emily to stand straight, ready to back away as the evil inside of Charlotte continued taunting her. "It was the fault of my pathetic sister and grandmother for putting their noses in my business by trying to look for me that day. As far as

Thomas—too bad his spawn lived. Somehow that little bastard survived."

Emily thought of Walter at that moment, never realizing he was also in danger. Emily wanted to scratch Charlotte's black eyes out when she suddenly heard a voice calling her name. Both Emily and Charlotte turned their heads toward the grimy window.

Charlotte stood on the opposite side of the table, glaring at Emily. Emily heard her name called again in the distance. She thought the voice sounded like Rick's. How can that be? she wondered.

As though Charlotte could read Emily's thoughts, she laughed again. "Well, well, well, if it isn't lover boy coming to the rescue. How convenient. He's a fool just like you, and now I can kill two bleeding hearts with one stone."

The voice got closer as it continued to call her name. If it was Rick, which Emily thought impossible, she knew she needed to escape the shack as quickly as possible. Emily darted to the door but couldn't open it. She frantically twisted the knob, but the door seemed to be sealed shut. She could hear Charlotte's evil laugh as she approached Emily from behind. Charlotte was now steps from her.

"You're going to die in here trapped like a rat," Charlotte taunted. "As soon as he goes over the threshold, you and lover boy will be mine to kill."

Emily felt rage take over every part of her body as Charlotte was now within arm's reach. Emily turned and lurched towards her, shoving Charlotte into the table and knocking over the candle into the pile of straw used for bedding. The straw immediately ignited into flames that shot to the ceiling. Charlotte darted towards the fire, trying to douse the flames with her shawl.

Smoke billowed through the shack like a speeding train straight into Emily's lungs. She coughed and dropped to the floor to stay low where the smoke was less thick. The fire caught on to the old, decayed wood quickly. Emily crawled to the door again. "RICK!" she screamed, grabbing the doorknob with all her strength to open it. Emily felt faint and fell to the floor next to the door. Pain shot through her lungs with every cough. She inched her way to the window with little success and heard Charlotte yelling.

"You can't get out, Emily," Charlotte mocked. "You're gonna die just like that pitiful little whore of Thomas's. You'll cease to exist like poor, old Lily Spencer and my weak, pitiful sister, Kathleen." Charlotte laughed again like the insane, demonic person she had become.

Emily lay limp. She barely heard the blood-curdling scream from Charlotte as she yelled her last torturing words: DIE! YOU CAN ALL DIE AND GO TO HELL!" Charlotte became engulfed by the inferno.

Emily resigned herself to the fact that she, too, would die a fiery death. Tears rolled down her face from the smoke and from the overwhelming sadness of never seeing Rick again. Then, with all the air she had left, she spoke her last words. "I love you, Rick." Then all went black.

Chapter 19

INTO THE ASHES

Sometime Earlier

RICK ENTERED THE HOSPITAL and stopped at the information desk, where a nurse sat behind a large desk with smoke lingering in the air from her cigarette. She was fully dressed in white, sporting a large nurse's cap on top of perfectly placed finger waves.

"Can you tell me where the emergency room is?" Rick asked.

The nurse took a long drag of her cigarette, blowing smoke through each word. "It's through those doors," she said in a raspy voice as she pointed to her left. "At the end of the long hallway," she added while tapping the ashes into the ashtray.

"Okay, thanks, and ah..." Rick hesitated, then leaned in towards the nurse. "You might wanna give those up. They cause cancer."

The nurse gave him an indignant look, and Rick darted towards the doors that lead to the long hallway. He walked briskly down the hall and saw several people in the waiting room. He peeked into a small window of a large door with an Emergency Room sign over the top and saw two nurses standing together in conversation. He pushed the door open and stepped into the emergency area, which got the attention of the two nurses. "Excuse me, I'm looking for someone."

The nurses looked up at Rick. "You're not supposed to be in here, sir," one of the nurses said in a stern voice.

"Yes, I know, but I'm looking for a redheaded woman, petite with emerald-green eyes and a man named Billy Easton." Rick craned his neck around the corner, hoping to find Emily and a man he only remembered from a photo. "I believe Mr. Easton's daughter Beth is in here," Rick added.

"You must leave now, sir," the bossy nurse said. "You'll need to go out into the waiting area, and I will retrieve Mr. Easton for you."

Rick reluctantly left the emergency room and felt a gnawing in his gut when only Billy's name was mentioned and not Emily's. He paced back and forth in front of the big door when suddenly, a tall, well-built man with dark hair opened the door, almost hitting Rick in the face.

"Whoa, sorry there, fella. Are you the guy that wants to speak to me?" Billy asked.

Rick stared at Billy for a second. The man before him looked remarkably like Lucas Easton. Same dark eyes, same familiar expression. He momentarily became lost for words and then stuck his hand out without thinking. "I'm Rick Miller, Emily's husband."

Billy said nothing and didn't offer a handshake back. Rick could see the shock on his face. Most likely similar to his own a second ago. "Your daughter…how is she?" Rick asked, breaking the awkward moment between them.

Billy seemed to regain a small portion of his composure. "Alive—at least, thanks to Emily." Billy took a step forward, tilting head with a look of bewilderment. "How…how did you get here? I thought Emily was—"

"The only time traveler?" Rick said as he finished Billy's question. "It's a long story, but for now, is Emily around? I stopped at Grace Stanford's house, and she told me Emily was here." Rick noticed that Billy's shoulders stiffened as he looked to his right towards the waiting room and avoided eye contact with Rick.

"No, no, she…she…" Billy stammered. "She left less than an hour ago."

Rick was pretty good at reading people's postures and facial expressions. Billy was stalling, and he also knew that Billy was holding something back. "Where the hell is she? I know you know something."

"She insisted. I told her I couldn't protect her," Billy said, gesturing toward the long hallway for more privacy as Rick followed. "She insisted on returning to the swamp. Only she can save my daughter."

"WHAT!" Rick barked. "You let her go into that swamp by herself with no protection!" Rick grabbed Billy by the arm. "What the hell is wrong with you? I know what you are, Billy. Isn't it your job to protect?"

Billy pulled his arm away from Rick, pushing him against the wall. Although Billy was the same height and build as Rick, Billy had the strength of much younger arms. Billy's features tightened on his face. He clenched his jaw as if holding back the fury pent up inside him.

"I didn't let her go. She had to go. I can't help her DAMMIT! There's a curse on that swamp that kills Witches and Guardians. It killed my stepmother, Lily Spencer, and Kathleen, Beth's mother, and now, it has its evil clutches on my daughter." Billy loosened his grip slightly but still held Rick against the wall. He narrowed his eyes. "You think I like it? It's tearing my guts out letting Emily go. I wish to God I could kill that bitch Charlotte myself. Destroy that disgusting curse, but I can't. My powers are rendered useless at the water's edge. I tried to keep Emily from going in there. All I'm left with is to trust Emily's powers to stop this whole nightmare." Billy finally let go of Rick and took a step back. "Emily is the only one who can end this."

It was beginning to make sense to Rick. Billy would suffer the same fate as Lily and Kathleen if he were to go into the swamp. He could protect Thomas and his family and little Beth, too, as long as he was nowhere near the surrounding area of the swamp. Billy Easton had his work cut for him with Charlotte's deadly curse. A curse he could not stop and a curse he had kept from Thomas. But still, Rick felt a mix of irritation and anger. Billy had let Emily go alone. It sickened him to think that Emily was about to face death from a swamp that kills. But she wasn't a Witch, and he was not a Mystic Guardian, an advantage in their favor, he hoped.

Rick took a step forward and pressed his finger on Billy's chest, speaking in a steady, firm voice. "You might not be able to go in that swamp, but I can." Rick turned abruptly and began walking away when Billy called out. "Rick?"

Rick stopped and turned slightly without saying anything.

"There's an old shack off one of the logging trails," Billy said with bleak sadness in his eyes. "And I want you know that Emily means something to me, too."

Rick nodded. He knew Billy was powerless. He had felt the same way many times before, but now, the power was in his hands. He had no doubts that he would lay his life down in a second if it meant saving Emily from the clutches of an evil Witch and a curse that had a hold on little Beth. Rick turned and walked away quickly to once again fight another battle. Only this time, it was Emily's life hanging in the balance.

Rick navigated on a path covered with a thin layer of snow alongside the edges of the marshland engulfed in darkness. Only small amounts of the light from the moon pushed through the gathering clouds, casting enough light for him to follow Emily's footprints. At least, he hoped they were hers. The prints were small, about Emily's size. "They're hers all right," he said out loud. Rick could hear only the creaking of branches caused by a tiny breeze moving through the hollow spaces. Snow owls hotted near an opening ahead. Snow flurries drifted down through slits of light from the fading moon. Rick continued following Emily's footprints until they veered off next to an old broken sign that read *Cemetery.*

As he approached the wrought iron fence, a trail of blood spotted the blanket of snow that led to an old oak tree. Rick raced over, finding a small pool of blood and another set of tracks that led back out. "EMILY!" he yelled. "She has to be close," he said, glancing down at a broken gravestone. He squatted in front of it, touching the streaks of blood running down from the jagged edges. The blood was fresh, most likely Emily's, and then he looked closer at the stone.

"William Easton. Well, old boy, you wouldn't happen to know where my wife went." Suddenly, Rick heard a howling wolf. It was as if the wolf was trying to tell him what William Easton couldn't—the next direction he needed to go. The snow started falling heavier. Rick knew he had to hurry before Emily's tracks got covered up.

Her footprints led Rick to a logging trail that she clearly was on, and he wondered if it led to the shack Billy had mentioned. "EMILY!" he called again but heard no answer. Rick walked up the incline at a fast pace. Every bone in his body screamed danger, and then he saw a large amount of smoke billowing over the top of the trees. As he got closer, he spotted a structure burning out of control. "EMILY!" he yelled louder, and that's when he heard his name being carried through the air by the smoke—it was Emily's desperate voice.

Rick rushed through the narrow, wooden walkway, coming upon the blazing shack. He ran to the porch, not yet touched by fire. "EMILY!" Rick frantically yelled as he pounded on the door. He felt adrenaline shoot through every part of his body. With great force and by harnessing all his strength, Rick stepped back, lifted his right foot, and kicked the door. It didn't budge, so he tried again, kicking even harder until it crashed open, revealing the entire inside swallowed up by flames.

The horror of Emily being consumed by fire was more than Rick could bear. No matter what it took, even if he had to walk through fire himself, nothing would stop him from getting to Emily. Rick was about to enter when the old lady's voice popped into his head. *Don't go over the threshold.* Rick looked down to see his foot touching the doorsill when something else caught his eye. He looked slightly to his left and saw someone else's foot. "EMILY!" He reached in enough to grab what he prayed would be Emily's ankle and dragged her across the infamous threshold.

"Oh, my God, Emily?" Rick swooped her into his arms, carrying her several feet from the inferno.

He dropped to his knees. "Emily, can you hear me?" Rick wiped the black soot caked over her eyes and mouth. "Please, please don't leave me!" His desperate pleas went unanswered. He laid her on the ground and began mouth-to-mouth resuscitation. "Emily, come back to me," he begged and then continued his life-saving measures.

Finally, Emily sucked in air and coughed uncontrollably. Rick lifted her into a sitting position. She coughed violently. Her hand clenched her stomach, and suddenly she lurched towards Rick, vomiting all over his field jacket.

Chapter 20

OASIS

THE BURNING SMELL SCORCHED her throat and blurred her vision. Emily could vaguely hear Rick's voice. She felt him scoop her into his arms, cradling her like a small child. She tried catching her breath and then coughed some more but less urgently. Rick buried his head in her neck. His kiss felt desperate yet warm. Her eyes were beginning to come into focus. She could see the shocked look on Rick's face that must have mirrored her own shock at seeing him there. "Rick? Is that really you?" Emily asked, still feeling confused.

"Oh, sweetie. I thought I lost you," he replied.

"Am I dead?" she wondered out loud.

"No, sweetie. You're alive." Rick kissed her forehead as he repeated, "I thought I lost you."

"But...if I'm not dead then...how are you here?"

Rick kissed Emily's cheek this time and gave her one of his handsome smiles. "Because a new Witch was born in a new century on the darkest day."

It didn't take long for Emily to process what Rick was saying. She touched his face to make sure he was real. "Our granddaughter?"

"That's right," he said, caressing her cheek.

As Rick ran his hand down her cheek, Emily suddenly realized something was different. She took his right hand, studying it as she gently touched each finger, astonished at what she saw.

"But how?" Emily asked.

Rick smiled and kissed her hand that was holding his new miracle. "Let's just say it was a gift from a couple of really good Witches."

"You mean, Sylvia and Meghan?"

Rick just nodded. That's when Emily discovered she had puked all over the front of his jacket.

"Oh, no! I'm so sorry," she said, trying to wipe away the disgusting mess, but he grabbed her hand and kissed it.

"Emily, it's okay. I don't care about that. All I care about is that you're alive. I thought I lost you forever. I don't know what I would do if that happened."

The two looked into each other's eyes, neither wanting to look away for fear that the other would vanish from sight. Rick gently kissed her. Their tears mingled with their merging lips when suddenly a loud popping sound caused them to look towards the now smoldering shack. Rick helped Emily to her feet, and they stood, watching the remaining sparks shoot up through the trees. Emily went over in her mind the evil that had consumed Charlotte's body and soul along with the flames. "Charlotte's dead," she said, still feeling the burning sensation in her lungs.

"Good," Rick replied with a cold tone to his voice. "She can go back to the hell she came from."

Rick put his arm around Emily, kissing her forehead once again. He pulled her close and held her in a long embrace. They kissed again long and gently until Rick spoke. "Come on. Let's go home."

As the two walked towards the wooden walkway, Emily couldn't help but wonder which home that would be.

Later that evening, Emily's eyes remained closed in Grace's bathroom in the same bedroom that she and Rick shared in another time. The two sat in a large tub with clawfoot legs, an old-fashioned style bathtub and one that didn't exist in the future.

She bathed in the warmth of the water and in the strong arms of her lover. Time stood still as she felt his soft breath upon her cheek and nestled her back against his chest. She felt his hands move over her body as they reacquainted themselves with one another. His gentle touch moved across her breasts, stirring the passion that grew with each stroke of his hand. She felt his yearning beneath the water and pressed her nakedness against his body as she felt him become harder. For the moment, though, he seemed content to hold her tight in his arms. Both souls were now cleansed from dirt, grim, and the wickedness that had tried to consume them. The evil experience was now replaced with a love she longed for: the love of her best friend, her soulmate, and the hero who had saved her from certain death.

A short time later, he carried her to the bed, and his strong body covered hers. She thought he was gentle, not wanting to cause more pain to her leg. She had missed his touch and how he aroused all her senses as he entered the place inside her, the action for which she hungered. He slowly made love to her and controlled each movement to last. They made love into the night until exhaustion finally took over, and they fell asleep in the comfort of the soft blankets. Neither one had dreams. Only peace and calmness filled their minds.

Morning came as the brightness of the room interrupted Emily's slumber. She opened her eyes, expecting to find Rick nestled beside her. When she saw he was not there, she turned towards the window where she saw him. The morning sun cast shimmering light on Rick's silver locks as he sat in the rocking chair, taking in the new day. Emily quietly got up and wrapped the blanket around her nakedness.

"Rick?" she whispered, coming around to his side and sliding onto his lap. He held her like a child and kissed her cheek, yet Emily could see a faraway look in his eyes. "What are you thinking?"

Rick brushed pieces of her hair out of her eyes with his restored hand and remained quiet. His gaze was intense as he seemed to take in each part of her face. "I just miss you, is all," he finally said.

She took his hand, kissed it, and then looked at it closely, examining every inch with amazement.

"I don't understand. How did you get your hand back?" I know you said the Witches did it, but..." Emily voice trailed off.

"I wondered that myself." Rick held his hand up and wiggled his fingers. "Then I remembered something Sylvia said to me."

"What's that?" Emily asked, still caressing his hand as they locked their fingers.

"When I insisted that she send me back in time, she said there would be consequences to time travel. I could end up someplace else. I could be older, younger, or..." He gave her a crooked smile. "Dead—all of which hadn't happened. But then..." Rick let go of Emily's hand, moving his fingers again. "I thought if this is my consequence, well, who am I to argue with that?"

"So, after I disappeared, Sylvia and Meghan got their powers back?"

"Yup and found a time travel spell in that magic spell book of theirs."

"Geez, between a published book, a hidden diary, and a magic spell book? I'm not one bit surprised they found a time travel spell." Emily ran her fingers through Rick's hair. "So, our granddaughter's birth caused Sylvia and Meghan to get their powers back and in turn caused me to go back in time to destroy the curse—exactly what Rebecca said would happen."

Rick took a deep breath and let out a long sigh. "And Grace telling us that Beth was back to normal is further proof."

Emily put her hand up to her mouth and giggled. "Poor Grace, did you see the look on her face when she caught sight of us walking in the door last night?"

Rick let out a little chuckle. "Yeah, she must have thought we were the creatures from the black lagoon." Rick ran his hand down Emily's cheek. "You had to see the look on Grace's face when I handed her a letter from her beloved Thomas before I went looking for you."

Emily recalled that on the way home the night before, Rick had told her how he had ended up in Pearl Harbor with Thomas. He had said little else, and Emily didn't press the subject as they were both processing what had just happened to them. She wondered if he would say more now. "So, Thomas is okay then?"

"Yup, fine as wine, just like your lips," Rick said, kissing her softly.

Emily gazed into Rick's deep blue eyes, and she became more serious. "Nothing could be scarier than what I saw in that shack. It was as if the devil himself had jumped into Charlotte's body and took over. There was no remorse over Lily and Kathleen's deaths. She mocked the fact that Billy's powers were rendered useless to protect Beth. She seemed to relish the fact that he couldn't go into the swamp and that he was unable to save Beth." Emily regarded Rick's expression and wondered if Thomas had told him about Billy.

"Did Thomas tell you—?"

"About Billy and how he's a Mystic Guardian?" Rick said, finishing Emily's question.

"I guess he mentioned it then."

Rick just nodded. "And I found out from Billy about Lily and Kathleen's deaths."

"I'm glad you know," Emily said. "Charlotte had this overwhelming hatred towards Laura Green and gloated about how pleased she was when her curse killed Laura."

Rick sat up straight, almost dropping Emily on the floor. "You mean Charlotte killed Laura?"

"Not only that, but she was also enraged that Walter lived."

"Walter?" he said, tilting his head to look at Emily and then pointing downward to the floor, indicating the first floor. "You mean that Walter?"

Emily nodded. "Yeah, you know—Walter."

"Our Walter? Or the little boy downstairs playing with his toy trucks."

"Yes, Rick," she said, kissing his nose. "Our Walter and little Walter are one and the same and now he's Grace and Thomas's Walter."

Rick sat back in the rocker, still holding onto Emily. "So, Laura is the girl Thomas had a love affair with."

"Thomas told you about Laura?"

"Yeah, not her name or much else. He said the affair was brief and then she disappeared. I remember you telling me Laura Green was born during the Spanish flu outbreak and then later became Walter's mother. So, if that's the case, then what you're telling me is that the Walter who died in our time and the little guy downstairs is Thomas's real son?"

Emily nodded again.

"Well, I'll be damned," Rick's eyes shifted to Emily. "Thomas had mentioned a son, but his name is Matthew. Wait. Thomas doesn't know about Walter, does he?"

"No, but Grace does. She took the news well enough."

Emily continued to tell Rick how Lucy fled with her pregnant daughter after a terrible encounter with Charlotte. Months later, Laura died giving birth to Walter, which Emily now knew was caused by Charlotte's death curse. Six years passed. When Lucy was diagnosed with stage four leukemia, she knew she had to bring Walter back to town, so his real father could raise him.

"So, Charlotte had it out not only for Laura but for Thomas, Beth, and Walter as well?"

Emily laid her head on Rick's shoulder without answering. She thought about her awful encounter with Charlotte.

"Charlotte watched Thomas and Laura having sex one day in the shack," she said finally. "I think that's when she completely lost her mind. Both Billy and Lucy told me that Charlotte is pure evil." Emily held onto Rick with a fearful grip. "They both witnessed her demonic behavior, and I saw it for myself. She spit her hateful words out of her mouth like a dragon shooting fire. I've never seen anything like it, and I never want to see it again."

Silence fell between them. Both Emily and Rick wanted to forget the flaming hell they had encountered. Emily relaxed again as she held Rick's magical hand. She caressed his fingers with a lingering stroke, which triggered a wave of lust in Rick, and he pulled Emily closer. He reached beneath the blanket wrapped around her, moved his hand over her breast, and kissed her neck. Within seconds, Emily could feel his erection growing beneath her. Both were aroused by one another's touch.

Emily held onto Rick as he rose from the rocker, carried her to the bed, and placed her gently down. Rick slid alongside her, unraveling the blanket, revealing Emily's full nakedness. They held each other tightly, and she felt his soft lips pressed against hers as he kissed her deeply. He kissed her ear and then whispered, "I'll never let go, Emily. I'll never let anyone hurt you. It's why I followed you through time, took that chance not knowing where I would end up. All I knew was, I couldn't leave you behind."

Emily touched Rick's cheek and ran her fingers across his lips. "I love you, Rick," she whispered back. She kissed him as she ran her hand down to where his heart nestled warmly in his chest. She could feel it beating faster from her touch as she said, "You truly are my hero."

It was late morning before Emily and Rick emerged from their oasis. They found Grace in the kitchen watching Matthew and Walter eating an early lunch of peanut butter and jelly sandwiches. The house felt warm and inviting, as always, with Grace humming a tune to the children while kneading fresh dough for a loaf of homemade bread. Emily and Rick stood in the kitchen doorway, taking in the Norman-Rockwell-type scene, when Walter looked up as he chewed his sandwich.

"Hi, mister, "he said, pointing to his ball and glove on the table. "You wanna play catch?"

Grace turned around. "Now, Walter, don't talk with your mouth full." Grace then looked at Emily and Rick with a delightful smile and a twinkle in her eyes. "Well now, I see our guests have risen from their slumber. I hope you slept well."

Emily glanced at Rick as though they were a couple of teenagers who just got caught making out in the family's car parked in the driveway. Rick gave Emily a wink and strolled over to the table, taking a seat next to Walter and tousling his hair. Emily poured cups of coffee for her and Rick and then gave Grace a side look. "We slept just fine. And thank you so much for your wonderful hospitality."

Rick picked up Walter's glove, squeezing his fingers inside the child's glove as far as they would go. Emily noticed a look of recall on Rick's face. He had told her once that, when Walter was dying, he had thanked Rick for playing catch with him. Rick looked over at Emily as his mouth turned up in a weary grin, both recalling the same memory. He glanced down at Walter and picked up the baseball. "Well, buddy, I'll tell you what. You do as you're told and eat up all your sandwich, and then I'll play catch. What do yah say?"

Walter nodded and ate faster.

"Me, too, mama. Me, too, mister. Play ball," Matthew chimed in.

Rick looked at Matthew sitting in his highchair and reached out his hand. "Same deal go for you too, little buddy." Matthew's eyes lit up as he put his hand out to touch Rick's.

"Give me five," Rick said, tapping Matthew's palm.

Matthew laughed as Walter stuck the palm of his hand out. "Give me five, mister," Walter said.

"Okay, buddy, but only if you call me Rick—deal?"

Emily and Grace looked on with amusement. Emily liked watching Rick interact with the children. He would have been a good father to Derek if not for his misfortune of being wounded in war and drowning all the good parts of himself by drinking. She wondered about the pain of missing out. In a way, she had felt the same pain of not being able to have children. She thought that the whole missing out part, whether self-inflicted or not, had to be the same for them both.

Emily sat by Rick as Grace took out two plates kept warm in the oven with scrambled eggs, bacon, and homemade jelly smothered on toasted, fresh bread.

"Oh, Grace, you didn't have to do that. I'm sure just toast would have been fine," Emily said, giving Rick a please-agree-with-me look.

"Grace, you have been more than generous, and I thank you," Rick said in a formal voice as he picked up his fork. "I have to tell you the truth, though, eggs and bacon are my favorite, and that, ma'am, makes it very hard to resist." Rick took a mouthful of eggs when Walter spoke up.

"If you eat up all your eggs, mister--I mean Rick. Then I'll play catch with you. Is it a deal?" Walter said, sticking his hand out.

Rick smiled and patted the palm of Walter's hand. "It's a deal."

"Listen, Grace. Rick and I were thinking about going to see Beth at the hospital today."

"Oh, she's not there," Grace said, offering Rick another piece of toast.

Rick put his hand up. "No, thanks. I got more than enough."

"Where is she? Is she home already?" Emily asked.

"Bright and early this morning, and according to Billy, Beth is already asking for her favorite dessert for supper tonight."

"I got an idea," Rick offered, downing the last bit of his breakfast. "Why don't we go over to Billy's house, that is—" Rick winked at Walter. "After playing catch?" Rick got up and put his plate in the sink. "That way we can swing by Marion's to bring her car back."

"Sounds like a great idea," Emily chimed in. "And I could look in on Beth there."

Grace looked at Rick as her eyebrows came together. "Didn't you tell me last night you had left Billy's car in the park?"

"Yup, and on the way to Marion's, we can stop at the park to pick it up and bring it back to him." Rick added.

Grace grabbed the last of the dishes off the table. "Well, then, you'll need a ride home from Billy's. Just give me a call later, and I'll come pick you up."

"Great. It's settled then," Rick said, grabbing the ball and glove off the table and patting Walter and Matthew on their backs. "Well, little buddies, let's get to it then."

Twenty minutes later, Emily stood by the kitchen window, the same window she remembered looking out of on many occasions when thinking of good times and bad. Her thoughts wandered as she watched Rick play catch with the two boys. These were the good times.

The house felt like an oasis. A safe place filled with only good. Her memories of so much love had filled each room throughout time and space. But it was here in 1941 where she could rest safely and without fear. She had, after all, no blood relative left in her own time. They existed here and now. Staying was a thought that was so appealing. But that would mean she would never see her granddaughter, and Rick would never see his son again. She knew they didn't belong here, yet here was where they were, and she felt protected with a sense of well-being and in a place where she could stay forever.

Emily's thoughts immediately dissolved when she heard Grace calling out in a loud screech. Emily raced to the entrance hall by the front door. Grace stood frozen with her feet planted in place, pressing a letter against her chest with happiness written across her face.

"What is it, Grace? Is everything all right?"

"I got another letter from Thomas."

"That's wonderful, Grace."

"There's also another one," Grace said and handed the second letter to Emily. "From Rick."

Emily looked at Grace as though she would have the answer to a riddle that needed to be solved. "That's strange. I never thought I'd get a letter from Rick."

Grace scanned the front of both letters. "By the postmark on the letters it looks like Thomas and Rick sent them on the same day. I guess Rick was faster getting here than the post office," Grace offered, and then looked longingly toward the living room. "I just... I'd like to..." Grace stammered.

Emily knew Grace was itching to read Thomas's letter in private and offered her a pleasant grin. "Of course, Grace, enjoy."

As Grace hurried off to the living room, Emily went upstairs to that safe oasis that had held both her and Rick in warmth and comfort throughout the night. She sat on the bed and took the letter from the envelope postmarked December 8th. Although Rick wrote about saving Thomas's life, the great sorrow between the lines made her wonder. Rick was a true hero in Emily's eyes, and now a hero once more in a war he was never meant to fight.

Chapter 21

MAKING AN AMENDS

AFTER RETRIEVING BILLY'S CAR and dropping off Marion's, Rick and Emily made their way to Billy and Marlene's house. "I guess they don't live too far from the Maple Ridge hospital," Emily said.

Rick nodded. "Well, I'm sure it's for convenience seeing that Billy's wife works there."

"You're right," Emily added. "And with her constantly taking shifts, being close to Billy and the children, no doubt, are pretty important to Marlene."

Rick turned onto a well-manicured street where each home mirrored one another. It was a brand-new community built for people with money, with its upscale neighborhood and all the conveniences of Maple Ridge at their fingertips. The Stanford farmhouse was considered the countryside in 1941 where homes sat on more than one acre of land separated by wooded areas, but in the future, not so much. The neat, well-kept neighborhood that he and Emily were driving through at the moment would change drastically with the years slowly claiming its beauty. As a building inspector, Rick remembered giving a few citations in this neighborhood for shoddy renovating attempts.

"Well, here we are: number 427," Rick said, pulling into the driveway.

Suddenly, the side door of the house burst open with Marty running at full speed toward the car. Rick noticed he was wearing a Boston Braves hat, a pair of Converse black-and-white, high-top sneakers, and a look of excitement.

On Marty's heels was Billy coming out while throwing a coat

on. "Marty, get yourself back in the house before your mother has your hide," Billy yelled.

Marty knocked on the passenger side of the car door where Emily was sitting. She rolled her window down, giving Marty one of her pleasant smiles. "Hi, Marty, I'm so glad to see you, too," Emily chirped.

Just then, Billy's big hand came into view, grabbing Marty by the shoulder. "Do what you're told, young man."

Marty made a moaning sound. "Gee whiz, Dad," he complained and then went back into the house.

As Rick and Emily got out of the car, she noticed Rick exchanging we-need-to-talk glances with Billy. Rick had briefly mentioned to Emily that he had had words with Billy at the hospital before coming to her rescue in the swamp and that he needed to clear the air between Billy and himself.

Emily smiled at Billy as she hugged him. "I'll go inside and talk to Marlene while you two say whatever it is that needs saying."

Rick came around, kissed Emily's soft cheek, and watched her walk into the house. He had noticed the sweet strawberry scent from the warm bath they had shared the night before, and he felt an immediate desire for her. All he could do for now was smile. The rest would have to wait for later, he thought.

The two men entered the garage, where Billy had a big carpentry bench with assorted tools and what looked like several projects started. Rick picked up a hand drill with a wooden handle that featured a metal crank and iron drill bit. "Oh, man, the last time I saw one of these was at an antique shop," Rick said as he studied the tool.

Billy let out a humorous grunt. "I'm sure in your time the tools are much more sophisticated."

Rick raised his eyebrows. "Sophisticated? I'd say. Much more power, as in electric, no cranking and some, believe or not, cordless." Rick gave Billy a weary smile as he set the drill down. "But tools are not what we're here to talk about, am I right?"

Billy fiddled with a screwdriver, mindlessly moving the saw-dust around on the bench. "I hated the fact that I couldn't save my daughter." He raised his head and looked Rick straight in the eyes. "And Emily."

"Look, Billy, you don't have to tell me how bad it feels to be rendered helpless. While fighting in well, a future war, I lost some guys on a scouting run. Two heavily armed vehicles got blown up under my watch. I saved a couple of guys, but I also lost three others. I spent twenty years beating myself up over it. I know this is a different situation, but yeah, I know how you feel."

Billy said nothing, so finally Rick put his hand on Billy's shoulder. "I'm sorry for being such an asshole to you."

"Nay, you were just worried about Emily." A slow-building smile came across Billy's face. "I'd say by how you two looked at each other a few minutes ago, there's a pretty intense romance going on." Billy then crossed his arms and became more serious. "Feelings like that would cause any man's emotions to run high; and if it were me, I'd sure as hell would've plowed over anyone that got in my way."

"Well, Billy, I'll just have to be a little more discreet with my affection for Emily, but there are no guarantees," Rick said with a bit of humor. "Besides, when you have two soldiers fighting the same battle, as you and me, when one gets wounded, that's when the other guy takes over. To win that battle, having each other's backs is an absolute."

Billy walked over to a window that looked out towards the house. Rick could see the tension as his head dropped, and he released a slow breath. "You okay, Billy? Are we good here? I mean between us?"

Billy abruptly turned with his eyes filled with confusion. "Emily told me she was married to my grandson. And now—to you." Billy rubbed one eyebrow as he seemed to be looking for the right words. "Did…Emily get a divorce or…" Billy hesitated and then shook his head as if rethinking his line of questioning. "Never mind. It's probably best I don't know." Billy returned to the workbench, staring at the sawdust as Rick took two steps towards him and spoke softly. "But you do want to know something, am I right?

Rick couldn't help but feel sorry for Billy. He would never want to know the fate of his own granddaughter or anyone else he loved. Yet Rick knew that Billy had already figured out that something had gone wrong and felt he needed to offer Billy some sort of comfort.

"I can tell you this much," Rick began. "Emily loved your grandson with all her heart. She would never have left him. Your grandson lived a lifetime with her and loved Emily throughout all those years. And he was my friend. He helped me out more times than I could tell you. Your grandson was the kind of guy you could count on no matter what."

Rick went and stood by his new friend. "Billy, we're all going to die. Some sooner, some later, but nobody gets out of it."

Billy turned to face Rick. "So, the best friend marries the grieving widow?"

For a second, Rick thought Billy was angry, but then he saw a smile forming on his face. "And…I'm glad it was you," Billy clarified with a friendly pat on Rick's arm.

"I appreciate that, Billy."

"Hey, I heard you also were a good friend to Thomas. Even saved his life," Billy said as his demeanor became more relaxed, giving Rick a look of appreciation. "He sent me a letter. I got it this morning."

Rick thought for a moment, and the memory of J.J. came rushing back. The knot in his belly twisted, but he managed to speak through the lump in his throat. "I might have saved Thomas, but...I couldn't save everyone."

"Yeah, I know about that, too. Sorry for your loss."

Rick nodded, not wanting to talk about it. To Billy's credit, he quickly changed the subject. "So, you told Thomas about the curse?"

"Yes, I did, and I reassured him that between you and me, we'd both make sure Grace and Matthew would be safe."

Billy's features softened. "And Emily?"

Rick looked out through the garage window at the side of the house. He took a deep breath and then exhaled slowly. "As far as Emily, she's done with what she was sent here to do. If there are any more battles to be fought—it will be me doing the fighting."

Chapter 22

SAFE AND SOUND

MARLENE PULLED THE BANDAGE OFF Emily's leg as gently as possible. When she touched the area of the gash Emily had suffered the night before, Emily winced with pain. Emily had hoped to avoid such discomfort by taking matters into her own hands. She had cleaned the wound and applied the ointment Grace had given her to soothe the affected area. Then Emily had wrapped the cut well with a clean bandage. Rick had even kissed her leg more than once as he tried comforting her, but Marlene meant business.

Marlene sat on a short stool in her kitchen with Emily's leg resting in her lap as she assessed the wound thoroughly.

"I see it's a bit swollen, not bad enough where you would need stitches, but you'll sure have a nasty bruise for a while. Other than that, you did a good job of cleaning it." Marlene gave Emily a considerate glance. "But why wouldn't it be in good shape? You are, after all, a good nurse."

"I appreciate the compliment, but I'm sure anyone could have cleaned and wrapped their leg without that much fuss," Emily said.

"Well, Emily, you know what they say: give credit where credit is due."

With that, Marlene began to re-wrap Emily's leg. While she worked, Marlene lifted her brown eyes at Emily, which showed a hint of mischief.

"Billy told me everything," she said and then lowered her voice to a whisper. "Time traveler?"

"I assure you it's not all it's cracked up to be, but I'm grateful to have Rick with me this time," Emily said and then sighed. "I don't have to experience this alone, which is comforting to say the least.”

“He’s quite handsome. I can tell how much you love him by how your face lights up just mentioning his name.”

Emily leaned forward. “Very good observation, Nurse Easton.”

“I’d say my observations and my medical skills are spot on,” Marlene declared as she finished wrapping Emily’s cut.

Emily was about to stand up when Marlene took hold of her arm. Her demeanor suddenly changed, and Emily could see an inkling of shame in her expression.

“I’m sorry. I was awful to you in the hospital. My behavior was borderline abusive. I should have trusted you, I—”

“It’s okay, Marlene,” Emily interrupted. “A mother will do anything to help her child, and at that moment, I’m sure you felt completely helpless.”

Emily stood up, tucking her arm under Marlene’s. “Now, enough of all this fuss over me. Let’s go see Beth, shall we?”

The two women went into Beth’s bedroom, where she was playing with her favorite doll.

“You have a visitor. It’s Emily. She came to check on you,” Marlene said, fluffing Beth’s pillows and caressing her head while adding a gentle kiss.

Beth’s room was pretty. The pink rosebud wallpaper matched the comforter draped across Beth’s legs. Beth snuggled her beloved doll in her arms.

“Hello, Beth. I see you’re doing well.” Emily sat on the side of the bed, patting Beth’s hand. “Your dolly must have missed you terribly.”

Beth looked shyly at Emily. “She did. Heidi cried all night for me.”

“Aww, poor little Heidi.” Emily reached up, offering a pat on Heidi’s porcelain head as if the toy would come to life at any moment.

Marlene sat on the other side of the bed. “Beth named her dolly after Shirley Temple. The little girl who played Heidi.” Marlene caressed Beth's hair. "This past October, the Maple Ridge movie house had featured old Shirley Temple movies for their Saturday afternoon matinees. I told Beth I'd take her to see one, so, Beth chose the Saturday when *Heidi* was showing. Isn't that right, honey?"

Just then, Emily heard Rick and Billy enter the house, stomping their boots on the carpet. Marty asked Rick something she couldn't hear, but Rick's inaudible response caused the trio to break out in laughter.

"We're in here," Marlene yelled.

Billy came in and then Rick, who leaned his shoulder against the door frame. Marty darted past both men, hopping onto Beth's bed.

Emily got up so Billy could take her spot on the bed next to Beth. "How's my little darling today?" Billy asked.

"Good, Daddy," she said, hugging Billy.

Emily glanced over at Rick and hoped he could read the I-miss-you-already message in her eyes. Rick winked at Emily with an I-can-take-care-of-that-later twinkle.

"It must have been terribly difficult being away from each other and not knowing where either one of you was," Marlene said.

"Yeah, it was, but we found each other now," Rick said and then looked at Beth. "And now we found Beth healthy and happy, which is all that matters."

Emily stood next to Billy, who was still sitting by Beth. "May I ask you something, Beth?"

Beth looked at Billy and then at her mother as if seeking permission to speak. Marlene nodded.

"I saw you speaking to an elderly lady in the park," Emily began. "You know, the one with the buckskin shawl."

Just then, Rick spoke out. "I saw that lady on the way to the hospital yesterday. She practically walked out in front of my car as if on purpose. I had all I had to do to stop in time. Otherwise, I would've hit her."

"You didn't tell me about that, Rick." Emily said.

"Well, Emily we had more important things to discuss besides crazy old ladies walking out in the middle of the street."

"I know who you're talking about," Marty piped up."

"What is it, son?" Billy asked.

"That old lady talked to me and Walter in the park."

"Walter?" Both Emily and Rick said simultaneously.

"Yeah, she was nice. She gave us some candy canes that were in her basket," Marty said.

"Then she told us not to go near the swamp," Beth added.

Emily knelt next to Beth's bed. She felt the pain shoot through her wound but tried to cover it up in front of the child. She took Beth's hand, glanced up at Billy, and then back at Beth. "Then why did you go into the swamp?"

Beth looked scared, as though afraid of giving the wrong answers.

"It's all right, honey. Answer Emily's question," Marlene encouraged.

"Because...because I heard a voice call for me."

Emily felt a chill go up her spine. She, too, had heard haunting voices she would just as soon forget. But she also knew that the ghosts from the past never really go away. They linger in the shadows of time and space.

Emily squeezed Beth's hand gently. "Beth, what did the voice say to you?"

"It was a lady telling me not to pay attention to the old woman."

"What else did this voice say?" Emily asked.

"She told me she wouldn't hurt me and how she wanted to give me a new dolly."

"Why that little bitch," Billy abruptly mumbled under his breath and then checked his words. "Sorry, baby girl."

Emily knew who Billy was mumbling about, and fortunately for everyone, Charlotte was nothing more than dust now.

Beth clutched her doll as Emily stroked the blond braids of Beth's Heidi doll. "You don't have to worry about that any longer, Beth. That person is long gone and will never ever return. That person can never hurt you again. Do you understand?"

Beth nodded and gave her doll a hard squeeze.

Marlene put her arms around her daughter. "I think Beth has had enough for today."

"Of course," Emily said while struggling to stand.

Rick and Billy jumped into action, each extending a supportive arm around Emily. She squeezed her eyes shut as the sharp pain persisted. When she opened her eyes, she saw that everyone looked concerned, and she felt almost embarrassed. "I...er...guess my leg is bothering me more than I thought."

Later, Emily and Rick sat nestled together on the couch in the living room. Marlene and Billy brought in hot tea and homemade biscuits courtesy of Grace. Emily could relax knowing that Marty was in the next room playing with his baseball cards and that Beth had fallen asleep tucked safely in her bed.

The living room was bright, decorated in the Art Deco style featuring shimmering wallpaper with a gold leafy pattern over a creamy white background. The furniture was upholstered in a soft tan fabric that had a hint of the same gold leaves shown on the wallpaper. A side table displayed a porcelain figurine of a man formally kissing a woman's hand. Beside the figurine was a clean glass ashtray sitting on a white doily. A welcoming fire blazed in the fireplace where Billy and Marlene sat. Billy had put on a record with an orchestra softly playing uplifting music, but an orchestra wasn't the only thing playing in the room.

Emily was playing the conversation over in her head from a few minutes earlier as she sipped her tea. That's when her curiosity couldn't wait any longer, and she turned to look at Rick. "The old lady that walked out in front of your car, what happened after that?"

"Well, I got out of the car to see if she was okay and then she said something strange to me."

"Strange? How do you mean?" Emily asked.

"She told me not to go over the threshold, and then she went on her merry old way to the other side of the street." Rick scooted to the edge of the couch and leaned forward, resting his arms on his legs. "Here's the thing," he began, addressing everyone in the room. "When I kicked the door open to the burning shack, I was about to go in when I heard the old lady's voice in my head say, 'Don't go over the threshold.' Not only that, but when my plane landed in Boston, I woke from a dream about Emily struggling in icy water as she was screaming 'Don't go over the threshold'."

"Charlotte had said something about going over the threshold too," Emily added as she looked into Rick's eyes. "I think it had something to do with the curse. It must have trapped me in the shack because when I tried to escape, I couldn't open the door."

"Maybe this elderly woman was warning you, Rick." Marlene suggested.

"Or saw something using the powers only a seer has," Billy added.

Emily perked up hearing the word "seer." You're aware of seers then?"

"I am and there's only one old woman that I know who has those powers." Billy gave Emily an apologetic glance. "Sorry, Emily, but I'm not the only one in this town keeping secrets. I made a point to respect other people's secrets for that very reason." He turned to look at Marlene. "And I'm sorry I didn't tell you sooner, sweetheart."

Marlene gave Billy a reassuring pat on the leg. "I understand, my darling. You just thought you were protecting me."

"You were saying, Billy, about the seer?" Emily asked.

To my knowledge, the old woman you described as wearing a buckskin shawl is a kind, elderly lady."

"Well, buddy, spit it out. Who is she?" Rick probed.

Billy leaned in closer with his focus directly on Rick. "Her name is Nora Miller. She was married to one of your ancestors. A man named George Miller."

Chapter 23

THE ENCHANTED COTTAGE

EMILY AND RICK LEFT BILLY AND MARLENE'S HOUSE with still enough daylight left to find more answers to a growing number of questions. Billy had insisted they take his car and that he would have Marlene drop him off at Grace's the following day to retrieve the vehicle.

They drove slowly over the Shady Brook Bridge, searching for a small cottage Billy said Nora Miller had lived in for almost fifty years. He told them it was beyond the Magic River, off the beaten path, and hidden on the edge of the forest deep inside the park that led into the mountains.

Emily had hoped this forest was much friendlier than the swamp and felt slightly at ease when Billy had assured her the cottage was nowhere near that area. They wanted to learn more from this mysterious seer and why she warned Beth not to go into the swamp. Emily concluded that Nora had to know something.

The large park took up thirteen acres of land just over the Shady Brook Bridge. On the north side of the park stood the Maple Ridge nursing home. The bridge and the swamp were to the south. To the east and over the river was the town of Maple Ridge, and on the west side was a forest filled with spruce and pine trees and where they were headed.

"I can't believe that poor old woman walks this far. It must be at least a quarter of a mile into the park," Emily calculated.

"Yeah, well, it's probably why she's still alive. Anyone who walks that much could easily live well past one hundred," Rick added.

Emily saw a small opening through the pine trees that looked like an entrance. "There," she said, pointing.

"That must be it." Rick pulled into the unplowed opening with small footprints leading ahead.

They slowly drove along the narrow, snow-covered road when suddenly it opened to an entranceway draped with a large trellis covered with dormant rosebuds. Rick pulled over, and as they got out of the car, Emily saw a stone cottage just ahead. She tucked her hand nervously under Rick's arm. He looked down at her with a reassuring grin.

"It's okay, sweetie. This time we're doing this together. I won't let anything happen to you."

She pulled him closer and stood on her toes to kiss him on the cheek. His gaze rested on hers, and he squeezed her hand and said, "Come on. Let's go see the seer."

They walked under the trellis and entered a front yard filled with empty flower beds. Emily imagined the garden in full bloom and how beautiful it must be in the warmth of summer. Up on a small hill was a rock wall leading to a cascade of stones with melting water tricking down under paper-thin ice into a pond in the center of the yard. The same stones covered the exterior of the cottage. Smoke drifted leisurely from the chimney, making the scene not only look cozy but enchanting as well. Still, Emily clung to Rick as they approached the door.

"Well, here goes nothing," Rick said, giving a gentle knock on the door.

The brass doorknob jiggled as the door slowly opened. There stood the withering old woman wearing a knitted shawl this time. Her thin, gray hair had a braid twisted into a bun pinned neatly in the back. Her lips sucked in, and when she smiled, Emily noticed several missing teeth.

"My, my. To what do I owe the pleasure?' the woman asked in a faded voice.

"Hello, ma'am. Are you Nora Miller?" Rick asked, still holding Emily tightly.

"I am," Nora responded with a slight nod.

"We thought you could give us some information about the swamp." Rick added.

"Ah, yes. Come in, won't you?" She presented her hand in a welcoming gesture, allowing them to enter the cottage. "I have been expecting you both."

Emily felt the blood chill throughout her body. No more than twenty-four hours ago, she had heard Charlotte's words – *"I've been waiting for you."* – ring in her ears. Feeling not quite as threatened by the elderly woman as she had been with Charlotte, Emily chased the sinister thoughts away. Emily was also well aware that Nora was a seer with the powers of knowing the future, and apparently, she knew they were coming.

As Emily and Rick walked into the small room, they found themselves in another enchanted scene with a little Christmas tree next to a charming stone fireplace. The walls were rustic, with exposed beams on the ceiling, and the room smelled of wood and pine with a mixture of chocolate and freshly baked bread.

"Won't you have a seat? I will bring refreshments," Nora said in a low, weak voice.

"Oh, you don't have to go through any trouble," Emily said, gesturing with her hand, indicating to stop. "We're just hear to talk with you if you don't mind giving us a minute of your time."

Nora put her hand on Emily's arm. Her hand felt warm and inviting, causing any fears Emily may have had to evaporate. "No trouble, dear. I'll be right back." She had wise, kind eyes that seemed to have the ability to penetrate the soul.

The elderly woman was small with a hunched back, and she shuffled slowly toward what looked like a tiny kitchen.

Rick leaned in, whispering to Emily, "At least we know she doesn't have enough muscle to take our heads off."

Emily nudged him in the side and whispered, "Can't you be a little more serious?"

Just then Rick rose and walked over to look at a leaded-glass window in the wall behind Emily. He touched one of the panes that featured a design. "Emily," he whispered while waving his hand for her to come over. Emily approached the window, squinting her eyes to see the design better.

"Why does this look so familiar?" she asked.

"Remember? The old wooden box Thomas's grandfather hid in the basement of the farmhouse," Rick said.

Emily did remember. Sam Stanford, her two-times great-grandfather, had received the box from Rick's great-great-grandfather. The box lid displayed the Miller family crest, as did the leaded-glass window in front of them.

"It's the Miller family crest," Rick confirmed.

Emily looked closer, and sure enough, one pane of glass had symbols of three wolves, which signified perseverance, and the medieval steel armor, which represented the military. Then, something else caught Emily's eye. To the left of the window was a painted portrait of a Native American girl, and Emily's mouth dropped open. "I can't believe it! Rick, look!"

Emily recognized the image in the portrait. It was Catori, the Indian seer she had met in 1776 and again in the dark prison of Salem in 1692. The memories startled Emily. An ice-cold chill ran through her, causing her to shiver. Rick seemed to notice her reaction and quickly put his arm around her.

"What is it, Emily? Do you know who she is?" Rick asked as he, too, studied the portrait.

"My husband's four-times great-grandmother," the soft, withering voice said from behind.

Rick and Emily turned their heads simultaneously, finding Nora carrying a tray with homemade bread, jam, and three mugs filled with piping hot cocoa.

Rick darted over, taking the heavy tray from her. "So, she's your ancestor, then?" Rick asked while placing the tray on a table between a rocking chair and the couch.

"She's your ancestor and my inspiration."

Although Emily was aware that Catori was one of Rick's ancestors, clearly, the knowledge had slipped his mind at the moment.

"Yes, that's right. I suppose she is," Rick said as Emily noticed his mind had caught up.

Emily recovered from seeing the image of Catori and sat by Rick as Nora gently lowered herself into the rocker with an unfinished crocheted scarf hanging over the arm of the chair. "Now, my long and far away travelers," Nora began as she leaned slightly forward in the rocker. "What can I do for you?"

"What did you mean when you said Catori was your inspiration, and how did you obtain a portrait that looks remarkably like her?" Emily asked.

"I painted her myself, dear. I spent some time meditating on her, and she showed herself to me in a vision. So, I painted her. I was also able to tap into her powers. Needless to say, my dear, the vision and the experience were quite successful." Nora glanced at another painting near the entrance to the kitchen that showed a meadow of wildflowers. "I do many landscapes as well, many of which I have donated to the Maple Ridge nursing home."

Emily had seen almost every painting when she worked in the nursing home and never saw Nora's name on any of them, and as for Nora's vision, Emily thought it was strange. Nora wasn't a blood relative to Catori, yet she seemed to possess her powers.

"Wow," Rick said. "I didn't know there were artists in the Miller family."

Nora chuckled with amusement. "There is much more than that in your bloodline, Richard Miller. Because of your great courage through time, you now have the vision of your ancestor Catori. You dream and see of what is to come." Nora shifted her gaze to Emily and then back to Rick. "Courage as well as passion for another has ignited the flame that burns within you, causing those visions."

Rick looked at Emily with adoring eyes and squeezed her hand.

Nora then focused on Emily. "You, my dear, are from noble ancestors. Mostly kind, giving, and with a hidden power of time travel that none has ever known." Nora leaned forward, resting her hand on Emily's. "But it was you who was chosen when the last of your bloodline came to pass. Those powers were discovered by a very powerful Witch. This dynamic Witch then tapped into those powers to right a wrong she had caused to so many. You, too, showed great courage through time. And now, my dear, there is a very powerful Mystic Guardian that has called upon those time travel gifts to right another wrong as well."

Emily had known she was the last of her bloodline, and it was she and she alone, appointed with the extraordinary task of defeating not only one curse but now two. Nora's claim of a powerful Mystic Guardian confused her.

"I know the Witch you are referring to, and I know only one Mystic Guardian, Billy Easton. Is that the powerful Guardian you just mentioned?" Emily asked.

"There are things I cannot say." Nora reached for her mug of cocoa and took a sip. Emily could tell that Nora could see the confusion on both her and Rick's faces. "Yes, well..." Nora said with hesitation. "He will reveal himself to you in your own time."

Rick snorted. "Guess that means we're going home...I'm mean to the future, that is."

Nora seemed to enjoy Rick's witty observations. She smiled warmly at him with a look of appreciation in her eyes.

"Tell us about Beth," Emily urged. "You warned her not to go into the swamp. Did you know something was going to happen to her?"

"Yes, dear, I did, but you were also there and saw me, which led you toward the situation that was about to unfold."

"Why couldn't you have stopped Beth?" Rick asked with a slightly irritated tone.

"Oh, my dear Richard, I do not have the power to prevent, only to warn."

"Like you did on the street walking in front of my car trying to get yourself killed?"

Emily shot Rick a glaring look. The old woman rocked slowly and rhythmically in the chair and said nothing. A lull fell over the conversation. All eyes turned to the dying fire, and Rick stood to put another piece of wood over the smoldering embers.

"So, what you're saying is, you knew that I would be able to help Beth," Emily finally said.

Nora remained quiet, and Emily wondered if she was going into a trance.

"Can you at least tell us what you know about Charlotte?"

Rick, still annoyed, returned to his seat next to Emily. She could see he was doing his best to stay level-headed.

"I brought her food every day to keep her alive. Her curse has no power over me," Nora said with her eyes still closed.

Rick was ready to say something, but Emily pulled on his arm and shook her head to urge him to stay silent. Nora didn't move a muscle and appeared as though she were dead. That's when Emily noticed something, which caused her to flinch and cover her mouth to hold back the disbelief. Rick looked at Emily with a what's-wrong? expression. Emily grabbed Rick's arm, pointing discreetly at Nora's wrist. Rick's face turned two shades of white. He jerked his head towards Emily as his mouth fell open. Under Nora's sleeve was a brown, heart-shaped mark. The same mark borne by an accused Salem Witch—Sandra Easton.

In a trance-like state, Nora spoke: "Charlotte had cursed the swamp to keep out all those who possess magical powers. Her curse not only kept them away and killed Lily Spencer and her granddaughter, Kathleen, but it was Charlotte's own curse that had trapped her inside the old dwelling. She could not go over the threshold. If she had, she would have died, leaving the spell unbroken, the Spencer Witches without their powers, and a death curse to remain forever."

Nora suddenly opened her eyes and gave Emily a haunting

stare. "Charlotte had been waiting for you, Emily. You see, my dear, it is upon the time traveler's death that an evil Witch could escape her own curse. But the curse would cease to exist if the time traveler killed the evil Witch."

Rick abruptly stood and his anger exploded. "What do you mean! Emily almost died in there. She almost burned to death. You're a seer! You must have known this. Why couldn't you have warned her!"

Nora reached out with both her hands. Emily yanked on Rick's sleeve, indicating for him to sit. As Rick retreated to a sitting position, Nora held Rick and Emily's hands. Her voice became rich in understanding.

"No, Richard, Emily had to save Beth, and then you saved Emily."

"Nora? Why do you have the same mark on your wrist as Sandra Easton, the Witch who had cast the first death curse? "Emily asked as she turned Nora's hand over.

"This too, my dear, shall be known in your own time."

Less than an hour later, Rick turned right over the bridge as he drove slowly and quietly back to the old farmhouse. Emily settled into the silence. She suspected that Rick was still annoyed over Nora's lack of warning over Emily's possible demise. Nora Miller had filled in the blanks and added new information, yet the mystery persisted. Only two things remained unsolved: Nora's claims of tapping into Catori's powers and why she had the brown, heart-shaped mark on her wrist. Nora left both Emily and Rick with more uncertainty. However, Emily was glad she had no knowledge of how much danger she had been in when confronting Charlotte.

Emily looked over at Rick as he gave her a slight grin. He reached out his hand, and she took it willingly and kissed it. Emily was also glad Nora had intervened with Rick by warning him not to go over the threshold. They were both in peril, yet nothing had stopped either of them from saving a life. She closed her eyes and tried to forget, but the shadows of doubt had a way of creeping in along with the elusive voice of a man that had remained another mystery.

Later that night, Emily and Rick held each other in bed. She felt his touch linger over her breasts as she traced her finger over his cheek, circling his lips. No words were needed. Their bodies had a language all their own. The room felt warm by the burning log that glowed in the fireplace. Its light was enough to cast a flickering glow over their naked bodies. She felt herself tremble in ecstasy as he responded to satisfy his own urgent need. Each gazed at the other as they both reached the peak of pleasure with a sensation of warmth and love nestled between them.

They held each other for a while; neither one had fallen asleep. Emily wondered if it was their need for one another or all the strange mysteries that had kept them awake. She rested her chin on Rick's chest and looked into his distant stare. Her eyes then drifted to the nightstand when she suddenly remembered Rick's letter that she had tucked under a book. Emily returned her attention to Rick's stare and wondered if he was thinking about Pearl Harbor.

"I read the letter you sent me."

His gaze then lowered, resting on Emily. "Oh, yeah. So, ah, what did you think when you read it?"

Emily sat up, pulling the blanket around her shoulders to stay warm. "You missed me," she said, batting her eyes with a flirtatious grin.

Rick sat up, giving Emily a slight smile. "Yeah, there's that, but I mean, what did you think about Thomas, your grandfather?"

"Well, I wish I could have met him, and it sounds like you two did some male bonding."

"Yeah, just like the good soldiers we are." Rick rested his elbows on the pillow behind him as he sighed. "You had to see him, Emily. He was smart and tough. He didn't run away from the fight. He had no intention of leaving anyone behind. Thomas felt the need to be with his men no matter what, and then..."

Emily scooted closer to Rick, resting her hand on his chest. "And then, there was your grandfather."

He gave Emily an intense look. "Did you know that Thomas was best friends with J.J.?"

"J.J.?"

"That's what Thomas and all the other guys called my grandfather."

"No, I didn't know that, but I did know they were serving together in Pearl Harbor. I got that information from both Grace and Marion."

Rick's expression hardened, and he turned toward Emily. "I couldn't save him. I tried. God knows I tried. Thomas and I were making a run for it. We ran towards the sandbags where there was a machine gun." Rick's face showed resolve. "Those bastards needed someone to shoot back at them. Anyway, Thomas and I got to the sandbags just as J.J. jumped on top of us, and then…one of the enemy planes dropped a bomb just feet from us, killing my grandfather."

"Oh, Rick, I'm so sorry." Then suddenly, Emily remembered something. She sat up straight, feeling almost stunned. It was the last column she wrote for the *Maple Ridge Gazette* before she traveled back to 1941—an article about Rick's grandfather saving two men in Pearl Harbor and how he got killed.

"Wait. So, what you're saying is, those two guys your grandfather saved that day were you and Thomas?"

"Yup. That's what I'm saying."

Emily sat there with her mouth open. She hardly knew what to say. She already knew that time travel had always been on a collision course with the ghosts of the past. Now, it was happening to Rick. She glanced at him, feeling strange. Emily could feel time pulling at her. She saw the same look in Rick's eyes, and she imagined that they had the same thought. Then Rick said, "Maybe it's time for us to go home."

Emily crawled back into Rick's arms, and he held her tightly to him. "There's just one problem," she sighed. "How?"

Chapter 24

THE EMERALD TEAR DROP

It was now Saturday, December 13th, and Grace held her weekly gathering of friends and family. The woman had congregated in the living room with talk of new recipes, the latest fashions, how to rear children, and the looming threat of war coming to the home front. Emily was glad Marion Miller was able to be there. It was good for her to be around people, and Rick was pleased to see her again.

Nora hadn't come. Marion said the commotion would be too much for her and that Nora was the type who preferred keeping to herself. However, Emily had not gotten that impression from Nora. She had been very welcoming to both her and Rick.

Later, Emily sat on an iron garden bench near the river, breathing in the cold air. Her mind felt tired and wanted to be alone to mull over everything Nora Miller had said during their visit with her in the old cottage. What bothered her the most was the disturbing voice still calling her name from beyond the Magic River. Nora had also revealed that a powerful Mystic Guardian had called upon the time traveler's gift to right another wrong from a second death curse. Emily wondered if the voice she'd been hearing all along came from this powerful Mystic Guardian.

She looked over her shoulder and saw Rick and Billy in conversation, standing by a pile of firewood that Grace most likely sent them out to gather. She imagined Rick was talking Billy's ear off about the old farmhouse and how he wanted to restore it to its original glory. Watching the two men made her feel calm and safe, but the unknown began to creep back in when she turned her attention toward the river.

A few minutes went by and then she heard a commotion and looked towards the house again and saw Rick and Billy go inside as each carried an armload of firewood. She, too, decided to go in and freshen up before dinner.

Emily went through the kitchen into the hallway and noticed the basement door was ajar, with light coming from underneath. Billy and Rick were probably rummaging around down there, she thought. She then glanced into the living room to tell Grace she'd be right back after she freshened up, but Grace was nowhere to be found. Emily took the stairs and entered the bedroom at the top, seeing Grace sitting at the vanity, rummaging through a jewelry box.

"Oh, I'm sorry. I can come back." Just as Emily was about to leave, Grace stood and held a small box. Emily could see sadness in her eyes as Grace stared at the box in her hand. Her gaze then shifted to Emily.

"Emily, please stay." Grace opened the box, taking out a gold and emerald teardrop pendant surrounded by diamonds. Her eyes softened as though a memory came into focus. "Thomas gave this to me on our wedding day," she said, caressing the tiny stone as though yearning for that moment to come back. "He said it matched my eyes. I...I have to admit that I hardly wear it. Except, of course, on special occasions. I dare say there's not many of those these days."

"It's beautiful," Emily said.

"I would like you to have it, Emily," Grace said.

"Oh, Grace, I don't know why you would want me to have such a sentimental item. Especially a wedding gift from your husband."

"You know,..I always thought I would hand this down to my daughter and she to her daughter after that. But as you can see, I have only Matthew."

"You're still young, Grace. You could have more children and possibly a little girl."

Emily knew that was never to be, yet felt she had to say something to make her grandmother feel better. Emily stood in front of Grace and touched the emerald in her hand. "Grace, something like this should be given to someone close to you."

Grace's eyes were thoughtful as she smiled. "There is someone else with emerald-green eyes that I think Thomas would be more than happy that I give this to." She reached over, placing the necklace in Emily's hand. "Our granddaughter."

Emily's mouth fell open. "But…but how…did?"

"Billy told me. Emily, you don't know how relieved I am. I felt a connection to you the moment I met you. You seemed like a part of me somehow. I felt like I knew you, yet we had never met before. And then, the strange way you showed up and…" Grace touched a strand of Emily's hair hanging down on her forehead. "Your hair, that red hair, the same green eyes as myself."

"I'm so sorry, Grace, that I couldn't tell you. You've been so kind to me and now to Rick as well."

Grace's posture stiffened as if she became acutely aware of something. "Rick…is…Marion's?"

"Yes, he is. But maybe it's best we—"

"Don't say anything to her," Grace said, finishing Emily's thought.

"Yes, and it's better that very few people have this knowledge. It can be a burden," Emily said.

"I suppose the burden falls more heavily on you, Emily. After all, you must know everyone's fate. You know all our joys and sorrows. The way we lived, when we…die—how we die. You must know all that right now as you stand in front of me."

Grace spoke very philosophically, and her sense of reality was commendable. Emily could see her eyes moist with tears.

"Even if I were alive in your time, I would be extremely old and at an age well past one hundred. Now, I doubt I'm even alive at that time. It's why I myself want to be the one to give this keepsake to you right now and before you go back to your own time where I no longer exist."

Grace was right. Emily did know her fate, dying of a heart attack nine years after Thomas's death and four months after her son, Matthew, was killed in Vietnam. Emily vaguely remembered her grandmother's sadness and had always wondered if she had lost the will to live, causing her heart to simply stop beating. Emily had been too young at the time to understand such sorrow. She would later find that out for herself after Lucas's tragic accident and how she, too, wanted to die, but somehow her heart kept beating. As far as knowing Grace's fate, it was one of those awful realities for a time traveler. She would have to compartmentalize, putting all those thoughts into little boxes, storing them away in her brain, and trying not to think about them.

Emily looked at the necklace in her hand. She put the tiny gold chain around her neck, hooking the clasp, and touched the stone where it now lay near her heart. She took Grace into her arms in a heartbreaking embrace as the two women softly cried. Emily knew she would never see her again once she returned to her own time. Then Emily leaned back to get a good look at Grace's face. She wanted to remember her just like this—young, beautiful, and full of life. Emily knew there was only one more thing to say. "I love you, Grandma."

Chapter 25

THE WAY HOME

EARLIER, RICK HAD WATCHED BILLY pick up one piece of firewood and cradle it in his arms. The two men glanced over to the river, where Emily sat motionless by the water's edge. "How is Emily doing? Is she still hearing that man's voice?" Billy asked.

"No, I don't think so—at least not since I've returned." Rick's attention remained on Emily. "I'm pretty sure she would have said something. Nora did tell her she would find the answer in her own time." Rick lifted one brow. "Meaning, in the future."

"Really? So, Nora knows about it?"

"She seemed to and a lot more." Rick ran his fingers through his hair while walking halfway around the wood pile towards Billy. "Did you know that Nora has a brown mark on her wrist shaped like a heart?"

"No, I never got that close to her, just cordial hellos. I did, however, sense her seer powers when I did encounter her, but that was about it."

"You do know what that mark means though, right?" Rick asked.

"Yes, it means somehow Nora is a Witch…something I didn't know," Billy said as he shifted the firewood in his arms and glanced at Emily bleakly.

"Nora also told me I now have the powers of a seer," Rick said.

Billy handed Rick the piece of wood he was holding and picked another from the pile.

"Wow, that must have been a shock to you," Billy said, making a noise in his throat. "And here I thought I had special powers."

"Yeah, well, being a seer is one power I would rather avoid tapping into. It's bad enough I'm carrying around eighty years of knowledge from the future." Rick looked over at Emily and shook his head. "She just wants to go home and...so do I. There are just too many paranormal events surrounding us, making us both uneasy." Rick gathered another piece of firewood off the pile and gave Billy a look of uncertainty. "The problem is, we don't know if it's possible."

Apparently in deep thought, Billy kicked the snow off the side of the pile. Rick could see his eyebrows turn in as though trying to figure out a problem and then he finally spoke.

"What I do know is this," Billy began. "Emily was sent here when a new Witch was born in a new century and then the Spencer Witches regained their powers. But what I don't know is—" Billy gave Rick a look of skepticism. "How did you get here?"

Rick balanced the firewood with one arm and firmly touched Billy's shoulder. "By those same Spencer Witches."

"They must have had to use a spell then. You're not a time traveler like Emily," Billy said.

"They did, from a magic spell book they found in an old chest."

A wide grin suddenly came across Billy's face. He bent down, grabbed two more pieces of wood, and took a step toward Rick. "Well, my friend, I think I might know the way home for you and Emily."

The basement still had that musty smell Rick remembered. An old brass light dangled from a wire, and when Billy yanked on the pull chain, the small space filled with a yellowish glow. Rick watched as Billy lifted old cans of paint and scrap wood from what Rick assumed were previous projects.

He found himself staring at the slight indentation in the old brick wall, knowing it contained an old box dating back to 1776. The box was later placed in a hidden vault behind one of the bricks by Emily's great-great-grandfather in 1918. Rick would be the one to discover that old box in the future. The moment's unease caused him to try and focus on other things around him. Not much had changed. He recognized some of the old things that belonged to Billy or Thomas and that were still in the farmhouse's basement eight decades from now.

"Here it is," Billy said, dragging something sizable that a sheet had covered.

"What is it?" Rick asked.

Billy pulled the sheet off a large wooden chest. "It's a hope chest that was my stepmother's. Thomas has been keeping it down here to give it to Beth someday."

Rick watched as Billy popped open the cover and pulled out the same book Sylvia used when sending him back in time.

"*The Spencer Magic Spell Book*," Billy said, holding it up.

"Yep, that's it all right," Rick agreed.

The two men sat on a pair of old chairs as Billy thumbed through the ancient book. "Here," Billy said, pointing to a particular spell. "This must be it. It says the spell must be said in a whisper while harnessing another form of power." Billy looked up at Rick, "What do you suppose that means? Was there another source of power the Witches used?"

Rick stood and rubbed his chin. "Let me think." He walked towards the stairway in deep thought while running his fingers through his hair. "The Witches used each other," he finally said when another thought occurred to him. "Wait! They also used something called 'Magick' to tap into the magic that runs through the river." Rick glanced up the basement stairs and pointed. "They told me the Magic River possessed powers that any Witch could harness. That has to be the other source of power. I stood right in this very backyard next to the water when a swirling mist covered me. The next thing I knew I was lying in an airfield with World War II planes flying over my head."

"Well, then," Billy said with a smile. "If a Witch could use the powers of the Magic River, I don't see any reason why a Mystic Guardian couldn't do the same." Billy got up from the rickety old chair and gave Rick a pat on the back. "Sounds to me, my time travel friend, that we found our answer. When you and Emily are ready, just say the word. I just might be able to do some harnessing of my own."

Rick found Emily in the bedroom just before dinner. He told her how Billy had found *The Spencer Magic Spell Book* tucked away in an old hope chest and, within the pages, discovered a time travel spell. He told her that this sounded like their one chance to return to the future. Rick knew how painful the goodbyes were going to be. They had both felt time pulling at them as the future called them home.

At dinner that evening, he watched Emily's face as she looked at Walter, Matthew, Marty, Beth, and little Randy. Rick knew what she was thinking, and he felt the same sadness that he saw in Emily's eyes. Rick glanced at Marion, who had no idea that he and Emily were about to disappear, never to be seen again.

The thought of never laying eyes on his grandmother again weighed heavily on his heart. Rick would say his final goodbyes to his grandmother, and come morning, Billy would send them back to their own time. Emily had told him earlier that she had wished with all her heart to have spent time with Thomas and to have said a proper goodbye.

As they sat among the ghosts of the past, he looked at Emily and saw her fingers caress the emerald teardrop her grandmother had given her. She gave him a faint smile. He laid his hand on her leg to reassure her, and she placed hers over his to offer the same. They would be together, take this journey back together. This time, Emily wouldn't be alone, he thought. This time, he would be by Emily's side.

Chapter 26

THE SAD DETOUR

It was early Sunday morning when Billy, Marlene, Emily, and Rick gathered near the banks of the Magic River. Emily and Rick held each other close. Emily could vaguely see Grace in the kitchen window, waving as she watched. They had said their tearful goodbyes after breakfast. Emily had kissed Walter's precious cheek with the heartbreaking knowledge that he no longer existed where she was going. She held little Matthew in her arms as she smelled his hair and caressed his soft hands, wanting to remember him this way forever.

Rick had said his goodbyes to his grandmother the night before. He had given her an affectionate hug. Marion looked as though she didn't quite know how to take the sudden fondness but seemed pleased nonetheless. Rick playfully wrestled with Walter, Marty, and Matthew. The three boys laughed when they thought they got the best of Rick by successfully tackling him. He then held them close, telling each one he would miss them.

An inquisitive Marty asked, "Are you going back to the war?"

"No," Rick replied as he swallowed hard and looked longingly at Emily and then winked. "Just going on a long trip with my girl."

Emily was sure he had known the pain that comes with time travel: the same pain she had gone through many times before.

As they stood by the Magic River with Billy and Marlene, Rick looked at his hand. "Hey, ah,..do you think they'll let me keep my hand?"

Emily took his newfound hand, feeling each finger and then glanced up at Rick with the same hope and sadness. "I suppose there's only one way to find out."

"Are you both ready?" Billy interrupted in a soft voice.

Rick nodded and then turned to Emily. "I love you so much, Emily."

She kissed his hand and then his lips with no more words. She gave Billy a nod. No one said anything. Emily was sure only painful thoughts were running through everyone's minds as they shared this final farewell. Marlene held *The Spencer Magic Spell Book* as Billy read the incantation. Emily could hear his whispers of the words ever so faintly:

> *"A task at hand to save a soul. Eyes have seen a place of old. Powers take hold and descend on thee, as thee cast out evil that shall no longer be. Time will bring thee to thy loved one in need to say goodbye or never to leave."*

The mist floated off the river and swirled around Emily and Rick. A warm breeze whipped strands of her hair as she grabbed onto Rick with a tight grip. She could almost feel his body melt into hers as they both closed their eyes. It was then that the blackness engulfed them. Moments later, they were swept away.

The light pierced through Emily's eyelids. No longer was there darkness. A breeze moved something around her that gently brushed against her arms and legs. She was almost afraid to open her eyes, and she settled on lifting one lid at a time. She saw a blue sky and a tree branch fully in flower with cherry blossoms swaying in the breeze. She was no longer in the snow, and it felt warm. Springtime? she wondered.

All of a sudden, Rick crossed her mind. A shot of panic surged through her, with both eyes opening wide, she sat up and looked around. "Rick? Rick?" she called, moving her hand through the tall, green grass surrounding her. She heard a faint moan. "Rick? Is that you?"

Rick moved into view, sliding through the tall grass in an army crawl towards her. "Emily? Emily? Are you okay, sweetie?"

She reached for him as she felt herself tearing up. Both held each other tight.

"It's okay, Emily, I'm here, sweetie. I got you."

They lingered in each other's arms until Emily felt Rick's grip on her loosening. She saw his eyes blink several times, as he stared down at his hand. "Emily, look!" he exclaimed in amazement. "I still got my hand!" He let out a spontaneous laugh. "Can you believe it? I still have it!"

They both got to their feet and gazed at Rick's hand when something unusual caught Emily's eye.

"Something's wrong, Rick."

"What are you talking about? How can anything be wrong when I still have my hand?"

"You know that maple tree in our back yard? You know, the one with the swing on it? The one Thomas planted nine months before I was born?"

"Yeah, why?" Rick said.

"Look," she said, pointing.

Rick looked in the direction where Emily was pointing. There stood a tiny maple tree held up by two stakes. "It's barely bigger than a sapling. It can't be anymore than a year old," Rick said.

Emily looked around and saw an old shed that didn't exist in their future. Other than the shed, tall grass, and the baby maple tree, almost everything else looked the same. "Rick, I don't think we're back in our own time."

Rick stepped forward but tilted slightly to one side, trying to stay on his feet. Emily scooted next to him. "What's wrong, Rick? Are you okay?"

Rick put two fingers above his nose as he squeezed his eyes shut. "I hear something...a man with shallow breathing. I can see he's alone. He's waiting for someone." Rick jerked his head up and looked at the back of the old farmhouse. He took another two steps forward, saying, "I know what year this is." He turned to look at Emily. "We're in the year 1959."

With Rick beside her, Emily entered the house from the back and walked through the same hallway she had gone through in three different centuries. This time, she felt an overwhelming sense of sorrow, loss, and love that had surpassed distances and years. She looked at the wall and saw the picture of her grandparents, one she had looked at less than two hours before. But now, eighteen years later, it still hung in the same spot.

Then, another picture caught her eye, a photo Emily had never seen before. It was an image of a handsome, middle-aged man with a smile transcending all that would ever make sense in the real world. A picture of her grandfather, the mysterious man with a beard she had dreamed about long ago. Her focus settled on the front door. She had already said goodbye once to the young boy. He had been sick with the Spanish flu and had quickly recovered. But now? she thought.

Emily stepped onto the front porch. A man was slumped over in a chair, his chin touching his chest as a tiny bit of drool dribbled slowly down the side of his mouth. Emily felt the tears welling up in her eyes. She clutched her chest, and a hint of a painful gasp escaped through her breath.

"Oh, Thomas," she whispered, taking a step toward her grandfather. Her heartache had masked the pain of her wounded leg as she knelt beside him. "Thomas?" She spoke his name softly and gently touched his arm.

He raised his head in slow motion. Emily could see a shadow of a smile. "Oh, my...sweet Emily," he said with halting breaths. "Billy said you would come to say goodbye."

Emily took a tissue from the box on the side table and wiped Thomas's chin and mouth. "I've missed you, Thomas. I wish I could have seen you when I was in 1941." She put the tissue down and wrapped her arms lovingly around her grandfather, holding him for several moments. His body was frail, wasted away by cancer, and so weak he had no strength to hug her back. "I love you, grandpa." She leaned back, looking Thomas in the eyes. "I guess I've only known you as the little boy, haven't I?"

He reached over and touched the emerald pendant dangling from her neck. "Grace told me she gave this to you," he murmured. "I was so happy she did."

Emily put her hand over Thomas's as he held the tiny stone. "I will always cherish it." Emily couldn't stop the tears from rolling down her cheeks.

Thomas reached over and caught one of her tears with his finger. "Please, don't be sad for me, Emily. I've had a wonderful life. I held you in my arms but two days ago, kissed you goodbye, knowing that you would someday see me again through time and space." Thomas lowered his hand, and a hint of a smile began to form on his dry lips. "Now, tell me. How is our hero doing?"

Emily stood and lifted her hand towards the door. "Why don't you ask him yourself," Emily said with a broad grin mixed with tears.

Rick stepped onto the porch as Thomas turned his head slightly. "Hey there, old flyboy. Never thought I'd see you again."

Rick let out a chuckle as he pulled a chair alongside Thomas. "Thought I'd stop by to see how you're doing, buddy."

Thomas tried to sit up. Rick helped him while Emily placed a pillow behind Thomas's back.

"As you can see, I'm dying."

Rick leaned closer to Thomas. "I know, buddy, that's why we're here. So you don't have to be alone while doing it."

Rick glanced up at Emily. She knelt again between Thomas and Rick. She placed one hand on Thomas and the other on Rick's knee for support. The sorrow welled up once again, and her weepy voice gave away her broken heart. "How many more times must I say goodbye to those I love so dearly?"

Rick laid his hand over hers and gently squeezed. Emily could see his own sadness in his eyes. Thomas held Emily's hand. His touch was considerably weaker and as cold as ice. Emily could see the life beginning to drain from his eyes. It would be a matter of minutes, she thought.

"Thank you, Emily, for saving me. If not...for you, I would have died as a young boy." Thomas then turned his attention toward Rick. "How will I ever thank you enough for saving my life in Pearl? From the day I first met you, you...have been such...a good friend to me. You both have and..." Thomas tried hard to catch a breath.

Emily hugged him again and cried a torrent of tears. She felt Rick's hand rest on her back. His touch felt comforting, but nothing could take away the despair Emily suffered over losing the grandfather she held in her arms. "I love you, Thomas," she said again through the rushing tears. Then, within moments, he took his last breath.

Emily and Rick sat with Thomas for a while. She gazed out into the front yard. An old truck sat in the driveway, and then she realized she had seen it before in 1941 when it was new. Many times, Billy had loaded it up with lumber or other materials when something needed fixing on the house—fresh memories for her but old ones for those in the here and now.

The wind blew gently through the trees and whistled through the eaves above them. It reminded her that this had always been an old house filled with memories that only time travel provided. It had allowed her to enter into so many lives, especially the ones she had loved so deeply.

She took Rick's hand gratefully. He, too, seemed to be in deep thought as he absently gazed into the distance. Then suddenly, they both saw a car approaching and stood. It wasn't hard to miss, with its loud engine and beautiful red color. The bat-wing tail design made it seem as if the car could fly.

"Holy shit!" Rick said, walking down the front steps. "You see that, Emily? That's a 1959 Impala convertible. The last time I saw one those was at the New England car show a few years ago."

Emily came down the steps and stood by Rick as she tried to focus on the driver. "Who do you think it is?" she asked.

"You're not going to believe this, but I think it's Billy." Rick walked a few more steps forward as the car came to a stop in front of him. The gray-haired driver got out and, sure enough, there stood an older version of Billy.

"Hey, Rick," Billy said. "How are you, Emily?"

Emily remained silent, still feeling the effects of Thomas's death. Rick approached Billy with his hand out to shake his. Billy pulled Rick in for a manly embrace.

"You're not trying to catch up with me now are you, Billy, old boy?" Rick said, rubbing the top of Billy's gray hair.

"Nah. You're always going to be the old guy in this relationship," Billy said and laughed. Billy then walked over to Emily. He lifted his chin toward Thomas. "Is Thomas…?"

Emily's eyes filled with tears again. She nodded. Billy took Emily into his arms and held her close as she melted into the embrace.

"It's going to be all right, Emily," Billy whispered. "He's been so sick for a long while. We both loved him with all of our hearts."

"He only just passed away just before you got here," Rick said solemnly behind them.

Billy nodded. "I know."

"How did you know?" Rick asked

Billy looked over at Thomas's lifeless body and then at Rick. "I knew you were coming. I stayed with Thomas for as long as I could, then drove down the road, and waited. Let's just say it was the burden of knowing the future." Billy's hand gestured towards the Magic River. "Come on, we need to get you two home."

A few minutes later, all three stood by the Magic River. There was no time to waste. Neither Emily nor Rick wanted to get tangled up in another time period. Billy had said he could try once more to send them forward to their own time, but Emily needed to know how and why she and Rick ended up in 1959.

"How did you know we were here and just as Thomas was dying?" Emily asked.

"Nora Miller," Billy replied.

"Nora? What does she have to do with this?" Rick asked.

"She came to me one day and told me that the time travelers would take a sad detour. She told me the exact date and time." Billy stood before Emily and touched the tiny emerald she wore.

"Nora said that a keepsake will alter the time travelers' passage where three sad hearts will be together to say their last goodbyes."

"And you guessed that it was us?" Emily asked.

"It wasn't until Thomas revealed that Grace had given you the emerald necklace. He told me he had given it to Grace as a wedding gift. I just put two and two together and figured that had to be the keepsake Nora mentioned. Besides, you two are the only times travelers I have ever known. Then with Thomas dying, I knew what that last goodbye meant. So, like I said, it wasn't hard to figure it out."

Billy walked over to the small shed and stepped in. When he came out, he was holding *The Spencer Magic Spell Book*. He flipped through the pages, settling on one particular spell. "This is another time travel spell I found later on and most likely the one the Spencer Witches used on Rick."

"What was wrong with the other one," Emily asked.

"That one was to take the person through time, bringing them to their loved one in need, to say goodbye or to never leave. Well, you had said your goodbyes to all of us in 1941 except for one person."

"Thomas," Emily said.

"Yes, and now you have said your goodbyes to Thomas when he needed you the most." Billy pointed to the opened book. "This other spell I found is written similarly but with a different ending."

Emily came forward, peered down and read the spell:

> *"A task at hand to save a soul. Eyes have seen a place of old. Powers take hold and descend on thee, as thee cast out evil that shall no longer be. Return to thy rightful time, where loved ones await. Then hold them close in thy loving embrace."*

Emily lifted a brow. "It does sound slightly different."

"It does, and apparently it's all in the wording and makes sense," Billy added. "Between the spell book, the keepsake, and Nora's prediction, I was quite certain you would come here at this particular moment to say that painful goodbye."

Emily studied Billy's face. The lines on his forehead deepened, and she saw a slight glisten in his eyes as he bravely held back tears. The protective instinct of a true Mystic Guardian, she thought. Billy reached into his back pocket and pulled out a photo. He tried hard to hold onto his emotions when he whispered the name "Lucas."

"Lucas," she repeated, touching the picture. "I remember seeing this photo before. It was worn and faded, but it's the same picture." They both looked at the image adoringly and then Emily gazed into Billy's sad eyes. "He's just a baby right now, barely a year old."

Billy nodded as he returned the photo to his back pocket and swallowed hard, unable to speak. He didn't have to. Emily felt it, too. Knowledge of the future had an awful sting. She stood on her toes, leaning in towards Billy. "Give Lucas this for me." Then, Emily placed a gentle kiss on Billy's cheek.

Chapter 27

PAINFUL REALITY

It felt warm and soft beneath her on the couch with the smell of wood burning in the fireplace. Other pleasant aromas made her stomach growl. Soup? And a whiff of coffee? she thought. She opened her eyes. The ceiling looked clean, freshly painted, not dulled with smoke stains from the last time she saw it. Emily turned her head and saw Rick sitting across from her. He stared down, rubbing his wrist. She slowly sat up. His empty stare confused her.

What happened? Are we back home? she wondered. Her mind took its time comprehending. "Rick?"

He didn't say anything at first, but finally he lifted his eyes. "It's gone."

His voice sounded cold, even bitter. "What's gone?" Emily asked.

"My hand. It's—gone.»

Emily got up from the couch, still trying to get her bearings. She knelt in front of Rick and kissed the spot where his hand had been. "I love you just the way you are," she said and then tried to hold him. His body was stiff, and he barely looked at her. Rick was always affectionate towards her, but not now, she thought. She leaned back and saw on his face a looming shadow she had never seen before. "Rick? I know how bad this must feel for you."

Rick shot her an abrupt look. She tried to touch him again, but he flinched.

'No, Emily! You don't know how it feels!" Rick's eyes turned cold, and Emily could sense his anger.

"First, I have my hand back," he said as his voice built in fury. "Then they fucking take it away from me!" Rick got up, walked over to the window, and pounded his only fist on the wall next to the window, spewing rage. "Now I'm supposed to act like it never happened all because I went through the fucking *Twilight Zone!*»

Rick's mouth twisted with an expression of self-pity. He mumbled something incoherent. Something about drinking again, she assumed. The thought horrified her. Was she hearing things? Were her assumptions wrong? She didn't want to believe it.

Emily stood and took a step towards him; she could feel her own anger building. He had never spoken to her like that before. It was a side of him she had never seen. "So, everything we've been through—-our pain, heartache, the passion between us." Emily's voice became louder. "What? All that means nothing? You're going to go back to square one by drowning your sorrows in a bottle of Scotch!" Emily put her hand up to her mouth, immediately regretting her words.

Rick spun around. "What did you just say to me?" He walked towards Emily, stopping within an inch of her face. Their eyes met, both unmoving. All their love, hate, and anger rolled up into this moment. Then— Rick walked away. She flinched as the front door slammed and her heart sank.

Emily walked into the kitchen a few minutes later and saw Sylvia washing dishes. She must have sensed Emily's presence because she quickly turned around with a look of regret.

"So, I guess you heard that?" Emily asked, not needing an answer. She sat at the kitchen table and put her face in her hands. She felt the wave of tears coming and swallowed the lump in her throat. Emily felt a gentle touch on her arm, as Sylvia sat next to her.

"It will be okay. Don't worry. I imagine you both have gone through a lot," Sylvia said.

Emily looked around the kitchen when a thought occurred to her. "How did I get into the house? I don't remember any of that."

"Rick carried you through the back door. He had such a haunted look on his face." Sylvia shook her head and sighed. "He didn't give a single glance toward Derek or me. He walked right past us. His eyes were so dull, and he hung his head as if in defeat over something. Both Derek and I stayed quiet as he laid you on the couch. We both heard Rick's outburst. Derek just left, going out the back door." Sylvia leaned towards Emily. "I'm so sorry, Emily."

Suddenly, Emily thought of something else, "How long were we gone?"

"About eight hours. Why?"

"One hour means one day in the past. Rick and I have been gone eight days."

"Where did you end up?"

"Exactly where we needed to be." Emily took a long, weary breath. "I'm sorry, Sylvia, it's a long story, and I'm too tired and upset to go into it."

"I understand," Sylvia said, patting Emily's arm again. "You can always talk to me whenever you want. I'm here for you and Rick."

"That's very kind of you. Thank you."

"I'll tell you what," Sylvia said, getting up and taking a soup bowl from the cupboard. "I'll give you some soup, and maybe that will restore your mood. Well, at least slightly anyway."

The soup Sylvia placed in front of Emily did as Sylvia promised. The spoonfuls of broth, chicken, and vegetables that Emily sipped warmed and revived her. She was glad to have a caring friend like Sylvia and changed her mind, deciding to offer her good friend something from the past.

"I saw your mother," Emily said.

"You did?" Sylvia had excitement in her voice as she sat next to Emily.

Emily put her spoon down, smiled, and leaned towards Sylvia. "Did you know your mom had a doll named Heidi?"

"No, tell me about it—and her."

"Beth was sweet. She had wavy blond hair and a precious smile that would melt your heart. She loved her stepfather, who happens to be my late husband's grandfather."

Sylvia's eyes widened. "I don't understand. How did that happen?"

"His name was Billy Easton—a Mystic Guardian. The same Mystic Guardian that your grandmother, Kathleen, had asked to protect your mother, Beth."

"So, it's true. My grandmother, Kathleen, put my mother under the protection of a Mystic Guardian who had raised her?" Sylvia got up and walked towards the kitchen window. Emily could hear her sigh, and then Sylvia turned, and Emily noticed the recognition in her eyes.

"I remember this man," Sylvia began. "When I was very young, we lived in upstate New York for a while. I was so little. I barely knew him. My mother never talked about her parents. Mostly, I remember occasionally visiting a nice elderly man and woman. When I was fourteen, I went to his funeral. Afterward, I went with my mother to visit the older woman, never realizing she was, in fact, my other grandmother.

"Her name was Marlene, and it sounds like the man you remembered was Billy Easton," Emily offered.

"Yes, that's right. And not long after my grandfather—this Billy Easton died—Marlene died. I remember my mother being very sad for a while. But like I said before, she never talked about them."

"Why do you suppose your mother kept them from you?" Emily asked.

Sylvia sat next to Emily again. She rested her folded hands on the table. "It wasn't that she kept them from me, but it's possible that she kept them from my father. He was not an easy man to live with. Come to think of it, maybe my mother didn't want my father to know about her magical past or that she was a descendant of Salem

Witches. When my father died, we moved back to Maple Ridge. By then, I was eighteen and getting ready to go off to college."

Sylvia leaned back in the chair with her arms folded in front of her, looking mildly irritated. "I just wish my mother and grandparents weren't so secretive. My mother could've at least told me."

Emily gave Sylvia a side glance. "Believe me when I tell you, Billy Easton was the king of secrets and apparently your mother was too. But my best guess is: They didn't want you to have the burden of knowing too much. Trust me, Sylvia, that kind of knowledge is downright painful. But now, what we both know for sure is: The Easton family and the Spencer family are connected because of Billy's willingness to protect and adopt your mother."

"If Billy is a Mystic Guardian," Sylvia added, "Wouldn't your late husband be one? I know you said he gave no signs of magical powers in all the years you'd known him but…"

"None that I had ever seen anyway," Emily said. "I'd known Lucas practically my whole life. I imagine if he did have powers, he certainly had no knowledge of them nor was there anyone left alive to tell him otherwise."

Emily became quiet as she thought of all those she had loved and lost. She wondered how much she should tell Sylvia, especially about Charlotte. Then Emily realized that Sylvia, as well as herself, need not worry over people who were already dead. "There is something else," Emily said, hesitating.

"What is it?"

"Charlotte tried to kill your mother. She almost did, but I was able to intervene before that happened."

Sylvia's eyes blinked in disbelief as though trying to process what she had just heard. Emily took Sylvia's hand, giving her a light squeeze.

"But Beth was just fine. She lived her whole life. She had you, didn't she?"

Sylvia's eyes softened with an inner glow. "It sounds like my mother had that chance because of you."

The two women sat quietly for a few minutes as they appreci-ated each other's company. Emily could hear the snowblower out-side as Derek was most likely clearing the snow from the driveway. She was thinking about Rick's outburst and craned her neck to-wards the hallway, wondering if he had come back into the house.

"He's out clearing snow with his son," Sylvia said with the corners of her mouth turning up.

"How did you know what I was thinking?" Emily asked.

"You're forgetting. I now possess magical powers," she said, giving Emily a friendly nudge.

"Speaking of powers," Emily said, sitting up straighter in the chair. "Where are the other two Spencer Witches, and how is the little one?"

Sylvia got up, taking Emily's bowl. "Would you like some more?"

Emily waved her hand and shook her head. "No, thanks, but it was delicious."

"As far as Meghan and the baby, they're both fine and sleeping. Later today Derek will bring them to the hospital to get checked out, but otherwise they seem perfectly healthy."

Emily stood and walked over to the kitchen window. The snow was blowing, drifting across the yard as it whipped the swing hanging in the tree her grandfather, Thomas, had planted. Echoes from the past always had a way of following her. Emily could feel the exhaustion coming on and looked at Sylvia. "I think I'll go up and take a shower. I can check on Meghan and the baby before they go if you'd like."

"They've been up all night. I'm sure sleep has taken over until at least this evening, but yes, of- course, that would be great." Sylvia entwined her arm around Emily's and escorted her to the stairway. "You go on up and rest." She looked towards the front door and then back at Emily with empathy. "I'm sure he will be up soon."

Chapter 28

REGRETS

It was bitter cold from all the snow on the ground—a fitting place to cool off from his blow up at the one person he had vowed to love and protect. Rick had immediately regretted speaking to Emily so harshly and was glad the biting wind was cooling the anger that had strangely taken over his mind moments earlier. Rick watched as Derek used the snowblower and then noticed a broom leaning next to the front door. Rick grabbed it to clear the front porch steps. When finished, Rick caught Derek's eye and swiped his finger across his neck as an indication to cut the power to the snowblower.

"Hey, Dad." Derek shut off the snowblower and walked towards his father. "You…ah…okay?"

"Guess you heard my explosion."

"Yeah, along with half the countryside," Derek said.

Rick stood his ground and nodded slowly. "I see you've become a wiseass just like your old man."

"Look, Dad. It's none of my business, but that guy in there a few minutes ago sounded an awful lot like that guy I hated most of my life. Now, Dad, I know you've changed and for the better. You came back alive when Emily entered into your life." Derek took a step forward, letting out a heavy sigh. "You never had that with Mom. I'm beginning to think the only thing you did have with Mom was—well, me." Derek took another step, stood at the bottom of the porch, and looked up at Rick. "There is a love between you and Emily that's…well, in my opinion—epic.»

Rick chuckled. "Epic? That does sound about right." Rick sat down on the top step and looked at the spot where his hand had been. He could almost feel his fingers and how Emily caressed each one, causing one of those epic moments between them.

Rick let out a long breath. "Truth is, I knew guys that came home with no legs, no arms or…not at all. For me, it was just a hand." Rick shook his head. The shame of his actions began to sink in. "Worst of all, I can't believe I spoke to Emily like that. I'm such an asshole."

Derek sat beside his father and put his hand on his shoulder. "Nah, you're not an asshole, Dad. You're just a big jerk."

Rick gave his son a side glance. "Very funny."

The two men looked out over the mountain of snow that had accumulated within the eight hours of Rick and Emily's absences. Rick decided to change the subject. "I got to meet your great-grandfather, Joseph."

"Oh, really? So, it sounds like you traveled back to World War II."

"Yeah, just before. I ended up in a sugarcane field alongside an airstrip in Pearl Harbor." Rick looked Derek straight in the eyes. "On December 6, 1941."

Derek's face dropped. "NO SHIT! REALLY!"

"Yup, sure did. Anyway, it's a long story but to their credit, your wife and mother-in-law sent me to the right place at the right time."

"What do you mean?" Derek asked.

"I saved Thomas Stanford from getting killed. Although Thomas was five thousand miles from Maple Ridge, the curse may not have been. I also tried to save my grandfather, but…I guess some things can't be changed. It was like I was reliving Iraq all over again, only this time I wasn't hurt. In fact," Rick held his arm up. "I had my hand."

"You what?"

"My hand. It was completely restored as if nothing ever happened to it. But now…" Rick lifted his chin towards the house. "That was the source of my outburst a few minutes ago."

"Sorry, Dad. I guess I can understand your frustration now."

"It's still no excuse for speaking to Emily like that."

A gust of wind whipped tiny snow tornadoes across the front yard and back into the driveway. Rick looked over at his son, glad he could have such a meaningful and personal conversation with him, something he never had with Derek until recently.

"Anyway," Rick continued as he hugged himself to keep warm. "I thought about it good and hard, and I think I was supposed to be there to save Thomas, and Emily was there to save Beth."

"Beth? You mean Meghan's grandmother?"

"That would be the one, and it was Emily's deceased husband's grandfather, a guy by the name of Billy Easton, who had Beth under his protection. In fact, he and his wife raised Beth."

"So, this Easton guy was the Mystic Guardian?"

"Yup," Rick said. "It seems there are four families interconnected through time: the Easton, Stanford, Miller and Spencer families."

"Well, I guess it explains a lot, especially those cryptic messages in Lily Spencer's diary," Derek added.

Rick said nothing as he looked over his shoulder at the front door. He took a deep breath and got to his feet. "Well, ah…I suppose I should do some apologizing."

"You know what I think, Dad? I think if done properly things could become epic again in no time."

Rick squinted his eyes as the side of his mouth turned up in a slight grin. "How did you get to be such a smart ass?"

Derek stood and patted his dad on the shoulder. "I guess the apple doesn't fall far from the tree after all."

After returning to the house, Rick stood by the door to the bathroom, admiring Emily through the transparent shower curtain. He walked over, nudged the curtain open slightly, and watched as the hot water washed over Emily's back as she leaned against the tile with her head down. He thought she was on the verge of tears, wondering if it was simply exhaustion or the argument between them that seemed to cause the sudden emotions.

Rick loved her more than he had ever imagined and hated himself for saying such an awful thing to her. He also felt hurt at the same time, hearing the sting of truth about himself from the one person who had never judged him. He would never want to go back to his old ways. That was a time she hadn't seen or lived through, nor did he ever want her to.

Emily began to cry. His heart broke over her sudden rush of tears. She turned towards him as he held onto the shower curtain. He looked upon her with sadness yet took in the beauty of her naked body. She put her hands over her breasts as though embarrassed over her protruding nipples. The sight began to arouse him. Sex was not the only thing on his mind, though. Taking away the sadness from her green eyes was more important.

Rick stepped into the shower, fully clothed, taking her into his arms. She touched the fabric of his shirt sticking to his chest as the water saturated every inch of him. The warm water ran down and through the tiny spaces between them. He never wanted to let go; he wanted to hold onto her with all his strength.

He leaned back and brushed his hand over her cheek as the water trickled down, diluting her tears. He knew her pain as well as she had known his. Neither one needed to say a word as they drew closer together the only way they knew how. But now, it wasn't a lustful feeling but rather the need to let each other know they had shared the same sadness over their hurtful comments towards one another. They were both guilty of words neither one had meant to say.

Rick kissed Emily on her wet lips, and she responded by touching the one place on his body that began to grow harder, causing the urgent need to take her at that very moment. He peeled off his wet shirt and pants, then pressed Emily gently against the tile as he entered her. He felt both the warmth of the water and the heat inside of her that took but an instant for the encounter to turn into another one of those epic moments.

Chapter 29

A NEW MESSAGE

Seven months later

SUMMER WAS IN FULL SWING, and the only reminders of late winter and early spring were the cherry blooms blowing a blizzard of white petals into the early summer air. Emily sat on a bench Rick had built inside the gazebo, looking over the Magic River. She held seven-month-old Melanie in her arms and relished being alone with the baby.

Meghan was consulting with a client for another one of her interior design sessions. Derek was working, and Rick was helping to build a new platform for the live music and the official dedication of the park's rightful founder. The festivities were to occur the following day, July 16.

Emily hadn't returned to the park and figured it was best to stay away after what had happened that past December. She was glad all was quiet, thrilled to have spent time with her granddaughter, bonding over the winter and spring months. All was well until the icy grip of the ghosts from the past decided to haunt Emily once again.

Emily held Melanie's hand, amazed at the smallness, and admired the child's beautiful face as she slept peacefully. As Emily studied Melanie's hand, she turned it slightly, exposing her little wrist, and noticed something she hadn't seen before. The child had a spot on her wrist that looked eerily familiar. Emily had known only two other people who had it: the Salem Witch, Sandra

Easton, and Nora Miller. It was the same brown mark shaped like a heart.

Emily felt a heaviness in her gut when suddenly a brisk breeze blew through the gazebo, carrying with it a voice she had dreaded, a voice that had beckoned her before. Her adrenaline surged, and Emily felt her pulse throbbing in her neck. The shock she felt over discovering the mark on Melanie's wrist turned to irritation at hearing the voice that seemed never to give up.

Emily held tightly to the baby and focused her attention on the opposite side of the Magic River. Her gaze darted from one end of the river to the other. The wind whistled through the gazebo's roof; she refused to let her fear take over. The voice continued to call her, coming from the same place it had before, the swamp just beyond the Magic River.

"NO!" Go away! Leave us alone!" she yelled. Her outburst caused the baby to flinch and then cry. "Oh, I'm so sorry, my sweet little angel," Emily said.

She stood, placed Melanie in the carriage outside the gazebo, and headed to the house. Just before she went inside, she heard the voice again, causing a tingling sensation to go up her spine. This time, the voice had a message. "Emily...Emily, go through the invisible opening."

Emily pivoted around, taking several strides towards the river as she refused to be intimidated.

"Whatever you want, I'm not buying it, nor will I listen to you!" she yelled. "So, get away from my family and me!" Then Emily turned to go back to the house, stomping her feet with each step in defiance. She took the baby inside the house, ignoring the persistent voice haunting her.

A little while later, Emily sat in the room across from the basement entrance. This was the same room in which Melanie had been born and now served as a nursery. Emily had done quite a bit of babysitting in between writing for the *Maple Ridge Gazette*, and today she started working on a speech for the next day's dedication. As Melanie slept peacefully in her crib, Emily opened her laptop and jotted down thoughts about the true founder of the town park.

Emily had met William Easton when she traveled back to 1776. It was an encounter she had never expected. Although all her encounters were strange, she and Rick had simply called them being in *The Twilight Zone*. There was no other way to describe time travel.

"How can I write about this strange meeting with a man that has been dead for two hundred years without sounding crazy?" she asked the sleeping baby. "I suppose if it was written as a fairytale, it might be more acceptable. Hmm. What do you think, Melanie?" But Melanie had no answer, nor did Emily have any answers for herself.

She heard the front door open along with Meghan's voice in conversation with someone on her phone. Then Meghan ended the call with "Okay. I'll get back to you tomorrow." Emily figured it was one of her clients.

Emily walked out of the room quietly and closed the door. She looked at Meghan and put her finger to her lips, indicating the baby was sleeping. Then, the two women entered the kitchen, and Emily put on the tea kettle. "How was your meeting?" Emily whispered.

"I got the account, so I guess that means good."

With Meghan's unconvincing response, Emily was sure something else was going on. She sat at the table and patted the chair where she wanted Meghan to sit. "That's wonderful. I'm so glad your business is growing."

Meghan sat and crossed her arms, resting them on the table. "Me too," she said with less enthusiasm than Emily expected.

"What's wrong, Meghan?"

"I suppose a couple things are a little unsettling. Derek and I have had a hard time finding a good house to buy. They're all so expensive, and it seems every time we put in an offer on one, someone else outbids us. I'm afraid with my business still being new, we mostly depend on Derek's paycheck. It just feels like owning a home is a pipe dream at this point."

Although Emily knew that Derek made good money as a store manager, his paycheck probably wasn't enough with a wife and baby to support. Emily tried to be encouraging even though she knew there was more on Meghan's mind besides buying a house.

"I'm sure something will come along, Meghan, and like so many other things in life, it takes patience. What else is troubling you, honey?"

Meghan released a long sigh. "I think my daughter has the same brown heart on her wrist as Sandra Easton."

"You saw it too then?"

Meghan raised her eyebrows. "When did you see it?"

"This morning, and for the first time."

Meghan looked intently at Emily. "I know how Sandra Easton had misused her powers. I'm scared at some point Melanie might do the same and I won't be able to handle her. I guess I'm still haunted by what you told me about Charlotte and how her curse turned her evil. Emily, what does this heart-shaped mark mean anyway?"

"I wish I could answer that mystery for you Meghan, but I'm pretty sure Charlotte didn't have the mark, or at least I hadn't noticed one. As far as Sandra Easton, she was remorseful over what she had done. Charlotte was not. Brown mark or not, it seems it has nothing to do with a Witch being good or evil."

Emily took Meghan's hand and gave it a gentle squeeze. "Listen to me, Meghan, you and your mom are good Witches, probably the only Witches left. I think between you and your mom, you'll be able to teach Melanie how to be just as good." Emily smiled, giving Meghan a little nudge. "Besides, you've got me, and supposedly the time traveler has the powers to stop bad things from happening. You also have your own powers to keep things in check. From what I've seen, those powers worked out pretty well with sending Rick back in time and to the right place, I might add."

"Yes, well not without my mother or the powers of Magic River," Meghan said. "Anyway, what about Charlotte? She was so out of control that she killed her own grandmother and sister. You couldn't even help Charlotte from her own curse."

Emily knew Meghan was right. Charlotte did destroy herself, but that was not what bothered Emily the most. It was what Charlotte did to poor Laura Green and how her curse loomed over many others.

"No, unfortunately I couldn't," Emily admitted. "But this is the twenty-first century. We're not afraid to talk about it like they were years ago. We will all teach Melanie by telling her the truth about the consequences of what can happen when Witchcraft is not used for good. All of us have stories and real experiences to share with her. Experiences not written in some ancient book but rather she'll hear it from living and breathing people like us."

Meghan was about to respond when they both heard a commotion out back. A second later, Rick and Derek barreled through the back door in a panic.

Emily jumped out of her seat, annoyed. "What in the world? You're going to wake the baby!"

Chapter 30

VISIONS OF A SEER

Earlier, Rick worked on the wooden stage in the town park, pounding the nails with the hammer. He had no problem adapting once again to his prosthetic hand; however, he was thankful to be left-handed. All that mattered to him was that he and Emily had each other along with Derek, Meghan, and Melanie. Even Sylvia had been a good friend to Emily, which pleased Rick that she had another person to confide in. Rick looked up and saw Derek walking in his direction.

"Hey, Dad. How's the stage coming along?"

Rick jumped down from the platform, taking his hat off and wiping his brow. "We're getting there." Rick squinted his eyes from the sun. "Everything all right at work, son?"

"Oh, yeah. Just taking a break. Thought I'd check on all the progress. Meghan is going to have a booth for her interior decorating business. Thought I'd scope out a location for that."

"I see. Well, how about we scope one out together?" Rick took off his tool belt and tossed it on the ground. "Besides, my back could use a break just about now."

The two men strolled along the park's walkway where vendors were holding their spots in advance with orange cones. Rick glanced at his son's strained expression and the uneven stride in his step as Derek ran his fingers through his hair. Rick knew more was on his mind than finding the perfect location for his wife's booth. "So, what's really on your mind, Derek?"

Derek stopped in his tracks and darted a look at Rick. "Meghan. She wants to learn how to use her powers effectively, yet she's afraid of them at the same time."

Rick rubbed the back of his neck, unsure how to respond other than the obvious. "Why does she want to use her powers? Is there something she thinks she'll gain from it? Because I can tell you from experience that there are always consequences when using them, whether for good or bad."

Derek took in a deep breath, letting it out slowly. "Meghan saw something strange on the baby this morning. It appeared and then," Derek snapped his fingers. "Just like that, it disappeared."

"So, what was it?"

"A brown spot in the shape of a heart on Melanie's wrist," Derek said, pointing to his wrist.

Rick took a step back. "What? Do you mean the same brown mark as Sandra Easton and Nora Miller?"

Derek nodded. "It scared Meghan. She thinks if she knew how to use her powers better, she'd be able to handle any situation that might come our way pertaining to our daughter."

"Such as?" Rick hesitated and then realized where Derek was going with this. "Oh, yeah. Sandra herself cast a pretty bad spell as a teenager, causing all kinds of problems not to mention Charlotte's evil curse out of jealousy. So, yeah, I get what you're saying."

"That's right," Derek agreed. "And we don't even know what the mysterious heart-shaped mark means."

"I have to say, Derek, it's still a mystery," Rick said. Suddenly Rick felt a strange electric charge go through his body causing him to freeze in place. He felt paralyzed, and his heart was beating faster. The wind picked up unexpectedly. Then he saw a vision cross before him as if he were looking at a movie screen. He could vaguely hear Derek's voice asking him if he was okay. But the image in front of him had his undivided attention.

He saw Emily standing by the river. She was frightened yet at the same time angry. A halo of white roses formed over her head. She seemed to be pleased. Then a voice came rushing across the Magic River that scared her, a voice that said, "Go through the invisible opening." Rick felt the clutches of the spellbinding phenomenon gulf his entire body. Moments later, the vision that gripped him gradually released its hold and faded into a cloud of dust. He heard Derek's voice.

"Dad? Dad!" Derek yelled, shaking Rick's shoulder.

Rick looked at his son, feeling his jaw tighten. Every ounce of his mind and soul told him to run. "I got to get to Emily. Something's wrong." He pulled on Derek's arm. "Let's go. I'll drive."

Minutes later, Rick and Derek bolted through the back door and stood side by side like they were ready to pounce on someone neither could see. Rick saw Emily and Meghan's startled expressions from the pair's abrupt entrance, and no doubt the women saw the confusion on their faces.

Emily jumped out of her seat, annoyed. "What in the world? You're going to wake the baby!"

"Emily?" Rick said in a firm tone. "Did you hear the voice again?"

Emily's mouth dropped open. "What? How did you know?"

"Know what?" Meghan asked.

Derek sat next to his wife. "My dad saw a vision a little while ago."

Emily shot a look at Rick. "What vision? What did you see?"

Rick stepped towards Emily, close enough that he was sure she could feel the heat of fear radiating from his body. "You were frightened, and you were also mad all at the same time. There was a halo of white roses over your head. You became pleased until the voice spoke a message."

Emily gave Rick a curious look. "I've seen others do this before. Seeing things that would happen or had already happened, something they couldn't possibly know. Catori did it, and so did Nora Miller, and now—you?"

Emily placed her hand on Rick's chest, and he reached up and put his hand on hers as they both seemed to know what the other was thinking. "What was the message?" she asked.

Rick squeezed her hand a little tighter. "'Go through the invisible opening'.» They continued to stare into each other's eyes as Emily nodded slowly.

"What does that mean?" Meghan asked.

"I don't know," Rick answered without taking his eyes off Emily.

"White roses you said?" Suddenly, Emily gripped Rick's shirt. "Come on. Let's go. I might know the answer."

Chapter 31

THE HIDDEN CLUES

Emily stood at the edge of the forest not far from the orange cones and the tables covered with tarps. The preparations for the next day's dedication in the park had settled down, with most people gone for the night. Rick paced back and forth in the general location in question.

"There's got to be a hint of it somewhere in this area," he said.

Emily walked farther ahead and abruptly stopped when she saw an overgrown path. "I think this is it," she yelled to Rick.

They walked through the gnarly brush, staying on what remained of the old path.

"Watch yourself," Rick cautioned as he pushed away a pricker bush for Emily to duck under. The path was almost non-existent, thick with overgrown weeds and trees that had taken root in the center of what was once a small dirt path. One thing that did look familiar to Emily was the trellis just ahead and the entrance point to Nora Miller's cottage.

Emily and Rick reached the trellis, and Emily looked above her head in amazement. The trellis was covered with white roses in full bloom. She looked to Rick, who apparently was experiencing validation of his seer powers. "Was this what your vision was showing you?" she asked.

Rick walked over to Emily's side, as they both looked up. "I don't know, but it sure looks like what I saw." He took Emily's arm as they approached the cottage. "Let's see if the door is locked."

Emily glanced to her left and saw the same rock wall from 1941. Back then water had trickled down into a pond with moss and weeds growing between the cracks in the stones. Eight decades later no water ran to the pond. Dried mud filled the cracks between the stones, and slimy layers of green algae covered the surface of the pond. Some colorful flowers were still trying to bloom but were held back by the choking weeds and dead vines. The cottage was less than enchanting as it gave off a more eerie feeling, causing dread to seep into Emily's bones.

They lingered by the front door, now rotted from age. The brass doorknob had tarnished, and the keyhole was rusty. Rick walked over to an old flowerpot on the porch and grabbed a key from underneath that was as rusty as the keyhole.

"Let me guess. Your seer powers again?" Emily asked.

Rick gave her a curious look as if wondering that himself. "I'm not sure. It just came to me."

Rick looked at the keyhole, stuck the key in and with one turn, heard a click. "Oh, man, I hope we don't end up in *The Twilight Zone* again," he said as he pushed the door open.

Emily suddenly gripped Rick's arm. "You don't think something will happen when we walk in, do you?"

"Sorry, sweetie, I was just thinking out loud with *The Twilight Zone* remark." Rick looked at the half-open door. "I don't know if it's me seeing the future or not, but I think we'll be okay."

"Are you saying that to make me feel better?"

Rick looked at Emily, giving her one of his witty grins. "Maybe my seer powers are leading me astray after all," he said in a ghoulish voice. Emily suspected that his attempt at humor was a ploy to lighten the mood. She narrowed her eyes. "Seriously, Rick?"

"Come on. It's fine," Rick assured her.

Emily squeezed her eyes shut as they both stepped inside. She prayed they wouldn't be somewhere in a time that wasn't their own. She opened one eye and then the other and saw the same charming home of Nora Miller. Everything looked exactly the same only now covered in cobwebs. She brushed the cobwebs aside while Rick stood by Nora's old rocker and patted the upholstery, causing a cloud of dust to drift upward. "Well, looks to me like no one's been in here for years," Rick said.

Immediately, Emily became drawn to the painting of Catori still hanging in the same spot and covered with a sheet. Other artworks of Nora's remained in their places as well. She reached up and pulled the sheet, revealing Catori's mesmerizing brown eyes. She felt an enormous kinship towards the young Native American girl and wondered if part of Catori's spirit lingered among the shadows cast throughout the small cottage. Emily remembered the older Catori and her mystical chanting that cascaded over the Magic River long ago. She had told Emily that her name Catori meant *Spirit*. Her thoughts were interrupted by Rick rummaging through the drawers of an old desk in the corner. "What do you think you'll find in there?" she asked.

"I don't know. Maybe some old bills that might tell us who lived here last."

"I feel like we're invading someone's privacy—you know—trespassing?"

"Well, we are trespassing," Rick agreed. "But I think we're going to have to take our chances. This house may hold clues to that voice you've been hearing."

Emily looked around the room. "If I had to guess, and seeing how nothing has changed since the last time we were here, the previous owner had to be Nora."

"Hold on. I found something," Rick said, now sitting in a chair by the desk and flipping through old papers with brittle ends.

Emily peered over Rick's shoulder. "What did you find?" They both were trying to figure out the old writing on the paper.

"It looks like an old deed," he pointed to the upper corner and read the date. "June 18, 1872, Owners, George and Nora Miller."

"I suppose that makes sense, after all, Nora did live here," Emily concluded.

Rick continued rummaging through the pile of papers when he came across the transfer of ownership. They were shocked at the name of the new owner as Emily read: "Transfer of ownership from Nora Miller to Billy Easton on May 20, 1949."

Emily paced back and forth behind Rick trying to sort out the puzzle before them. "That was seven years after we left. Why would Nora leave Billy this property? Wouldn't the property technically stay with the Miller family?"

Rick put his elbow on the desk, rubbing his chin as if in thought. "Well, I'm not sure. Maybe Billy knew her longer than he let on. Nora might have had it set up to be transferred upon her death."

Rick stared at the old deed as if reflecting on another piece of the puzzle. "Still, I would think it would be my grandmother, Marion, who inherited the property. Instead, Billy was in possession of this property for over twenty years."

"Yes," Emily added, "twenty-three years to be exact. Billy died in 1972. Which begs the question: Who took over after that?"

He continued looking over the old documents as Emily strolled to the window. It's a shame, she thought, that no one had cared for such an enchanted place all these years. Emily tried to imagine how beautiful it could be all cleaned up. The flowers seemed to be itching for air, wanting desperately to be free from the chokehold of weeds and gnarly vines that diminished the color and beauty of the delicate florals. Then it occurred to her that there was another person who should have known about this place. She turned and regarded Rick as he concentrated on the stack of papers. He looked tense, borderline concerned. She walked over and put her hands on his shoulders, massaging the knots near his neck.

"I do know that Lucas's father, Marty, was killed in a motorcycle accident in 1969 at age thirty-five, so that counts him out," Emily deducted. "But what about Marlene? Wouldn't she be part owner as Billy's wife?"

"I suppose so. Did Lucas ever say anything to you about his grandmother, Marlene, owning other property?"

"No, he never really talked about them. Although I do remember him telling me once that his grandmother lived in the same house for over thirty years. Probably the same place you and I visited in 1941. She must've not known about Billy's ownership of the cottage and most likely that was another one of Billy's secrets. And believe me, I'm well aware of how good Billy was at keeping secrets."

Emily stopped her massage treatment and sat on the edge of the desk in front of Rick. "Did you know he reluctantly told his wife that he was a Mystic Guardian?"

"Really? Why?"

"Something about a pact that Billy and Thomas had, not wanting to burden their wives with all the Witch and Guardian stuff. And then I came along. Not that I said anything to Grace or Marlene but with all the strange things happening and Marlene being so inquisitive, I had encouraged Billy to be honest with his wife."

Rick took Emily's hand and kissed it. "And I know how persuasive you can be."

"I do try my best, Mr. Miller." Emily countered. "So, anything else new in those old papers?"

"Well, let's see here," Rick continued to go through the old papers. "Wait. There is something: a tax map with numbers but no location."

Emily leaned over Rick's shoulder again. "What name is on that one?" she asked.

Rick put his hand flat on the map and tilted his head to look at Emily. "Billy Easton."

Rick rummaged deeper in the drawer of the desk. "Hold on, there's another envelope with the date August 1972." Rick opened the envelope, and Emily saw his body stiffen.

"What? What did you find?"

"A newer deed to the cottage, and you're not going to believe whose name is on it."

Emily squinted as she read the name: "Richard Douglas Miller. How is this even possible, Rick?"

Rick turned in the chair and gave Emily a hesitant look.

"Emily? I hadn't said anything to you, but one day I looked in the town office's assessment rolls. This cottage is nowhere to be found in the town records. It's as if it never existed."

Emily rubbed the base of her neck, baffled over the official nonexistence of where they stood at that very moment. "That's really strange, and you know what else is even stranger? Billy died one month after signing over this cottage," Emily paused and then set her bewildered eyes on Rick, "And to a fourteen-year-old."

"Maybe this is the invisible opening then," Rick suggested.

That prompted Emily to wander around the room in thought. Suddenly, Lucas entered her mind. It always surprised her how the thought of him would catch her off guard. She still missed him terribly and suspected those feelings would never completely go away. She returned to where Rick sat at the desk.

"Lucas never told me anything about his grandparents. Why do you think that is?" she asked without expecting an answer. "If it wasn't for Ancestry.com, I'd begun to think I had conjured them all up in my mind."

Rick rubbed his forehead. "Well, if it makes you feel any better, Emily, I saw Billy and the rest of them with my own eyes, so you didn't conjure them up. As far as Lucas, if he was anything like Billy, they're experts at keeping secrets."

Emily and Rick searched the house for more clues and found none. It was as if time had stood still. The furnishings were the same: a now-tarnished candle holder Emily remembered seeing, still sat on Nora's fireplace mantel. She looked in the kitchen cupboard and found the same mugs they had drunk from more than eighty years earlier. No one could have lived here since Nora, she thought. But how could they? It was undocumented, perhaps even unreal. Magic undoubtedly hovered over the cottage. It was easy to believe. Nora was magical, and so was Billy. Did they somehow put a spell on the cottage to protect it from the outside world? Emily returned to Catori's painting. She stood before the image, admiring it. Emily felt Rick place his hand on her shoulder, as she continued to study the image. "What are the odds?" she asked mostly thinking out loud.

"What do you mean?"

"Quincy Miller and Catori naming their son George. What are the odds that six-generations later there would be another George Miller, who was married to a woman with the same seer powers as Catori.

Emily reached up and touched the edge of the painting as though it were a cherished treasure that had followed her through time like an old friend.

"You want to bring it home and hang it in the farmhouse?" Rick asked.

She turned around and put her arms around Rick, hugging him. She felt his hand caress her hair as he kissed the top of her head. She looked up into his eyes, releasing an appreciative sigh. "I suppose technically the painting is yours."

"No, sweetie, the painting is ours."

There was nothing more to be found at the cottage. It had only added more questions than answers. For now, unraveling the historical puzzle left behind by the ghosts from the past would require further clues. Emily wondered if those clues would reveal themselves at some point.

That evening, Emily sat at her desk upstairs in her office, writing her dedication speech for the next day. She watched as Rick hung the picture of Catori over the mantel.

"How's that? Is it straight?" he asked.

"Perfectly."

Rick stood back, looking pleased with his handwork. He walked over to Emily, leaned down and gave her a soft kiss.

"Now, what's that for, Mr. Miller?" she asked playfully.

He kissed her again. "Why do I have to have a reason to kiss my own wife?" He glanced down at her computer screen. "Besides, it looks like you have more work to do on your speech. As far as the kiss, it'll just hold me over until you're done, Mrs. Miller."

Emily sighed. "Regarding the speech, I'm afraid I'll have to fill in the blanks with more research." She looked at Rick. "There is no way for me to know every detail of William Easton's life."

"You know what, sweetie? I believe you'll figure it out." Rick kissed Emily on the forehead and began to walk out of the room when he glanced back. "I'll make us tea and then you can read your speech to me. Deal?"

Emily flashed him a smile as she nervously rubbed her arm. "Deal."

Emily was only halfway done with the speech and had to do more detailed research on William Easton. Her mind kept getting distracted by the unsolved mystery of Billy's impeccable timing in signing over the cottage to Rick and then there was the tax map with numbers but no location with Billy's name still on it. Also, Emily was still concerned over the haunting voice she had heard that morning, which now had a message attached. Was the cottage the invisible opening or had she missed something else? There were so many nagging questions, but for now, Emily had to finish writing her speech.

She had begun with the Easton family and decided to dig deeper. Emily traced back one generation after another until she saw something that stopped her cold, just as Rick walked in, balancing two cups of tea on a tray. She looked up in disbelief.

"What's wrong, Emily?"

"Lucas's four-times great grandfather was a man named Mitchell Easton."

Rick put the tray down on Emily's desk. "What about him?"

"According to this," she turned the computer screen toward Rick, "he was Nora Miller's father."

"What!" Rick looked at the screen as Emily pointed out the ancestral trail.

"Before she married George Miller back in 1868, Nora was an Easton." Emily's mind flashed with sudden recall. "Wait a second.

I remember that young couple. I caught a glimpse of them that day when the family gathered in the living room, the day Lillian Miller Green gave birth to her son back in 1864. The couple left before there could be any introductions."

"And it does explain why Nora left Billy the cottage," Rick added.

Emily looked up at Rick. "Don't you see, Rick? It's not just that. Nora had the Easton bloodline. She had the powers of the Mystic Guardians like Billy and Witches like Sandra Easton." Emily hesitated. The pieces of the puzzle were beginning to fit. "She must've chosen to take on the seer powers as well and most likely after she married George Miller."

"She could do that?" Rick asked.

"I'm not sure. I suppose Nora could do whatever she wanted to since she was an Easton. She did, after all, have the same brown, heart-shaped mark as her ancestor Sandra Easton."

Emily continued to puzzle over the new revelation on the screen. So many scenarios began to swirl in her head. She offered one to Rick.

"What if Louis Miller is not your two-times great-grandfather. What if it was George, his younger brother?"

Rick went over by the window where Emily had stacked a pile of books on a chair. Rick placed the books on the floor and set the chair alongside Emily. "Well, there's only one way to find out," he said pointing to the computer screen. "Follow the ancestral line starting with me and then go all the way back to Louis."

Emily followed the trail as Rick looked on. Suddenly it veered off leading straight for George Miller. "Look, Rick. Do you see what I see?"

"Yeah, you were right, Emily. It's not Louis Miller, but George Miller, who is my two-times great-grandfather."

Then it hit Emily like a freight train as she stood. Her legs suddenly felt weak. "Melanie!" she said. "Melanie! This explains why she has the Easton brown, heart-shaped mark. She has the

Miller, Spencer and now the Easton families in her bloodline."

"So, what you're saying is that Melanie has three magical bloodlines?"

Emily looked soberly at Rick. "Yes, and if I had to guess, Melanie is a complete anomaly, which means she might well be the most powerful Witch that ever lived."

Chapter 32

THE EASTON PARK SQUARE

It was a hot July day, as most days were in the middle of the summer, and the park was bustling with townspeople buying and selling their goods. If not for the coolness drifting from the swamp, the day would have otherwise been humid, and Emily was glad for the unusually dry air. She was nervous about giving her speech and felt more comfortable writing about people's stories than speaking about them, especially to a large crowd gathering in the park.

Emily and Rick strolled over to Meghan's booth, where they found Derek, Sylvia, and baby Melanie. "How's it going?" Rick asked, shaking his son's hand as Emily hugged Sylvia and Meghan and then picked up Melanie to give her an affectionate snuggle.

"How's my little sweetheart today?" Emily asked the cooing baby girl.

"She's been a little cranky this morning. I think she's teething," Meghan said.

"Well, all babies go through it," Sylvia said, holding Melanie's tiny hand. Sylvia looked at Meghan with a teasing grin. "If I remember correctly, you had such a hard time of it when you were Melanie's age that you kept me up all night."

"So, what you're saying, Mom, is that my daughter is getting revenge for her grandmother's sleepless nights?"

They all laughed at Meghan's comment. "You ladies keep chatting about all things baby," Rick said. "Derek and I are heading for that booth over there. Let's go, son." The two men walked to a booth with antique posters displaying every kind of automobile since Henry Ford's Model T rolled off the assembly line.

Emily returned Melanie to her mother. Emily caught Sylvia's attention and then lifted her chin towards the empty picnic table across the walkway near the hot dog stand.

"We'll be right back, darling." Sylvia said to her daughter.

Emily and Sylvia headed for the picnic table and took seats across from each other.

"You look so serious, Emily. What's going on?"

"I found out something yesterday when looking up the Miller ancestry. Did you ever hear of a woman named Nora Miller?" Emily asked.

"Yes, I've heard mention of her from Derek. She was Derek and Rick's ancestor. What about her?"

"Rick and I meet her in 1941. She was in her early nineties back then and living in a small cottage." Emily pointed in the direction of the forest. "Just beyond that tree line."

Sylvia's gaze followed Emily's pointed finger towards the general area near a line of pine trees.

"I never even knew there was anything or anyone living in there. From what I know, it's a pretty thickly wooded area."

"Here's something else you don't know. For some reason it seems to be undocumented in the town's official assessment rolls. It's as if the cottage is some kind of ghost dwelling."

"The invisible opening?" Sylvia speculated.

"I don't know, maybe. But there's more. Nora Miller's father was an Easton, and not only that Nora had the brown, heart-shaped mark on her wrist. I saw it for myself."

"It's funny that you're telling me this because I've been learning some pretty interesting things in that spell book about that heart-shaped mark. The book said that the mark is only present on the most powerful Witches. More powerful than regular Witches, Mystic Guardians, seers or…time travelers," Sylvia said and regarded Emily with a bleak expression. "I've been studying that magic spell book ever since I got my hands on it."

"I guess that explains Nora's claims of Charlotte's death curse having no power over her."

Emily looked across the walkway and saw Derek return to Meghan. Rick was farther down talking to one of the guys from the town office. Emily glanced back at Sylvia, wondering how to tell her about their granddaughter. Emily took a deep breath, letting her words out as she exhaled. "Sylvia, Melanie has the same brown mark. I caught sight of it once and then it vanished."

"I know. I saw it myself the other day," Sylvia admitted. "I didn't say anything because I thought my mind was playing tricks on me. Like you, I saw only a glimpse of it, and then it disappeared. But still, whether I was seeing things or not, it was one of the reasons I've been trying to find answers in the spell book."

"What did you find out?" Emily asked.

"I found a section about families with magic in their bloodlines that when merged produce the most powerful Witches and Mystic Guardians."

"Nora Easton had seer powers and by the mark on her wrist was also a Witch," Emily added. "Do you think she was capable of taking on the seer powers of the Millers?"

"Yes," Sylvia said. "Millers are seers, and Eastons can be both Witches and Mystic Guardians. Of course, it goes without saying that the Spencers are all Witches. According to the spell book, if there's a love strong enough binding those magical families, it would certainly give Nora the power to do that and much more."

"Do you realize that Melanie's bloodline is not only part of the Millers and Spencers but now the Eastons? Then there's *The Magic Spell Book* and what it has to say about the brown, heart-shaped mark, which means…" Emily looked towards Meghan as she fed Melanie her bottle.

Sylvia jerked her head in the same direction. Emily glanced at Sylvia, but she couldn't tell if Sylvia was in disbelief or experiencing a sense of dread. Clearly, the news of her granddaughter's extraordinary lineage was beginning to sink in. Sylvia hesitated and looked as if she needed to be somewhere important, and from Emily's observations, that somewhere would be with her daughter and granddaughter. "If you would excuse me, Emily."

She watched as Sylvia crossed the walkway and talked to her daughter. Emily was starting to understand Meghan's concerns over the extraordinary potential of little Melanie's powers. She could see Sylvia giving Meghan a motherly hug, and then Emily glanced over to see Rick approaching with something in his hand.

Sitting across from her, Rick set a large, folded paper on the picnic table and then reached for her hand. "Everything okay?"

Emily rubbed her temples and glanced at Rick. "Besides the butterflies in my stomach about giving a speech to hundreds of people, I'm perfectly fine." Emily pointed to the folded paper that Rick had placed on the table. "What's this?"

"It's a tax map with the same numbers as the one with Billy's name on it. " Rick unfolded it. "Unlike the other one, this map identifies the location."

Emily gave Rick a skeptical look. "Okay. What land did he own then?"

Rick looked past Emily toward the large dedication stone. "The swamp and the land that surrounds it, including the old shack."

"What?" Emily sucked in a breath. She could feel her heart pounding and looked over her shoulder as the haunting memories rushed into her brain. She felt Rick's gentle touch and heard his voice, pulling her back from her fears.

"Emily? It's gonna be okay. I know you're thinking about— that voice."

Emily remained silent, her thoughts jumbled.

"I was thinking," Rick said tentatively. "Do you think it was Lucas? I mean, you know, calling from beyond."

Emily's mind caught up to Rick's logical point. "No, it's not Lucas." The thought of Lucas easily brought on the lingering pain of loss and with a quivering voice she said. "I would've known his voice in a heartbeat." She felt Rick's hand tighten over hers, pulling her back from the loss that never quite went away. She gave Rick a weary grin. "Besides, the one I keep hearing sounds, well…proper."

"What do you mean by 'proper'?" Rick asked.

"Like someone from another century, and I don't mean the twentieth century." Emily stood looking toward the swamp while trying to tame her fears of another ghost from an unknown time. "It sounds—familiar."

Less than an hour later, everyone in the park gathered around the platform Rick had helped build for the renaming and unveiling of the dedication stone. Emily had avoided seeing the completed stone. Her reluctance to enter the park via the Shady Brook Bridge to avoid both the swamp and a restless spirit had kept her from seeing the stone ahead of time. When Emily and Rick looked for the old cottage the day before, they had taken the road on the other side of the park near the nursing home. But now, she found herself way too close to the place she had dreaded for so long, standing on a platform in front of a podium with a microphone.

Despite the cooler air from the swamp behind her, beads of sweat poured down her back. Although her heart beat faster with each passing minute, Emily knew enough to avoid the crowd's stares. Instead, she focused on Rick's face as he stood just below the podium. His presence calmed her. He gave her a slight nod and a reassuring wink that gave her the courage to begin the dedication. She read:

"My name is Emily Stanford Easton Miller. My ancestors came to Massachusetts as far back as 1689. Many years later, my seven-times great-grandfather, Augustus Stanford and his brother, Vergil, sailed from England across the cold waters of the Atlantic to join relatives in the nearby town of Salem. One day as Augustus traveled the countryside, he came across a run-down trading post called Maple Ridge on the banks of the Magic River. Although there were a few decent homesteads, most of the settlers lived in old shacks along the water's edge, trying to survive daily life. Augustus, being a savvy businessman, immediately saw an opportunity as he was fully aware of all the natural resources along the river. With Vergil's help, Augustus started a sugarcane factory, giving every able-bodied man work. In no time, the town grew and so did its trading post. Soon after, a school and library were built, and many more merchants moved into the thriving community."

Emily paused for a second, felt herself settle down, and saw the interest in the faces of the crowd that had gathered. She started to feel confident that her speech was a success, so she continued to read:

"Back then the Shady Brook Bridge was a mere wooden walkway barely wide enough for a horse and buggy to cross. The rickety old bridge led to a vast wilderness where men and boys hunted deer, bear, turkeys, and a variety of small game for survival.

Fast forward to 1776, when a twenty-year-old man named William Easton stood in this very spot armed with only a pair of cast iron cutting shears and a dream. His mission? Cut every shrub and clear every tree in a large enough section of the forest to create a town park. William spent years working hard cutting trees, and he donated the wood to the townspeople to build new homes and to heat them. He settled down with his wife and raised his family in Maple Ridge. When the park was completed, William became the park's caretaker until his death in 1850 at the ripe old age of ninety-four. He had dedicated his life to preserving such natural beauty, and today it's where we all stand to dedicate this park to the true founder, William Easton."

Rick came forward, taking Emily's hand as she stepped down from the podium. He escorted her over to the stone covered by a white sheet.

"With great pleasure, I present to you The Easton Park

Square." Emily grabbed the sheet, slightly pulling it as it dropped gently to the ground.

Resounding applause broke out with cheers and whistles. Emily and Rick finally got a good look at the stone adorned with yellow and orange flowers around the base and its inspiring message:

The Easton Park Square
Developed by the strong hands and loving heart of William Easton in the year of our Lord 1776. May the park's beauty give all who pass through a sense of peace and tranquility.

Chapter 33

THE GIFTS

The day was a blur. Many of the townspeople clamored to talk with Emily. She didn't necessarily like the attention, but it was a distraction from standing just feet away from the swamp. Rick had gone to check on Meghan and Derek, and a short time later, as the crowd grew thin, she finally had a reprieve from talking. Emily stood by the stone admiring its important presence and meaning. She was glad she had advocated for William, her late husband's ancestor.

Emily turned to walk away when she felt a slight breeze. It began to swirl around the stone, moving the yellow and orange flowers in a circular motion next to the base. The icy grip of terror shot straight through her as the voice suddenly drifted into her ears once again. "Emily. Emily. Go through the invisible opening."

She felt anger grow inside her. She had had enough. Her anger drowned out any fear she might have had otherwise.

She stepped to the side of the stone, looking into the swamp. "Who the hell are you?" she said firmly. The same swirly breeze parted a path for her to take. "You want me to come in there? So be it. I've had enough. Let's get this over with."

Emily walked to the edge of swamp that had caused so much pain, suffering, and even death to innocent people, and in her mind, she was ready for a showdown. She saw a green haze overshadowing the parted path, leading her, she had hoped, to the unknown voice. It had been a path she had taken before when trying to find Charlotte, and Emily had come upon the place where she had cut her leg—William Easton's gravestone.

Emily followed the parted path and eventually stood by the rusted old cemetery gate, hesitating to go in. All she could hear was the hollow sound of dead air sweeping through the trees until she heard it again, the message giving her instructions. "Go through the invisible opening." She stared at the gate. Could this be the invisible opening? she wondered. But I've been through this gate before. Then she heard the voices of others. They seemed to be coming from the cemetery. The sounds were happy yet mixed with sadness. Some even seemed excited.

"What is this?" she said out loud. The voices became silent. She heard only the creepy wind rustling bushes and dead branches. That's when Emily decided to go through what she hoped would be the invisible opening.

When she stepped through, she thought it was like walking into heaven. Sunbeams shone on every gravestone that was no longer broken or deteriorated. The light cast a glow that danced in the air, filled with translucent butterflies with colors she had never seen before. Birds with a shimmering shade of crimson through their feathers perched on the branches of trees that seemed to come alive.

"Am I in heaven?" Emily asked the voice that had summoned her there. She was pleased and felt an overwhelming sense of love beyond her understanding. Then she heard his voice again. The one that had been haunting her for what seemed like forever, only this time, it felt welcoming, happy. And then, there he was—William Easton. He looked the same as the last time Emily had encountered him almost two hundred and fifty years ago. She recognized the same dark brown hair and brown eyes that appeared thoughtful. He was young and handsome and stood as tall as a Mystic Guardian would when protecting those he loved.

"William? Is that really you?" Emily hardly knew what to say. Her thoughts ran wild, and she felt weakness in her legs, thinking she would fall over at any moment. "It was you all along that had been calling me?"

"Yes, Mistress Emily, it is I. Never had I meant to frighten you, only to call for your help in casting out a terrible curse upon my land. Land I spent my entire life caring for. I waited a long time. I waited for you to complete what my ancestor Sandra Easton had set out for you to do. And now you have done the same for me. You have broken the death curse not once but twice. A curse that had darkened this hallowed ground that trapped our souls with unending anguish for so long. It was you, Mistress Emily, who has freed us in the same way you had freed your ancestors from Sandra Easton's egregious curse. Therefore, I called you once more to thank you for honoring me and the Easton legacy with your dedication to this land and our resting place, which was always meant to be magical, spiritual and sacred."

Emily was utterly mesmerized by William revealing all that had been a mystery. All the puzzle pieces came together in a backdrop filled with color and beauty. William seemed to look over Emily's shoulder. She turned her head and was startled when Rick reached for her hand. She wondered for a moment how he had magically appeared, but everything about this moment was magical.

"Emily, are you okay?" Rick asked, taking another step towards her.

Emily took his hand and presented Rick to William. "This is my husband Rick—"

"Miller," William said, completing her introduction. "The war hero…Mistress Emily's hero…and now ours."

Rick pulled Emily closer, clearly his way of showing William that he would be the one doing the protecting. "You're the one who's been scaring the shit out of my wife?"

Emily gave Rick a slight poke in the ribs with her elbow. "William already said he never meant to scare me."

William moved towards them as if floating a mere inch from the ground. "We are all grateful to you, Mister Miller, for your part. You have proven to be a hero many times over."

Rick glanced around the area where they were standing.

"Who's 'we'? I only see you standing there. You got other ghosts you want to tell us about?"

Emily shot Rick a look but said nothing.

"I understand your anger, Mister Miller. It is completely justifiable. Mistress Emily has my deepest apology for my elusive tactics in getting her attention. My powers have been diminished for eight decades due to the evil Witch named Charlotte. But thanks to you and Mistress Emily, they have now been restored."

"Well, ah...then maybe you can tell us where we are," Rick said more calmly.

"It is the resting place of all Witches and Mystic Guardians that have passed through this land for over three hundred years. After Sandra Easton's demise in the Salem prison, her body was released to Rebecca Spencer who had been set free from the same prison. She arranged a place well hidden and undisturbed, burying her here. Sandra was the first, with many more who came after. Charlotte Spencer's curse afflicted and tormented the peaceful souls who dwell in this magical place. I had kept it sacred in my lifetime and before the evil curse took hold. Many after me had carried on the tradition and then passed on. Two centuries later, all the Witches had lost their powers over this evil curse until the time travelers intervened. You both showed great courage."

William seemed to be fading as if his time was up, but before he completely disappeared, he offered Rick and Emily one more thing.

"Mister Miller," William said in a voice of reverence. "For your heroism, you will be given a gift lost to you for many years. A gift known only by you, and all others will no longer have knowledge of your having this loss at all."

William then looked at Emily. "For your love and courage, Mistress Emily, you will now share in our magic and be granted the gift you had always longed for through all your sorrow and loss."

It was as if William were *The Wizard of Oz*, Emily thought, opening his black bag and giving Rick the medal for heroics and

Emily the badge of courage. They both stood there completely mesmerized as before their eyes William Easton disappeared in a sparkling mist. Complete silence filled the air.

Rick turned his head, scanning the magical graveyard with a sharp eye. "I suppose they're gone."

"Then you felt it too? I mean, that there were other ghosts present?" Emily asked.

Before Rick could answer, a sudden mist billowed up around him as Emily stepped back. She saw the look of amazement on Rick's face. "What's happing to me, Emily?"

"I don't know." Emily watched as the air swirled rapidly around Rick, encapsulating him in a dome similar to a snow globe. As suddenly as it came, it disappeared. He looked down in complete shock and then jerked his head up to look at Emily. "My hand! I have my hand back!"

"What? What just happened?"

Seemingly on the verge of tears, Rick held his right hand up. "Look, Emily, I have my hand!"

Emily took three steps forward and reached for his restored hand. They both stared at it in disbelief. They looked into each other's eyes as Emily felt herself merge into Rick's emotions. "Rick, I think this is your gift William was talking about."

Once again, a mist appeared, but this time by the edge of the cemetery. The heavenly birds started to sing and swirl around with an image forming. Emily wasn't quite sure who it was, and then the apparition became clearer as someone approached. Emily grabbed onto Rick and felt lightheaded from the shock. He held onto her as both were stunned at the sight of a man standing just beyond the swaying trees.

Emily let go of Rick. She recognized the man and walked toward him. He was a man she had loved with all her heart. A man she had grieved over with all her soul. Then his name passed her lips: "Lucas."

Chapter 34

MAGICALLY EVER AFTER

IT WAS AN OUT-OF-BODY EXPERIENCE. Emily saw herself lying in a bed of white roses. Am I dreaming? she wondered. The pain and loss subsided among the white roses—roses her beloved had given her a thousand times before, all gathered up in one place, ushering in enormous peace.

Somehow, the pain would always find its way in. Her heart had no more strength to pump the blood needed for her body to survive. She knew he was dead, never to be seen again. His eyes will never look into mine, she thought. I will never feel his arms wrapped around me or experience the love I still hold for him. How will I live without him? Emily's mind dreaded the thought of his struggle to breathe as the water took over his lungs. She wondered if he had thoughts of her as he took his last breath. Was he sad? Did it pain him as much as it had her, knowing he would never see her again?

And now, Emily thought, by some miracle, he stood before her. She could feel his touch once again. She could see the light in his eyes instead of a dead stare beneath the cold waters of the Magic River. Emily felt as though she was dreaming. Was she really seeing her beloved Lucas, manifested by the powers of all the Witches and Mystic Guardians that dwelt in this beautiful place? She touched his face and ran her thumb over his lips. It all felt real, as Emily remembered each detail on his face. The same thin lines on his forehead remained where she saw them last. He wrapped his arms around her once again. The surge of joy wiped away any pain hidden deep inside her for so long. Emily held onto Lucas's embrace but knew it wouldn't last.

"I wanted to come home to you that day, sweetheart. I want you to know that your face was the last thing I saw before a bright light appeared. I saw Jesus. It was amazing. He told me it was my time and that he would send someone to care for you."

Out of the corner of her eye, she saw Rick move away as though respectfully giving her and

Lucas privacy. She knew this had to be hard for him and was sure his heart sank at the sight of her and Lucas together.

Emily touched Lucas's arm. "Are you real?" she asked as an overwhelming rush of emotion billowed up inside her. "Oh, Lucas, I've missed you so much." A flood of tears ran down Emily's cheeks.

"I've missed you too, sweetheart, so very much," Lucas said. "Just know that I'm okay and how proud I am of your courage and for being so brave with what you have been sent to do. All along God has been looking out for you. You have saved many from the evils that lurk in this world."

"Lucas? Are you a Mystic Guardian?"

"Yes, Emily, but I never used my powers except to protect the last of the Stanford bloodline. In the beginning when we first met, I was there to protect you. Then I got to know you and fell deeply in love." Lucas placed his hands on Emily's cheeks and gently kissed her. "I devoted every part of myself and my powers only to you, my beautiful Emily."

"Why did you not tell me?"

Lucas looked over at Rick. "For all the same reasons Thomas Stanford had kept it from his wife, Grace." Lucas's eyes returned a penetrating gaze into Emily's. "And for the same reason my grandfather, Billy Easton, kept it from my grandmother, Marlene. To spare them the burden of these powers and what they bring. Mystic Guardians are always the protectors, even if it means keeping this secret from those they love the most."

As with William, Lucas began to fade. The mist crawled on

the ground toward him. He embraced Emily, which felt desperate to her. She saw tears forming in his magical brown eyes. "Emily, my sweetheart, know I will always be with you."

He kissed her deeply with what earthly presence he had left. Emily's tears welled up and a lump caught in her throat. She couldn't speak. Then she felt his grip loosen. His face became translucent, and Emily knew he was going.

Lucas looked towards Rick. "Take care of my girl for me." The echo of Lucas's voice reverberated off the mountains beyond the Magic River. Rick stepped forward and gave the ghost of Lucas a nod before the essence of his body and soul disappeared. "You got it, buddy." And without so much as a whisper—Lucas vanished.

Emily fell to the ground in a heap of sorrow. Her hands covered her face, and she sobbed uncontrollably as she let Lucas go along with any remaining pain that had lingered deep within her.

She felt Rick by her side, and he held her for as long as it took for the tears to stop. She had said her goodbyes once, she thought, in another cemetery where she had laid Lucas to rest. There, he had sent the white rose just after Sandra Easton disappeared into the mist as did Lucas moments ago. Yet somehow, there was a comforting acceptance this time, accompanied by an enormous sense of peace. No longer would she wonder what his final thoughts were or if he felt fear in taking his last breath. Lucas offered what her mind and heart had always longed for—closure.

That night, back at the farmhouse, the wind and rain hit the window of Emily's upstairs home office with force. Darkness filled each pane of glass. Emily leaned on the wide windowsill and peered out into the storm. Rick had put a solar light on the ceiling of the gazebo. Its faint glow reflected off the water ripples cascading across the river. There was no more mist, no haunting voice, only peace and a feeling of thankfulness.

Emily felt grateful to have said her last farewell to Lucas. She was also thankful to have Rick in her life. But something was different. It had nothing to do with Rick or even the miraculous experience in the ancient, magical cemetery. There was a shift inside her. Emily could feel the energy running through her body. She looked down at her hands as they began to tingle. A strange glow illuminated through her fingertips when she remembered something William had told her and repeated it to herself. "You will now share in our magic."

"Who are you talking to?" Rick asked as he came up from behind her and wrapped his arms around Emily's waist. He felt warm and inviting as always. She leaned back on his chest as they looked out into the stormy night. He kissed the side of her neck. It had always made her want him without hesitation. But at that moment, she held out her hands where the strange light glowed from her fingertips. "What do you suppose this means?" she asked.

Rick took her hand and touched the spot where the light was forming. She could see by his decisive nod that the knowledge from Rick's seer powers had kicked in with the answer. "Magical powers," he said softly, as if trying not to interrupt the moment of a fascinating phenomenon.

"The same magical powers that brought you to me in the swamp?" she asked.

"Yes." Rick sat on the windowsill, drawing Emily into himself. She felt the warmth and comfort as her body nestled between his legs. She moved a piece of hair off his forehead, causing Rick to reach up, take her hand, and kiss it gently. "It wasn't a vision at first. It…it crawled through my veins…fear, I thought, your fear. Then I could see your face, strained with whatever was in front of you. I felt your anger, your shock, and then your sympathy. I knew your feelings were all directed towards someone you knew. You wanted to be there, and that's when I heard your soul call to me. I knew exactly where you were, so I headed straight for the ancient cemetery in the swamp and towards the rusty iron gate, like it had some kind of magnetic pull. I knew you had heard the haunting voice again. When I got there, I saw nothing other than the long-ago graves with their decrepit stones. That's when I heard a voice saying—"

"'Go through the invisible opening'," Emily finished Rick's account of what had transpired.

"Yeah and that's when I knew the invisible opening was the rusty, old gate."

Emily ran her hand down Rick's cheek and was about to kiss him when she caught a glimpse of something just under her sleeve. As they both stared down at Emily's wrist, there it was, the brown, heart-shaped mark of a powerful Witch. Emily glanced at Rick and noticed a smile formed on his face.

"Well, Emily, it looks to me like you and our granddaughter now share the same powerful magic."

Emily walked over to the desk lamp and turned it on. She focused intently on the mark she had seen before. First, on Sandra Easton and Nora Miller, then Melanie, and now... Emily rubbed the spot to see if it would wipe off. She wondered if she was dreaming again and then looked up at Rick as she took a step forward. "If I do have these powers," she said. "I think I know the first thing I want to do with them."

"Careful what you wish for. Remember?" Rick warned. "There are consequences whether for good or bad."

The joy in Emily's heart burst forth into a bright smile. She reached up, cupping Rick's face. "Not to worry, you'll see. But first, I need to talk to Sylvia. After all, she's the one with the magic spell book."

Three days later, Emily stood anxiously near a pine tree in the park with Rick by her side. They were waiting for Derek, Meghan, Sylvia, and little Melanie to arrive. There was a storm brewing with thunderclouds looming overhead. No one else was in the park except for a couple of hardy runners and several sparrows perched on the tree branches, waiting for the oncoming storm.

The rumbling from the sky caught Rick's attention, and he looked up. "You couldn't have waited for a better day, Emily?" he complained.

"When I looked at my phone, it said it wouldn't rain until this afternoon," she said just as Derek's car came into sight. "There they are!" Emily gave them a vigorous wave.

Meghan was the first to get out of the car with little Melanie in her arms. "So, what's the big surprise?" she asked.

"You'll see," Emily said, giving a thumbs up to Sylvia who stood next to Meghan.

Meghan looked sternly at her mother as they gathered next to the pine trees. "I know my mother well enough to know when she's keeping a secret from me."

"And you would be correct, Meghan, to say your mother has been keeping something from you, but it's not her fault." Emily glanced at Sylvia with appreciation. "I told her to keep this secret."

"What secret?" Derek asked as he opened the trunk of the car. "Hey, Dad, can you give me a hand with Melanie's stroller and diaper bag?"

Emily saw the side of Rick's mouth turn up into a mischievous grin as he walked towards the back of Derek's car. "How about two hands," Rick said holding both hands out. Derek showed no reaction to Rick's restored hand and handed him the diaper bag. Rick's mouth hung slightly open, and he returned to Emily with raised eyebrows.

Emily leaned in towards Rick speaking in a low voice. "Guess William Easton was right when he said how all others will no longer have knowledge of the loss of your hand."

Rick looked down at the handle of the diaper bag dangling from his right hand. "All this magic is going to take some getting used to, that's for sure."

Emily patted Rick arm. "Wait till you see what's coming next."

Emily cleared her throat and addressed Derek first. "Before I give you the answer to that secret, Derek. I wanted to thank Sylvia for helping me find the right spell. And there's something else." Emily turned her wrist over, showing them the magical brown heart. Meghan looked at the spot with disbelief showing on her face. Derek reached for Emily's arm, and he squinted at the spot. "How did this happen?"

Emily then turned to look at everyone. "It's a long story. Everything that has happened to all of us has not gone unnoticed by the world of magic. I have received the powers of the Witches and Mystic Guardians from my late husband's ancestor, none-other than William Easton. And before you ask, the answer is yes, the same William Easton this park is named after."

Sylvia added to Emily's short explanation. "Emily came to me for help in using her new powers." Sylvia glanced at Emily with a smile. "She needed a specific spell called 'Transformation'.»

Derek and Meghan looked at each other with confusion. Rick walked over to Derek and patted him on the back. "What Emily wants to do is give you a place of your own," Rick told the couple. "A place Emily and I had been to twice. Once in 1941 and recently in this time period."

Emily then picked up the explanation. "Sylvia discovered in the spell book something extraordinary. That what you're about see has always been invisible to the outside world. A place where you, Meghan, and Melanie can live. A place of enchantment where you can live magically ever after."

Rick glanced upward as the thunder rumbled, and the sky started to open up. "Best get to it," he said, giving Emily a nod.

Emily turned toward the big pines and outstretched her arms with the palms of her hands up. The light shone from her fingertips, and the trees and brush suddenly parted with a clear path leading into the woods. She turned her head and flashed a wide grin at her family. "Come on. Let's get out of the rain."

If magic had its rightful place in the world, this would be it, Emily thought. She wasn't sure how it would look but was sure how she wanted it to be. She felt great satisfaction when they all reached the trellis covered with white roses. Everything had turned out perfectly. No thunderclouds or a threatening storm hovered over them, only a blue sky with sunshine and a warm summer breeze in the air graced the mystical place before them all. A place that not so long ago was in ruins. Now, the cobblestone cottage was like new, as if each stone had just been laid, or perhaps, Emily thought, was restored simply by her new magic.

Emily felt Rick standing beside her. He put his arms around her, and they held each other close. They looked on as Derek and Meghan's eyes lit up like two small children who had entered a place that only existed in a fairytale.

It was over, Emily thought. Peace now filled the air. "I wonder if it's even possible to do a story in the *Maple Ridge Gazette* about all this without people thinking I've gone completely out of my mind."

Rick gave Emily an affectionate kiss on her forehead. "Well, sweetie, if anyone can do it, you can."

Emily turned to face Rick and felt an overwhelming sense of contentment with only one thing left to say. "I'll love you till the day I die, Mr. Miller."

Rick gazed into Emily's green eyes, and she could see that he was holding back tears of his own. "I'll love you too, Mrs. Miller, till the day I die and beyond."

Three Months Later

The Maple Ridge Gazette
A Halloween Special Edition

To all the children of Maple Ridge

"A Place Called Magic"
by Emily Miller

Once upon a time, there was a time traveler who turned into a Good Witch, and she used her powers only for good. This Witch had traveled far to fight evil and to tell everyone she met

that their Creator loved them in order to break
a deadly curse.

She met her ancestors during this magical
time, and those encounters filled her heart with
love. It was a time that was not her own, and
she was sad to say goodbye to so many. When she
returned to her time, the Witch met her prince,
who was brave and strong, and she fell madly in
love with this man, who was a hero.

Then, one day, the powerful Witch cast a
spell, transforming a forgotten place into a
magical place. This magical place was filled with
beautiful white roses that covered every part
of a small courtyard in front of an enchanted
cottage hidden deep in the forest. There was a
pond in front of the cottage with a stream of
water trickling down from a rock wall, causing a shimmering effect as sunlight danced off
the water, captivating all who saw it. Frogs
sat on their lily pads as they watched the
crystal-clear water glistening in the sunshine.
Translucent butterflies landed on the purple and
red bushes as songbirds sang their bewitching
sounds. Colors burst from every kind of flower,
but the white rose had its domain over the
courtyard. That is, until one day.

There was another Witch, years younger,
with very tiny hands and delicate fingers. Light
darted from her baby fingertips, casting a daz-
zling light upon the white roses. Her little
hand touched one white rose, and then suddenly,
every rose in the magical courtyard turned pink.
The older Witch was amazed at the child's power.
The older Witch embraced the younger Witch. It
was then that the older Witch knew that all
would be well and that she and her hero prince
along with their family would all live Magically
Ever After.

Epilogue

She looked to the sky and saw a white dove fly overhead. It was a sign that had always appeared before the magic began. "I miss you, Grammy," she sighed.

The gate was still as rusty as she remembered. Then she stepped through the invisible opening. Her eye gazed upon the large gravestone as the enchanted resting place came alive with beauty. She reached out to a butterfly as it landed next to the brown, heart-shaped mark on her wrist.

"It's me...Melanie," she whispered to the translucent blue and white butterfly. "Tell them that I am here."

The butterfly lifted its wings and flew away to dance to the melody of the songbirds gathering nearby. Melanie rested one hand on the large gravestone as she held out the other. A swirling spark ignited in the palm of her hand as a pink rose and a white rose appeared. She placed them on top of the stone.

"Hello, Grammy and Grandpa. I just wanted to let you know I'm going to have a baby—a little girl. Mom and Dad are so overjoyed. They were beginning to believe I would never have a child. Now the wait is over, and they will be grandparents just like you were to me." The breeze began to pick up, carrying a voice Melanie longed to hear.

"We love you, too, our beautiful Melanie."

Melanie looked towards the sound of her grandmother's voice. Her heart raced excitedly as it always had each time she visited the magic cemetery.

"I came here today to tell you I'm going to name my daughter after you, Grammy." Tears welled up in Melanie's eyes. "I miss you both. I love you and Grandpa so much."

Then, came the voice of her grandmother: "Tell baby Emily that I will always be with her as I have always been with you."

Her grandmother's voice faded, and the cemetery became silent once again. Melanie blinked the tears away from her eyes and then read the inscription on the stone.

EMILY STANFORD EASTON MILLER
BELOVED WIFE
DOB MARCH 15, 1958

RICHARD DOUGLAS MILLER
BELOVED HUSBAND
DOB JULY 10, 1958

THEY BOTH DIED AS THEY LIVED
HOLDING EACH OTHER IN THE COMFORT
OF THEIR LOVING EMBRACE
ON DECEMBER 24, 2058

—WILL FOREVER BE REMEMBERED FOR
THEIR COURAGE THROUGH TIME—

I dedicate this book to all my descendants.
May there be one to carry this story forward
so that new generations of readers can take
this magical journey to a place
somewhere in time.

Stanford Ancestors

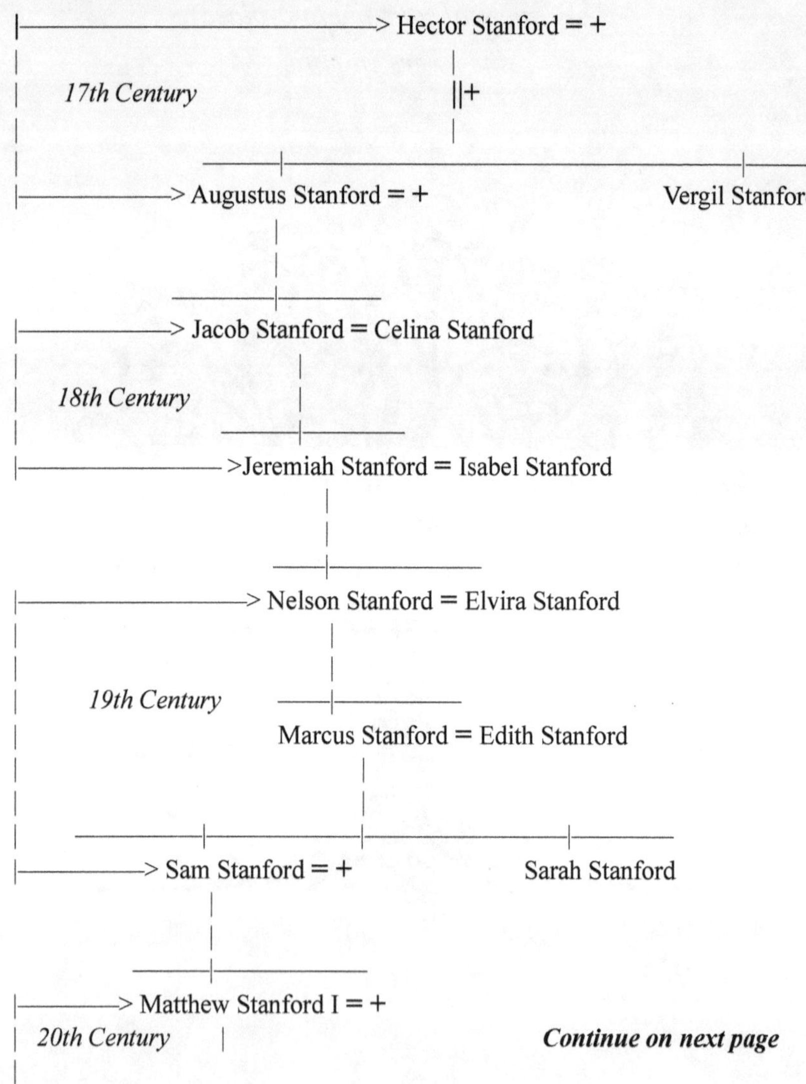

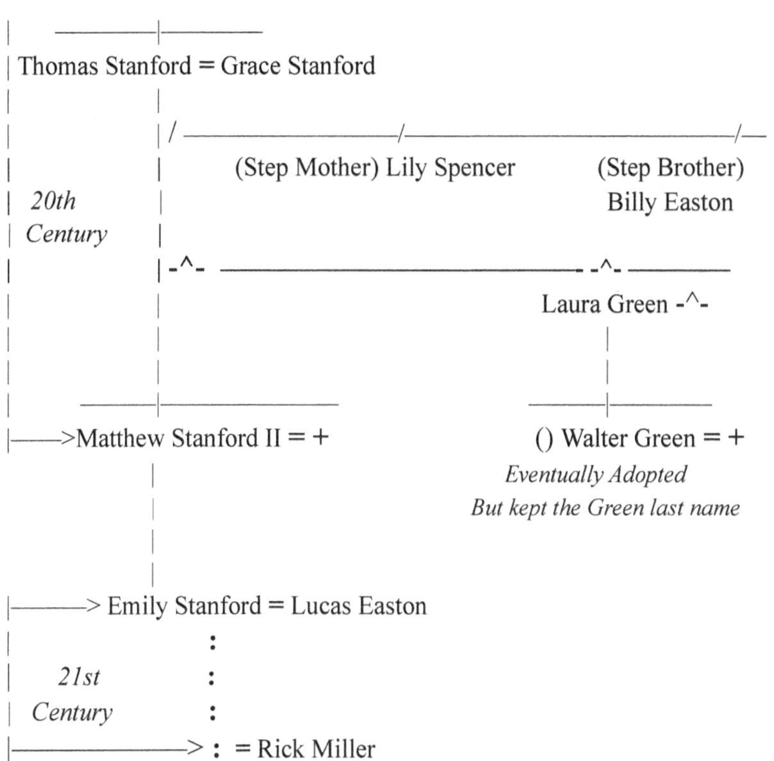

Thomas Stanford = Grace Stanford
20th
Century
(Step Mother) Lily Spencer
(Step Brother) Billy Easton
Laura Green -^-
—>Matthew Stanford II = +
() Walter Green = +
Eventually Adopted
But kept the Green last name
—> Emily Stanford = Lucas Easton
21st
Century
—> : = Rick Miller

Key
= Married
+ Name not mentioned
|| Skip Generation
() illegitimate child
: Re-Married
-^- love affair
< Divorced

Miller Ancestors

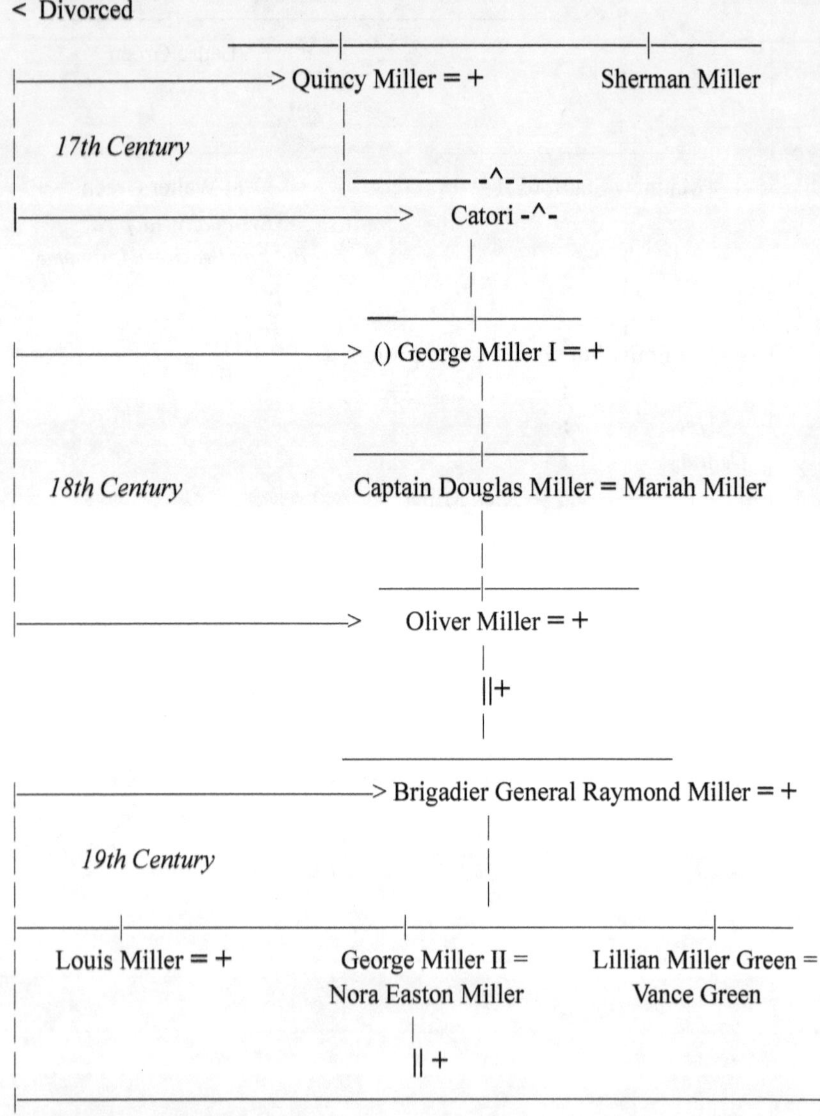

Continue on next page

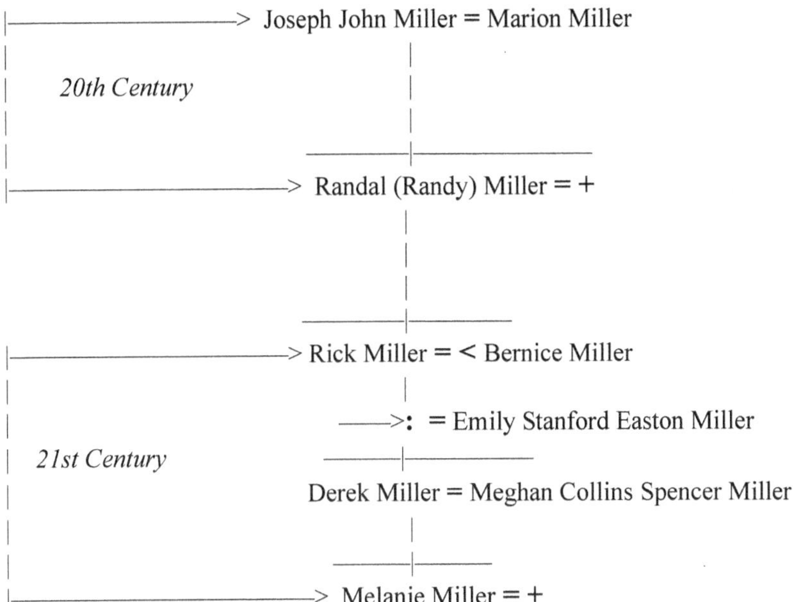

|————————————> Joseph John Miller = Marion Miller
20th Century
|————————————> Randal (Randy) Miller = +
|————————————> Rick Miller = < Bernice Miller
——>: = Emily Stanford Easton Miller
21st Century
Derek Miller = Meghan Collins Spencer Miller
|————————————> Melanie Miller = +

Easton Ancestors

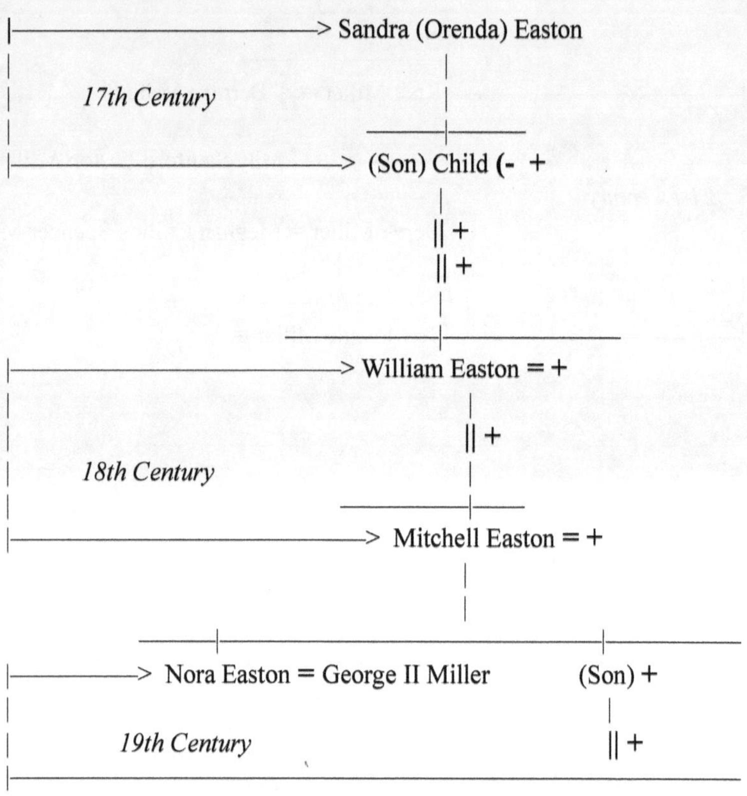

Continue on next page

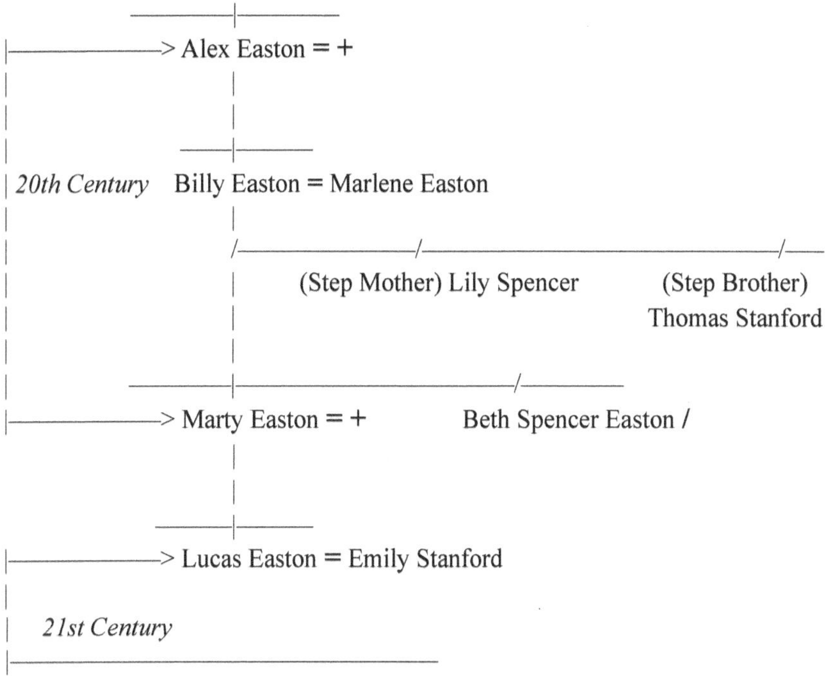

> Alex Easton = +
20th Century   Billy Easton = Marlene Easton
(Step Mother) Lily Spencer   (Step Brother) Thomas Stanford
> Marty Easton = +   Beth Spencer Easton /
> Lucas Easton = Emily Stanford
21st Century

Key
= Married
+Name not mentioned
|| Skip Generation
/ Step Family

Spencer Ancestors

17th Century

|——————————————————> Rebecca Spencer
| || +
|—————————————————— || +
                                               || +
                                               || +

|———————————————> Lily Spencer = +

19th Century

(Stepson) Thomas Stanford   (Stepson)
                                                  Billy Easton

|——————————————> (Daughter) +

|——————————> Kathleen Spencer = +   Charlotte Spencer

20th Century

|——————————> Beth Spencer Easton = +

|——————————> Sylvia Spencer Collins = +

21st Century

Meghan Collins Spencer Miller = Derek Miller

|———————————————————————> Melanie Miller = +

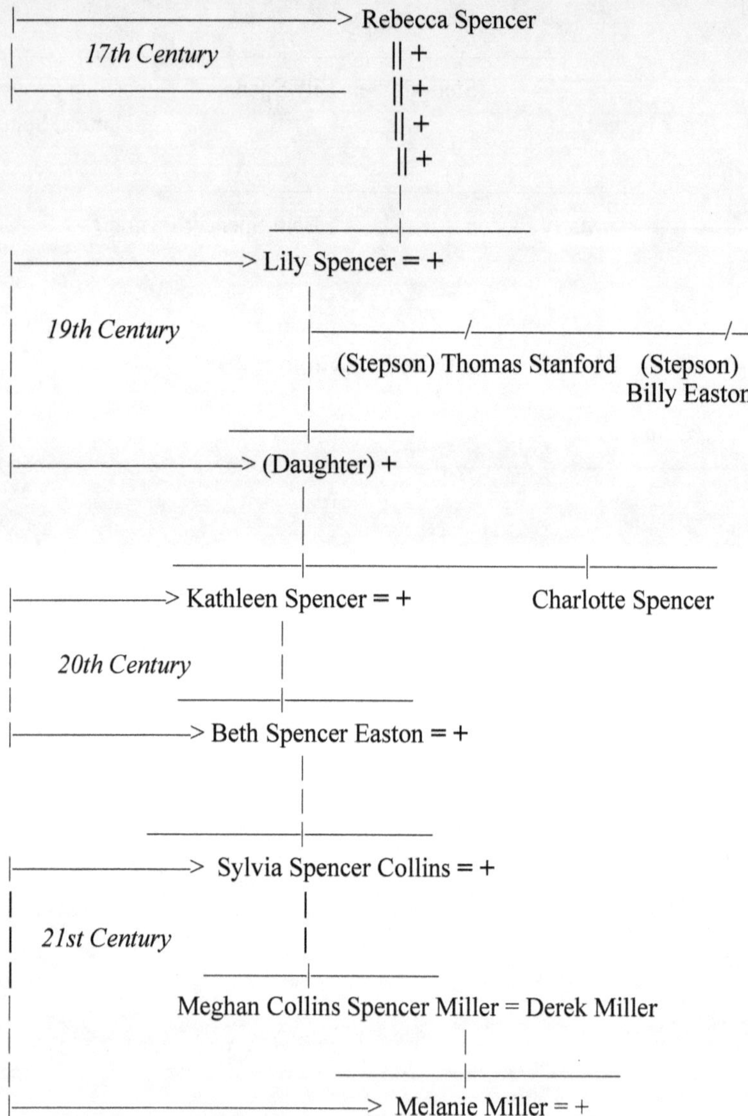

Key
= Married
 -^- Love affair
+ Name not mentioned
() illegitimate child
/ Step Family

Green Ancestors

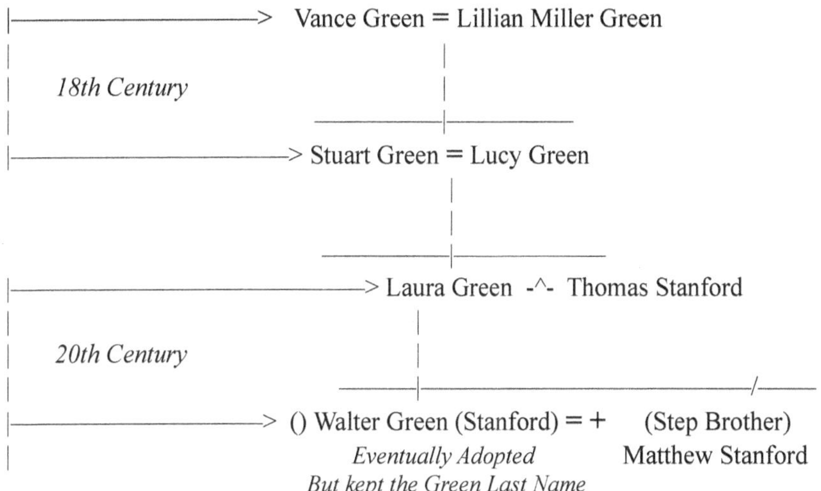

Acknowledgements

I want to acknowledge the men and women whose courage and sacrifice inspired me to write parts of this epic story featuring the **Greatest Generation.** They were a generation who had grown up during the Depression and looked to seek only the American dream for themselves and their family. When Pearl Harbor was attacked on December 7, 1941, the American dream was threatened, prompting men and even boys as young as sixteen who lied about their age to enlist without fear or favor to fight for our freedoms. May we never forget their courageous victory in fighting this evil and appreciate all those who kept up the war effort at home, for without the greatest generation, we would be living in a different America and a world inconceivable to us all.

I want to thank **Barbara Fournier,** the author who wrote the *Reese Clayton and Emerson Lake series.* Barb came to one of my book signings, and we connected immediately. We had two things in common: We were both retired hairstylists who had became authors. Barb offered her support and showed me the ins and outs of the author world. She pointed me in the right direction by telling me how to get my novels into more bookstores. Barb also introduced me to a community of talented local authors. Thank you Barb for your helping heart and kind friendship.

A book doesn't become a great novel unless it has two elements: a good storyteller's creative mind and a skilled editor's expertise. Those editing skills belong to **Pauline Bartel** (*Bartel Communications, Inc.*) Pauline was there from the very beginning. She taught me how to be a good writer through editing each of my books.

Thank you, Pauline, for making me a better writer and helping me to shape this novel into a polished story that reads effortlessly.

I would like to thank my publisher, *The Troy Book Makers*, for all the help in producing my book, from formatting to font design to *Jessika Hazelton's* talent in crafting a great book cover.

I'd like to thank my family for all their support since the day I told them I would write a novel, yet I never imagined I would have written three to date. Thank you for listening to me chatter on about my fictional little town of Maple Ridge and how I talked about the characters as though they are actual people. Well, they are real to me. They're just living inside my head.

I sincerely thank all my readers for giving my work a chance. I am so grateful for the many reviews, whether from direct messaging, Amazon or Goodreads. All those kind words have inspired me to continue in my writing journey.

Most importantly, *I would like to thank God*. None of this would be possible without his love. His love guided me many times when writing about these fictional characters who could easily be like real people who might have existed somewhere in time. I also drew inspiration from God's word.

"Be strong and courageous. Do not be afraid or terrified because of them, for the Lord your God goes with you; he will never leave you nor forsake you."
Deuteronomy 31:6.

Courage was never absent from Emily and Rick
when fighting the good fight to cast out evil.

Check out the first in this <u>Two-Part Magic River Series</u>
and read how Emily and Rick's story begins.

Also by Ann Marie: *Spiritual Journey of an Ordinary Girl*

You can order Ann Marie's books at
your favorite bookstore or find them on <u>amazon.com</u>
Publisher; The Troy Book Makers: order copies at:
<u>www.shopTBMbooks.com</u>

Visit Ann Marie's website: <u>annmariepichewriter.com</u>
Follow Ann Marie on social media:
Facebook : **Ann Marie Piche - Author**
Instagram: **annmarie_inspiredwriter**
Goodreads: **Ann Marie Piche - Author**
https://youtube.com/@annmariepiche7673

Please support Ann Marie by leaving a review on:
Amazon, <u>shopTBMbooks.com</u> and Goodreads.